CALCULATED SABOTAGE

CALCULATED SABOTAGE

THE CALCULATED SERIES: BOOK 3

K.T. LEE

VERTICAL LINE PUBLISHING

Copyright © 2018 by Vertical Line Publishing, LLC ALL RIGHTS RESERVED.

No part of this publication may be reproduced, distributed, sold or transmitted in any form or by any means, without prior written permission, except for statuary uses, the use of brief quotations in a book review, and other quotations with appropriate reference.

K.T. Lee

www.ktleeauthor.com

Publisher's Note: This work of fiction is a product of the writer's overactive imagination. It is not intended to be a factual representation of events, people, locales, businesses, government agencies, or rocket science. Names are used fictitiously and any resemblance to actual people, living or dead, is completely coincidental.

Calculated Sabotage/ K.T. Lee - 1st ed.

ISBN 978-1-947870-07-9

Book cover design by The Book Design House

The Calculated Series

Calculated Extortion (Prequel Novella)
Calculated Deception (Book 1)
Calculated Contagion (Book 2)
Calculated Sabotage (Book 3)
Calculated Reaction (Book 4)
Calculated Entrapment (Book 5)

For my family

1

QUINN KING RAISED HER GUN AND LOOKED DOWN THE SIGHT. SHE relaxed her shoulders, let out a breath, and squeezed the trigger. The bullet passed through the center-chest X and the paper target fluttered. It had been six days since Rory, her friend and sometimes-partner, had been murdered. It had been four days since her boss had officially rejected her request to find her friend's killer, reminding her that Rory's death had not yet been ruled a murder. It had been three hours since Quinn had decided to investigate her friend's death independently, orders be damned.

Quinn shut her eyes tight, then opened them. She fired again. The bullet passed through the same neat hole in her target as the previous rounds. Quinn emptied the rest of her magazine into the X on the head of her target. She reloaded her weapon with a fresh magazine, pulled the slide to chamber a bullet, and slipped the Glock into the holster on her back.

Quinn removed her ear protection and rolled her neck. The range master nodded at her, a small grin of admiration sneaking across his face. He knew her as Amy and had asked her out a few times. He was clearly former military and just attractive enough to not be obnoxious about it. He seemed like good people, but she just didn't need the complications right now. She had work to do and it would start with a flight across the country.

Contrary to popular mythology, even "lone wolf" CIA operations officers were expected to work well on a team. Quinn met Rory shortly after she started at the CIA, and they'd hit it off immediately. Rory had the charm to recruit foreign assets, and Quinn was the patient, strategic one. Some might call Quinn paranoid, but careful often looked like paranoid to the untrained eye. Within a few months of meeting, Quinn and Rory began to work on most of their operations together. However, it wasn't always practical to work on a team. Which was how Rory ended up dead and how Quinn ended up sorting through the wreckage. She rubbed a hand down her face. She considered putting a few more bullets through the holes on her practice target, but before she could reach for her gun, her phone buzzed against her hip. She didn't need to look at the name to know the Director of Special Operations was calling. The only people who had this number were Rory and DSO Dan Floyd.

"Hey, boss." Quinn absently rubbed her neck and scanned her surroundings. The crowd was pretty thin today, but the pops from the guns firing around her kept her from fully focusing on the call.

"How are you holding up, Falcon?" Dan's voice was carefully neutral.

"That's my name this month? Hm. I like it."

"I was thinking Bluebird, but it's too cute. You scare me a little, Falcon."

"Ha. Like anyone could scare you." When asked about his own reputation, the DSO would only shrug and say he could neither confirm nor deny the stories. He scared the bejesus out of the new operations officers. Quinn respected him, and what's more, she liked him. As long as he didn't coddle her.

"You're awful calm if you're in the middle of a shootout. Are you at the range again?"

"Yes, sir."

"You want to talk about it?" Dan's voice softened.

"No, sir. Not unless you've changed your mind." Quinn shifted her weight and put her free hand on her hip.

"We have a team on it, Falcon. Look, I can get you in with a counselor. What you're feeling is perfectly normal."

"With all due respect, you'd have to drag me in unconscious, sir. However, now that you mention it, I think I need to take some vacation time soon." Quinn turned around to check her back. Still just a bunch of cops and civilians practicing their aim. Their targets had more scatter than hers.

"I was afraid of that. I haven't authorized you to investigate Rory's death. Or pick up where she left off. Even on your own time. As I recall, I told you no. Multiple times."

"I have some ideas."

"I rejected your request for your own sake. You chase this down, I'll have to fire you."

Quinn raised her eyebrows. She wasn't under the impression she was irreplaceable, but she was good at her job because she knew when to call a bluff. "You're a real cut-up, sir. So, I need to take that vacation. To spend as I choose. If I happen to see something fishy going on while I do some sightseeing, I'll let you know. I've done some research of my own. I'm thinking of heading out west, maybe going to visit some mountain towns."

There was a long pause on the end of the line. If Quinn was there in person, she'd see Dan's jaw tighten and nostrils flare, just slightly. "We've got analysts digging into the evidence and checking security video. You're not the only person upset we lost one of our own. I need you away from this."

"Then you're going to need to be a good shot to take me down. C'mon, sir. Let me take this on. You need someone who can get in there and get the job done."

"You know there's a chain of command, right?"

"I call you 'sir.' Will you put me in charge, sir?"

Dan sighed. "If you show one sign of not being able to handle this, I'm pulling you. I'll take you into custody if I have to."

Quinn grinned. "Deal."

"We'll get you some information by tomorrow. Take your time coming up with a plan for this one. The last thing I need is to lose you too. I'll be in touch."

"Sounds great, sir. Thank you, sir."

Quinn cleaned up her things, tossed her target, and waved goodbye to the range master. Then, she went back to her apartment to pack. She couldn't bring Rory back, but she could make sure her friend hadn't died in vain.

2

CAM MITCHELL'S PHONE BUZZED. HE LOOKED AROUND THE tastefully decorated reception, but everyone was focused on the couple sharing a dance under strings of lights. He slipped his phone out of his pocket. It was a message from Morgan Grady, his boss at the Special Operations Group at the CIA. *Come to my office when you're back in town.* He tucked the phone back in his pocket and considered what Morgan might have in store for him. He'd flown to Minnesota for the weekend to see his best friend and fellow operations officer, Tyler Scott, get married. Tyler's new wife, Dani, leaned her head on his shoulder while cameras around them clicked. Tyler had met Dani when she helped them stop a plot to release a bioweapon, and their relationship had quickly blossomed into the kind that would very likely last a lifetime.

It was possible Morgan had questions about the report he submitted about his trip to Moscow. He'd written it in his hotel room, just after his plane landed in the States and a few hours before the rehearsal dinner. He'd flown to Russia to meet with local sources to see if the politician behind the bioweapon had anything else up his sleeve, but Dmitri was nothing if not careful. Cam's report didn't have much useful information in it. However, it was unusual for Morgan to reach out on a weekend for something that could afford to wait. If it had anything to do with Tyler and Dani, he should probably check on it before they were out of the country on their honeymoon. It wasn't long ago that Dmitri had orchestrated Dani's kidnapping when she traveled to Europe for a conference. Cam slipped away through a side door and pressed Morgan's name.

Morgan answered on the first ring. "Good evening, Cameron. How are Dani and Tyler?"

"Happily married. I think Dani will really like it in D.C. She's pretty excited she landed a job at the National Institutes of Health."

"I bet. They didn't waste any time getting married."

"Well, her parents are pretty conservative and they wanted them married before they moved in together. Tyler said he didn't need any more time to decide."

"That's sweet. I told him to take a few weeks off. After everything they've been through, they deserve it."

Cam checked his surroundings. All of the partygoers were still inside. "My flight is tomorrow morning, but I can get back sooner if it's urgent. Is this about my trip?"

"No, it's something new. I'd rather not go into details over the phone. We have a situation we'd like you to look into. Dan is managing this one personally. Can I tell him you're in?"

Cam raised his eyebrows. The Director of Special Operations usually left the running of operations to the people who worked for him. "Always, ma'am."

"Thanks, Cam. Enjoy the rest of your evening."

Cam ended the call and returned to the celebration. Tyler eyed him and Cam returned an easy smile. Tyler had a honeymoon to go on – he didn't need the stress of the next op weighing on him. And if Dan was in charge, he probably couldn't talk to Tyler about it anyway. With any luck, Cam would be flying solo on this one. Their last op had included people from both the CIA and FBI. While it had been a productive cross-agency collaboration, it had gotten a little crowded for his taste. A little quiet time on a solo operation would be just what he needed to recharge.

. . .

After an early flight to Washington Dulles, Cam drove directly to Langley without stopping at his apartment. Morgan's door was cracked open a fraction and Cam tapped on it before he walked in. She looked up at him and smiled. It didn't reach her eyes. "Great. You're here. How was the wedding?"

"Good. Tyler and Dani are on a plane headed to an island in the Pacific."

"Sounds nice. And how was Moscow?"

"Uneventful. Dmitri has been laying low. None of our sources know anything."

"We'll get someone to keep monitoring our sources over there in case something pops. Right now, I need to move you to something more urgent. Would you mind shutting the door?" While Morgan Grady was just over five feet tall, her presence was commanding. Her short hair was styled to perfection and she wore her trademark, impeccably-tailored navy suit.

Cam closed the door and took his seat across from Morgan. He raised an eyebrow. "How bad is it?"

"We added another star to the Memorial Wall."

Cam was a polyglot, an officer valued for his fluency in multiple languages and dialects. However, there was only one word in his arsenal appropriate for the situation. "Fuck."

"Agreed, Cameron."

"Please tell me I get to go rain hell on whoever did this."

"That's the idea. Quietly, of course. We need you to help find the person behind our officer's death. It goes without saying that this will be a tightly controlled operation. Dan reached out to me and he'll be heavily involved, along with one of his operations officers. Technically, since I report to him, it's reasonable for me to involved. Practically, he asked me because he trusts me. We don't know why or how this individual was targeted. In fact, it's still possible her death was an accident and that we are overreacting."

"Yeah, it's technically possible, but you don't believe it, or I wouldn't be here." Morgan nodded and Cam crossed his arms. "Tell me about the officer who was killed." Morgan didn't make a big deal out of every operation. There was real work to do here.

"The operations officer's name was Rory Flanagan." Morgan slid a folder across her desk, and Cam flipped it open to a standard CIA employee photo. Rory had strawberry blonde hair, freckles, and an easy smile – she looked like the quintessential girl next door. "She was a natural at recruiting assets and had a good sense for people. She had as perfect of a record as you can in this business. No indication she'd ever been burned. She was working a case at a rocket company in Victoria, Washington, called Innovative Rocket Technologies. The house she was staying in exploded."

"On its own? Or did it have help?"

"Non-CIA accident investigators have pointed to a natural gas leak. Our people haven't been able to prove otherwise yet, which could just mean our criminal knows what they're doing."

"IRT is the company that just lost a rocket, right?"

"Yes, their most recent launch exploded shortly after liftoff." Morgan looked down at her notes. "Just over two months ago."

"Is that related to the officer's death?"

"That's one of the things we need you to find out. Rory was sent to get a closer look at the company because the failed rocket was carrying a government payload. IRT's track record up to that point was excellent and the circumstances of the failure had some of our people asking questions. Rory was just poking around the edges. Given what we know about her death, we have better than even odds that a criminal secured a position at IRT through legitimate channels. As you know, this occasionally happens." Morgan raised her eyebrows. Cam's collaboration with the FBI had started with just such a situation at a university. Their criminal did a good job covering his tracks, and if Cam hadn't had an inside source at the university, they might never have known what he was up to.

"So, our perp is someone working at the company and Rory got too close?"

"That's our working theory, but we have no way to be sure. Still, you and I both know that most criminals aren't going to take someone out on a hunch they're working for the CIA. It would draw more attention to them versus just getting out of Dodge."

"So, they must have something else planned."

Morgan nodded. "Rory's partner thinks the criminal is still at IRT, waiting to execute whatever plan Rory uncovered. She wants to get a closer look."

"I'll bet she does. I would too. Do I know her partner?"

"Unlikely. Dan is holding on real tight to her identity." Interesting. The CIA was notoriously secretive with last names and scrubbed most of the intelligence they collected, but Morgan's tone suggested something more. He crossed his arms and waited. Morgan folded her hands on her desk. "She's an operations officer with very few paper records. They recruited her as a college student when she was having some trouble with her university's paperwork. Found out her information wasn't entered correctly in the government's electronic systems and she's incredibly intelligent. She's quite good with a number of languages but not a polyglot. Understandably, they created records for her and quietly paid for her college. She's been with us ever since. I only know her by the code name they gave her for this operation. And I know the additional facts only because I've been read in on this. Please consider even that top secret. Her code name for this operation is Falcon. Dan or Falcon will provide you more information at their discretion."

Cam let out a low whistle. He'd heard of these people but always thought they were more legend than anything else. Apparently not. "Who else are we bringing in on this?"

"No one. The analysts who investigated Rory's death will not know of your involvement. Even Tyler can't hear about this one."

Cam crossed his arms. "And the CIA is still claiming they believe her death was an accident?"

"No, I'm saying we don't have the evidence to prove it was intentional yet."

Cam's eyes narrowed. If the CIA was keeping it this compartmentalized, they'd already concluded the operations officer's death was intentional. Worse, the Agency was treating this like it could have been an inside job. Of course, they wouldn't come out and say it. They'd give him the spiel that Morgan just gave him. He nodded. "So, what are our next steps?"

"We wait. The Director is calling the shots on this one. Falcon will make contact sometime in the next two weeks. Call me, verify everything checks out, and then it's off to the races."

"So our new ally is a control freak."

Morgan smiled wryly and leaned back in her chair. Silence filled the room.

"Yeah, I know. Pot to the kettle. So I jump when I get a call?"

"Or an email. I'll let you know if they send me any more information I can share."

Cam nodded and put his hands on his knees, ready to stand. Morgan raised her index finger and took a moment to choose her words. "One more thing. I need you to tell me if Falcon isn't up for this. Dan wants her on the op, but we don't usually let partners get involved after something like this."

"Why are they letting her in, then?"

"Apparently she's one of Dan's best people. And she threatened to investigate without us if they didn't put her in charge."

Cam chuckled, then turned serious. "I'd do the same for Tyler."

Morgan nodded. "I expect you would. That's why I didn't challenge Dan too hard on it yet. Watch your six, Cam. You'll be in the crosshairs of someone who already killed one of our people."

"Well, thanks for not insulting me by asking if I mind."

Morgan smiled. "I wouldn't think of it. Oh, Falcon will be bringing along a surveillance camera to install near the gas line where you'll be staying, along with all the normal equipment. Check it before you get home. Every night."

"Will do. That's smart."

"Careful out there, Cameron. That's an order."

3

Quinn rested her chin on her hand to take in the view of Mount Rainier through the airplane window. Her thoughts slipped back to the operation she'd be starting soon, but there wasn't much she could do about it until the plane landed. So, she stared at the mountains to relax. It didn't work. She tapped her finger against her chin and waited for the airport to come into view.

Mercifully, a few moments later, the plane dipped under the cloud layer, seemingly ever-present in this part of the country. While Seattle had once been a hub of the lumber trade, it was now the home of a booming tech industry. Just a two-hour drive from the airport sat the shiny new headquarters of Innovative Rocket Technologies, located in Victoria, Washington, a small town at the base of Mount Rainer. While their name wasn't particularly creative, their work was widely respected. IRT was one of many privately-owned companies born after NASA's own development budgets had been slashed. They'd also been the most successful company to date, even though their last rocket had exploded shortly after liftoff. IRT had reported that a faulty component was likely to blame, and they were now preparing for the launch of a classified government satellite. They eventually wanted to send people into space using the same rockets, but the satellite program was what

Rory had been chasing. Quinn compartmentalized IRT's other projects. For now, she only needed to find out who wanted to make sure Rory didn't know about their plans for IRT's next launch.

After the captain made the same announcement she'd heard countless times in other cities, Quinn unclipped her seatbelt. She stood and subconsciously ran a hand over the small of her back where her weapon rested on the rare occasion she carried on an op. Since this was going to be one of those rare occasions, her Glock was safely nestled next to the appropriate paperwork in her checked luggage. While the gun was an unnecessary complication if she ever got caught lying, the risk on this operation tilted the balance towards bringing it. It hadn't taken much convincing for Dan to approve her request.

Quinn filed out of the airplane and followed her fellow passengers to the baggage claim. Quinn had been recruited by the CIA during her freshman year of college, and she'd chosen a major they believed would bring value at the time, nuclear engineering. She'd initially had trouble deciding on a major but loved the thrill of solving problems that at first seemed impossible. For her, nuclear engineering fit the bill. While the world had evolved, and her role at the CIA had turned into something else entirely, her background in math and science would help her blend in on this operation. The engineer in her was excited to get a closer look at the company's work with Uncle Sam's full permission. However, her intellectual curiosity was overshadowed by her focus on the operation.

Rory's last update indicated she was looking for an internal source through the social network of the small community. She'd chatted up a number of employees from the Flight Navigation department at IRT at a local bar. However, somewhere along the way, Rory had made a misstep. Quinn would dig deeper into Rory's notes after she had time to make her own first impressions. To follow the trail without hitting the landmine that caught her friend, Quinn would come at this operation from a completely different angle.

While Quinn waited for her luggage, she sent Dan a message with her status and location. Dan messaged her back to let her know he'd sent the other CIA employees who'd been sniffing around the area home to avoid any potential of blowing her cover by association.

Good. This op would require every precaution. Dan asked her if she was still sure she wanted to be there alone, and she confirmed she didn't need or want backup just yet. Quinn wasn't about to drag someone else into this until she had some time to reduce the risk of the situation.

Within a few minutes, her luggage popped out onto the carousel, and she hefted the large camping backpack over her shoulder. It was only noon and there was no time like the present to get to work. Thanks to her friends in the right places, Quinn had a job interview first thing tomorrow to prepare for.

The following day, Quinn followed her GPS directions until the Innovative Rocket Technologies buildings came into view. Only one person was walking through the expansive parking lot at the relatively late hour of 10 AM. He was dressed in business formal, unusual for the jeans and t-shirt culture of the West Coast. He would either be a fellow interviewee or they had a pretty formal work environment here. She looked down at her own simple gray skirt suit and nodded approvingly. She found an empty parking spot, reached for the black leather folder that held the résumé she now knew by heart, and entered the building for her interview.

Quinn's approach would be necessarily different from Rory's. Instead of fraternizing with the locals, she'd be directly embedding herself in the company. Once she nailed the interview. She'd been someone else countless times, often not even speaking English aloud for months at a time. This wasn't like her last assignment in Moscow. It was Washington state, for crying out loud.

The large glass front doors opened smoothly and closed quietly behind her. Four individuals were in the lobby: the security guard manning the metal detector who looked oblivious but was watching her out of the corner of his eye, the receptionist with a welcoming smile, the man she saw in the parking lot sitting in the waiting area with his hands awkwardly resting on his knees, and finally, a tall man with broad shoulders and bold pinstriped shirt. Pinstripes wore a badge around his neck. As she got closer, she could just make out the name. Ben Hall. It was showtime. Quinn adjusted the bag on her shoulder and walked over to greet him.

Quinn stuck out a hand. "Hi, you must be Ben. I'm Quinn Givens. It's very nice to meet you."

Ben returned her handshake, firm, but not crushing, while maintaining eye contact. "Hi, Quinn. Thanks for making the trip. If you'll just follow me." His eyes seemed honest, but then, hers probably did too.

Ben led her through security and she placed her handbag on the belt. It was too bad she had to go in unarmed, but it was the nature of the business. She had a weapon that wouldn't set off the metal detector, but her pencil skirt limited her mobility too much to make it worth carrying today. And there was no reason to think she would need it. She hadn't been there long enough to make any missteps yet.

Quinn retrieved her bag at the end of the belt and followed Ben down a hallway. She would be playing the part of an aerospace engineer with a specialization in flight dynamics. While nuclear engineering shared some of the same math and science fundamentals as aerospace engineering, anything past sophomore year of undergrad aerospace engineering was out of her league. Fortunately, a couple of CIA analysts with the right background had put together a crash course for her to study before she arrived. She couldn't do the actual work proficiently yet, but she should be able to use the proper terminology without setting off alarm bells. It wasn't going to be easy to fake out engineers and scientists of this caliber, but interviews were usually more about if you could play nice on a team, rather than a bunch of pop quizzes. If she could bluff her way through the interview, the CIA had provided references who would convince Ben of her technical prowess. Ben led her to an empty conference room. Quinn settled into a chair and folded her hands on the table.

"So, Ms. Givens, why are you interested in working for IRT?" Ben looked up from a list of canned questions with blanks to fill in the answers. Perfect. As long as he didn't pull out an orbital mechanics textbook, she'd be fine.

Oh, I don't know. You have a killer in your midst, and I'm here to make sure they don't kill anyone else. She smiled, making sure it reached her eyes. Experience and training had taught her to hide the tell-tale signs of fake emotions. "I love the challenge and excitement of the work. Any new company in this space is going to have to innovate on their approach to be successful, and I think you guys are out front. I think IRT would be a great fit for my skills and experience." She rubbed her necklace to appear as if she was nervous rather than squarely in her comfort zone. It was infinitely harder to be cut out of the operation than to be put in charge of it.

Ben nodded and took notes on her answer. He didn't cringe or smile, just moved on to the next question. He wasn't impressed enough. Next time, she'd use fewer buzzwords. "Okay. How did you hear about us?"

For the first time in recent memory, Quinn paused when she didn't intend to. Rory's face jumped into her mind, unbidden. She pushed it away. "I had some professors in college who knew of the company and thought highly of it. Since you guys have a lot of launches lined up for the next few years, I thought I'd check it out for myself. I know the work is hard, but I'm willing to put in the time."

"And how did you become interested in the Flight Navigation team?"

My friend thought her killer was hanging out with you guys. "It's my favorite part of my degree. I found something I loved and just grabbed onto it with both hands. What's your favorite part of the job, if I may ask?"

Ben looked up from scribbling on his paper and his face relaxed. Ah, he didn't like the questions either. "I like working on hard problems. Enough people have told me it's too hard to build this kind of company from scratch, and it can't be done." He grinned. "I like proving them wrong."

Quinn smiled back. "That's one of my favorite things to do too."

Another hour passed as Ben ticked through the HR-provided questions. Carefully, Quinn learned his opinions and evolved her answers to match his until he was putty in her hands. Ben offered to give her a tour, and the interview transitioned into comfortable conversation. It'd just be a matter of time before she would get the job, thanks in equal parts to her heavily-padded resume and genuine enthusiasm. The Agency would make sure the work was done by some of the best at NASA, so IRT wouldn't be totally screwed over by hiring a fake.

Quinn was fairly confident that with their help, she could BS her expertise. Being someone else was old hat by now and she was as motivated as she had ever been. This time, she even got to speak English.

As the interview drew to a close, she began to realize that Ben needed someone urgently. She dropped a few hints that she was available to start as soon as possible if she was the right fit and crossed her fingers. Ben assured her he'd be in touch. With any luck, they'd call her back in weeks instead of months.

Satisfied but exhausted, Quinn grabbed her dinner from a busy Indian restaurant nearby and returned to her rented condo to recover. It was a newer complex, likely built to account for the growing population of people moving to the area to work for IRT. Before she exited the car, she skimmed through the day's video surveillance of the gas line at high speed. There had been no unexpected visitors. Good.

Quinn dropped her keys on the counter and took her take-out to the couch. She tore off a bit of naan and popped a bite of chicken tikka masala into her mouth. The creamy tomato sauce was the perfect comfort food. She took a drink of water and sighed. If the interview had gone as well as she thought it had, it was probably time to call in backup.

Quinn emailed Watchman, the operations officer that her boss had requested – no, required – that she bring in, to let him know where he'd be going. After pausing to consider her circumstances, she told him to meet her there in a week. She read over the email one last time and hit send. While she could ask him to come sooner, the extra time was defensible and would give her the chance to get the lay of the land before he arrived. She wasn't thrilled about putting anyone else in the same situation that had killed another operations officer. But, Dan wanted her to have some backup and orders were orders. At least he'd ensure her counterpart would be a good one. She finished her meal and considered her options for the coming days. She had a week to figure out how to stay in front of their criminal before Watchman arrived. It'd be unthinkable to lose anyone else.

4

Cam Mitchell added a few small items to his pre-packed duffle bag and zipped it shut. He always had a bag with the essentials ready in case he needed to move quickly. It was a habit that had been drilled into him in his SEAL days and one that continued to serve him well. The elusive Falcon had finally reached out via email and disclosed their ultimate location. Since Cam had no intention of twiddling his thumbs in D.C. until they officially started next week, he'd booked the first flight out of Dulles. There was no harm in going out early to sniff around for a few days until his new friend could join him. Maybe he'd even find a clue or two to help them crack this case a little early.

Cam grabbed a paperback off his shelf, the newest spy novel from his favorite author. He hadn't even cracked the spine. This author actually got about half the details right, which was light-years ahead of everyone else. It made reading a glamorous account of his unglamorous job more enjoyable and was less dry than the non-fiction book on the history of military aircraft he'd read on the last trip. The thick novel would keep his mind busy on the long flight until he could really get to work.

. . .

THE DAY AFTER HER INTERVIEW, Ben called Quinn to offer her the job. She graciously accepted and offered to start as soon as possible. Ben was pulling strings to get her in by Monday, which meant Quinn had less than a week to complete her crash course in orbital mechanics and flight dynamics. She hung up the phone and pulled the heavy three-ring binder out of her bag. Even with the thrill of the operation moving forward, after a few hours of studying equations, her brain began to protest the addition of any more information. She considered a visit to the gym at the condo complex, but she needed some private time to think without the added stress of watching her back while she pounded out the miles.

Quinn closed the binder and went to her second-favorite place to blow off steam – the kitchen. Soon, she was kneading bread dough slowly as she considered her problems. She'd initially wanted to make cream puffs for the delicious end result, but Pâté à Choux dough was made in a pan, and she needed to sink her hands into something. Watchman would arrive next week, and it'd be nice if she could get a head start at IRT so she could tell him where he would be most useful. Much of his background, like hers, was classified. His first name was Cam and Dan spoke highly of him. He knew very little about her and was addressing her only as Falcon. She'd give him more information about herself once she'd had a chance to size him up in person. She needed to have things under control when he arrived. Keeping it simple would keep everyone alive.

Quinn placed the mixture in a bowl to rise and scrubbed the dough out from underneath her fingernails. She went back to the couch and eyed the binder filled with equations. She sighed, then pulled out Rory's case file. Unfortunately, the tighter-than-expected timeline meant the only thing more important than mastering her new specialty would be digging into her friend's notes. Quinn had been hoping for an epiphany about the Flight Navigation team on her interview, but no one's behavior even got close to suspicious. She grabbed a beer from the fridge and checked the time. It was three o'clock. Close enough to five o'clock. She took a long pull before opening the manila folder. Copies of Rory's neat handwriting stared back at Quinn, and she took in an unsteady breath. Quinn told Dan she could handle it. And she would.

Because Rory had just started researching IRT, her notes were largely focused on what she'd learned by chatting up the employees at the local bar after work. It was almost certain that someone she'd met was behind it. Ben's name wasn't in the notes, but Rory had met several members of his team at trivia night. Rory had a number of meaningful interactions with a man named Chuck from Ben's team. While she hadn't gotten any classified information out of him, he seemed to love to make small talk. Rory had been waved over to their table one night by a friendly technical writer who seemed to be more style than substance – her name was Hannah. A badge photo of the stylish writer with a scarf, glasses, and perfect pixie haircut was clipped to the folder. Hannah worked in the Flight Navigation division and was also the unofficial team coordinator of trivia night, which was well attended by the employees of IRT. A third employee, Lindsay, had worked for IRT for several years but moved to a new position at another company during Rory's operation. Since it was likely that their killer had a vested interest in covering their tracks so they could stay in place, Lindsay was a lower priority than her former coworkers.

Quinn went to the kitchen to shape the dough into a loaf and place it in the oven. Theoretically, getting burned by a suspect could happen to anyone, but Rory was careful. She had an instinct for people that, until this operation, had kept her out of any real trouble. Quinn returned to the couch to study her notes one more time. All of Rory's interactions with the team had occurred at the same bar. It had to be where she got burned. Rory had gone back to the bar the night she was killed – what had she seen? Or heard? The oven timer beeped and Quinn jumped. She rubbed her eyes and looked away from Rory's notes. She had some time this evening to visit the bar in question. She dumped her still full, now room-temperature beer down the sink and grabbed a glass of water. It was time to get to work.

CAM THREW his duffel bag onto his temporary bed in the condo the CIA had rented for the IRT operation. Oddly enough, his new place smelled like bread. Oh, well. He'd smelled a lot worse on previous assignments. He pushed on the mattress with one hand. It was actually pretty okay. Cam checked all of the rooms in the simple condo for bugs before setting up his own security system around the perimeter – windows and doors were swiftly taken care of with a couple of stick-on sensors. Satisfied with his work, he unpacked the contents of his bag into the small dresser opposite the bed.

Falcon would stay in the neighboring condo for operational simplicity when she arrived the following week. Dan was sending her with a discreet camera that would be placed where the natural gas line was piped into their shared building. Once she showed up, they'd both be able to check the video feed to make sure no one tampered with the line while they were gone. In the unlikely event their perpetrator found him before Falcon arrived, he placed a high-sensitivity natural gas detector on his dresser and connected it to his security system. The smell was usually a pretty good tip-off, but there had to be some reason the operations officer who was killed didn't notice it. In that case, he'd be glad to have the technology backup. Cam checked to make sure the door connecting their two units was locked and added another alarm to the internal door for good measure. There was no reason it needed to be open for another week, and he didn't need to get himself killed making assumptions when he knew better. He'd open it whenever Falcon arrived, assuming she'd be willing to pull the secrecy stick out of her butt.

Cam checked his watch. Thanks to the three-hour time difference from D.C., it was still late in the afternoon on the West Coast. Victoria, Washington wasn't exactly a huge metropolis, so even if Falcon wouldn't be joining him for a week, he could get a feel for the place. There wasn't anything wrong with him playing tourist.

Cam pulled up a map on his phone and searched for local watering holes. There was a grand total of three bars, including one that doubled as a family restaurant. After skimming the descriptions and social media sites for each bar, he settled on the one that seemed the most popular, and therefore the most promising for spontaneous interactions with employees of IRT. It even had a nerdy name. They were running a trivia night this evening. His brother, Parker, had started off life as an engineer and was now seriously dating an engineering professor, Dr. Ree Ryland, who regularly took him to trivia nights. Maybe engineers liked trivia nights. It was worth a shot. Cam pulled fresh clothes out of his bag and lay down to catch a quick nap before it was showtime.

AFTER AN HOUR of sipping a chai tea and exploring the specialty shops in the small downtown, Quinn zeroed in on her target destination, Bar 1.01. A dusty part of her memory recalled from her undergrad coursework that 1.01 bar was equivalent to atmospheric pressure at sea level. She chuckled and shook her head. That kind of name would doom a bar anywhere else. This was definitely a town filled with science types. She paused to read a sign taped to the glass door before entering. Trivia night started in an hour. Bingo.

Quinn took a moment to tidy her hair in the glass reflection. Unlike her last operation in Moscow, where she had to take care with her makeup to give herself a more Slavic appearance, back here, she only had to look like herself. She ran a hand down her leg to check her knife. It was still in position under her dress. The knife was quieter than a gun and more easily concealed under her A-line skirt. Plus, Dan made it clear that she could only pack the gun when the situation was overtly dangerous. Going to a bar didn't really qualify. She was a spy, not a cop.

Quinn found a spot at the bar and asked for water in a martini glass with three olives, giving a conspiratorial wink to the bartender. He grinned and raised the glass in a small salute when he delivered her drink. She tipped him well and took in the mostly empty tables. She didn't have to wait long before the bar began to get crowded. While she observed her surroundings, she sipped at her drink and tried to push away the feeling that she wasn't on her A-game. It didn't matter, in any case. It wasn't her first solo operation and she was just here to observe. Anyone could sit in a bar.

BAR 1.01 WAS BIGGER than Cam had expected. He entered through the glass door. A trivia sign had been taped and re-taped to it countless times. Like every bar in America, the music was playing too loud. The sound drowned out the important noises from his surroundings, so he focused on what he could observe visually. Groups of people, mostly men, were gathered around small tables. The occasional woman was sprinkled into the mix, but the uneven ratios were noticeable, if not particularly suspicious, in a town with a lot of scientists and engineers. While it'd be nice to see things even up on that front, especially after hearing Ree's perspective on the topic, he was here to catch a killer, not play politics. He approached the bar, ordered a beer, and forced himself not to do a double take at the woman sitting at the bar. She sat on a barstool with her legs crossed at the ankles in a knee-length dress and flat sandals. She was sipping at a martini and making small talk with the man next to her, but something about the way she moved made the hair on the back of his neck stand up.

He could only see the woman's profile, so he moved around a barstool and tried not to make it obvious that he was getting closer. The woman threw her head back to laugh and…son of a bitch. It was Katarina Ivanov, the secretary of the politician they'd been investigating in Moscow. Her hazel eyes, olive skin tone, and straight brown hair were the final evidence he needed to confirm his assessment. Cam had believed she was an innocent bystander, but she was now sitting in a Victoria, Washington bar, flirting with a patron. Less than two weeks after a CIA officer had been looking for information in the same bar and was subsequently killed a few miles away.

Cam took a small sip of his beer and sat on a barstool, not quite close enough to hear their conversation, but as close as he was willing to risk for now. He rested his elbows on the bar behind him to ensure he was comfortable without putting his back to Katarina. An announcer took the stage, and after a reading of the rules, pencils and slips of paper were distributed to all of the tables. Katarina's companion leaned in and then gestured to the crowd of people in the bar. She smiled and took another sip of her drink. While she looked as American as apple pie right now, she was Russian and probably could hold her own drinking what looked like a vodka martini. Not that her poor mark would know what he was up against. Based on his unkempt appearance and nervous laughter, she was playing him. For information, most likely. And she was nailing it. Cam inched closer. Finally, when he was close enough, he stumbled and spilled his beer on her arm.

"Oh, no. I'm so sorry." Cam apologized first to Katarina and then to her date. Much like the mates of female spiders who kill them after they've served their purpose, Katarina's mark was blissfully unaware of who he was dealing with. "Could you grab those napkins?" Katarina's mark passed Cam a stack of napkins and he began to blot her arm. She smiled and tossed her hair, tipping her drink over in the process and throwing a hand over her mouth.

"Oh man, you are bad luck!" Katarina said with a brilliant smile and no trace of her native Russian accent. Oh yeah, it was her. He hadn't just seen her from afar, he'd studied videos of another undercover operations officer talking to her. At length. In perfect Russian. Eliminating traces of her native accent took work and very likely, some formal training. She smiled at him like he was no different from anyone else at the bar. However, he had an advantage. She had no idea who he was. Katarina was the missing link that would help him finally close his last case and, with any luck, would help him solve this one before Falcon even showed up.

"That's what I hear," Cam said with a wink. "Can I buy you another drink? I promise to stay out of arm's length." The man behind her seemed disappointed, but she whispered something to him, and he laughed, oblivious to the close shave he'd just had. Her mark looked between her and a group sitting at the tables. She gave him a friendly smile, and he left to join them, clearly unsure of the turn things had taken.

"A drink sounds nice. And you are…?" She reached out a hand.

Cam met her hand. Her hand was soft, but her handshake was firm. "Aaron. Aaron Todd."

"Ah, two first names. It's very nice to meet you, Aaron Todd. I'm Quinn Givens."

"Nice to meet you, Quinn Givens."

"Well, Aaron two first names, are you here for the trivia?" She tilted her head and gave him a charming smile. She wasn't flirting, exactly. Just warm and friendly. Damn, she was good.

Cam shrugged. "Not really. I was just passing through and came in for a drink. You?"

"I was. But I like good conversation better than trivia."

So that was how she was going to play it. Let him think his lively conversation and beer cleanup skills were reeling her in. It was a little insulting to the male of his species that it was that easy for her to find a mark. The bartender set two fresh drinks on the bar. Katarina lifted her glass and took a drink. "Thank you. What do you do for a living, Aaron?"

"I work at IRT. But the work itself is classified."

Katarina smiled. "Of course, I understand. I'm actually starting a job at IRT next week. Maybe we'll work together." He shrugged in response and she looked up at the ceiling, "Unless we already know each other. I never forget a face and yours is familiar." She was digging. Unless she'd seen him lurking outside of her Moscow building. It was unlikely she'd make the connection since he was clean-shaven now. Then, he had been sporting a thick beard and shapka, the traditional Russian cap that, along with the right kind of makeup and sunglasses, helped hide his features.

He blinked and frowned. "Did you go to high school in Seattle?"

She tapped her finger against her lips. "No. Maybe I passed you in the hallway when I interviewed?"

"That could be it."

"Can you keep my seat warm? I'm going to go to the ladies' room."

"Of course."

Katarina hopped off her chair, looking over her shoulder once before walking into the bathroom. He met her eyes with a wink and warm smile. Once she was safely behind the bathroom door, Cam pulled out his phone to send a message to Morgan. *In a bar with Katarina Ivanov. Perfect American accent. Opportunity to apprehend on American soil. Please advise.* Cam wondered how long Katarina would be in the bathroom. Anywhere between two and five minutes, most likely. Unlike many women who travelled in packs to the bathroom, she'd gone in alone. So she could be back more quickly than most women. His phone lit up with Morgan's response.

Find out what you can but do not blow your cover. We'll send in another team if needed.

Cam scowled. *No time for that. She just broke away to the bathroom. Might have recognized me.*

He could almost hear Morgan sigh as he read her reply. *Cameron, be careful. Keep a low profile, see if you can gain her trust. Bring her in for questioning if you're backed into a corner.*

Ah, permission. Cam cracked his knuckles, then his neck. For the first time that evening, he smiled a genuine smile. He took a drink of his beer while he waited for her to return. He forced himself not to check his watch, even as several minutes passed. Hopefully, she hadn't left through a window. That was pretty much the worst-case scenario.

Cam scanned the room for additional threats, but it was mostly just clusters of people scribbling on paper and bringing them to the scorekeeper, totally oblivious to the danger around them. No one seemed interested in what the newcomer at the bar was up to. Those slips of paper wouldn't be the worst way to pass intelligence. He took another sip of his beer and watched Katarina come back to the bar out of the corner of his eye. There were no obvious bulges in her outfit, although her skirt had a flare to it. The loose skirt could be concealing any number of things from a throwing weapon to a Glock. This bar in small-town America didn't exactly have a metal detector and he wasn't carrying tonight. Well, he didn't work at the CIA for the money.

Cam nodded at Katarina when she settled into her seat and turned his body, nice and easy, to face her. Keeping his movements smooth wasn't an easy task when he was ready for anything, but that's what he had trained for. It took him a moment to remember the name she used. "Well, Quinn, do you have any plans for tonight?"

Katarina paused and checked her phone. "It looks like I'm free."

"Well, I'm not a fancy guy and we haven't had the best luck with drinks, so what do you think about a walk outside? Unless you'd rather stay here a little longer?"

She looked him up and down once and said, "A walk outside sounds perfect."

Cam held out a hand and she took it. Just like that, they left the bar, looking every bit a couple testing the waters. Now he needed to make sure the Russian secretary with the flawless American accent tried to get information out of him instead of kill him.

Cam released Katarina's hand when they made it out to Main Street, which had quieted down to only a few fellow travelers. There were enough witnesses that if she got any ideas about killing him, she'd have to pull him into an alley first. Cam felt her slip her hand back into his and tug him towards the idyllic storefronts of downtown, interspersed by alleys. Okay. Maybe she was going to pull him into an alley. He redirected her closer to the parking lot. After a brief pause, she followed his lead.

He stopped when they reached the truck the CIA had procured for him. Cam thought he needed a matching cowboy hat and boots to go with it, but someone at the CIA thought it was versatile enough for the job. What job, he wasn't sure, but it got him from Point A to Point B. Tonight, however, the tall truck would come in handy. It would serve as a barrier between them and the bar entrance, blocking them from curious passersby. He was hoping to charm his new friend, but success wasn't guaranteed. He didn't need any collateral damage to civilians if she turned violent.

He took a small step to position himself so that Katarina was between him and the truck. It wasn't the best defense, but it would limit her mobility. A row of trees blocked them from any pedestrians on the sidewalk. The solitude was a risk to him, but his top priority was protecting others if he misread the situation.

Katarina leaned against the truck and crossed her arms. He took a step closer to her and she met his eyes. Intelligence sparkled beneath her feigned interest. Oh yeah, she was playing games. He just had to figure out which one. Cam's jaw clenched and he forced himself to relax it. Katarina ran her hand down the side of her dress. Her dominant hand. The same hand that held her martini glass that could have been filled with water, considering how unaffected she seemed. He closed the distance between them, and she began to move her hand towards the bottom of her skirt. Shit. Instinct kicked in, and before he'd fully processed the thought, he'd grabbed her wrist. She stilled for only a moment before stomping on his foot and head butting him in the face. He lost his grip on her wrist and she pulled a knife from under her skirt. Instead of stepping back, he stepped closer so she couldn't get enough space to swipe at him. Cam grabbed her knife hand again and pushed it behind her back, keeping a tight grip on her wrist.

"Damn it, you don't learn," Katarina said, under her breath. In a heartbeat, she used the momentum of his hand to spin into him, pulling his arm across her chest. She bent over, levering him on top of her back, and rammed his head into the truck. Cam maintained the hold on her knife hand, despite the impact. He blinked hard and leaned to the side to regain control of the situation. She jerked him back up and rammed him into one of the truck's side mirrors. He released his hold on her wrist and rolled off of her, taking care not to slip on the broken beer bottle he'd spotted while she was banging his head into his truck. Now free, she turned to run but slipped on the glass bottle he'd only narrowly avoided.

Before she hit the ground, Cam caught her, grabbed the knife and flipped her around so that her back was facing him. He kept the flat edge of the knife pressed against her stomach. Deadly calm, Cam said, "You have five seconds to explain yourself." He sucked at the blood oozing into his mouth from his lip.

"You blocked me in...and I...got scared. Let me go and I won't scream for help." Her voice held the right amount of manufactured fear, but her skillset had already blown her cover. Oh yeah, she was a pro.

"You know what, you should scream for help. But before you do, you should know I know who you are, Katarina. You were a secretary in Moscow a few months ago, working for a Russian named Dmitri. He kidnapped a friend of mine. Now you're Quinn Givens, all-American girl. IRT employee. No trace of your Russian accent."

"I have no idea what you're talking about," Katarina said through her teeth.

"Four seconds. Unless you want to yell. In fact, why don't you? I bet the American cops would love to talk to a Russian spy beating up bar patrons."

Katarina stilled. Good. Now she knew he was serious. "I'm not who you think I am."

"No shit. And I don't like murderers. Three."

"Look, I think this is just a misunderstanding."

"Tell that to my black eye and split lip. I'm not someone you want to bullshit, Katarina. Two."

Katarina let out a breath. "Please tell me you're Watchman."

Cam relaxed his hold a fraction. "Son of a bitch. Who are you?"

"I'M FALCON," Quinn hissed, "and I would appreciate it if you would stop making a scene." She forced more confidence into her voice than she actually felt and tried to still the slight shake in her hand. Not many people got the jump on her. Watchman had her cornered so fast that when he moved towards her dominant hand, she'd reacted out of pure self-preservation. He wasn't even supposed to be in town. It was a minor miracle she'd realized what was happening before one of them got seriously injured. Well, he didn't look so good, but he'd come out of it okay. She'd just wasted an entire evening defending herself from her new partner. A partner who was no small amount of pissed off and had blood oozing from his lip. Damn.

"I don't know how you know that name, but I don't like liars, Katarina. So, here's what's going to happen. I am going to put a pair of handcuffs on you. You are going to sit in the front seat of my truck and I will take you back to my place for questioning. If you make one wrong move, you'll never see the outside of a prison again. Am I understood?" Cam's voice was barely above a whisper but still managed to be more intense than if he was yelling. Quinn shivered.

Quinn scanned the parking lot. They were still alone. "Keep the knife as a peace offering, but I will not be handcuffed. I work for Dan. I sent you an email yesterday. I'd say I'm sorry for the misunderstanding, but my partner was murdered recently, and you can understand my caution."

"Is this normally how you introduce yourself?"

"No. I was very clear that you were supposed to come next week. Regardless, you know how to handle yourself. You pass. Welcome to the team." When he stilled instead of offering a snarky comment in return, she turned to face him down, eye to eye.

. . .

CAM CLENCHED HIS TEETH, unable to keep his nostrils from flaring as his blood boiled. *You pass?* This woman was insane. She'd been working on the ground alone after telling him to wait a week to show up! It was pure dumb luck that their scuffle had been relatively quiet. This was why he worked with Tyler. Cam suddenly craved some alone time, but they still needed to leave without anyone noticing, and speaking to her was required. "Get in the truck. Now. You have some explaining to do. One wrong move and you're done." Falcon sighed and climbed up into the passenger's seat. She buckled in and folded her arms against her chest.

Cam tucked Falcon's knife into the driver's side door. Just in case. It had some weight to it. It was a good thing it hadn't ended up slashing him during their altercation. Explaining that to their superiors would have been fun. He tried to get his bearings, but his blood was still hot, and his temper, normally almost impossible to provoke, still held an edge. It'd be better not to have a conversation until he calmed down. He started the truck and began to drive back to the condo. She had been playing him, alright, but not the way he thought. Once it was the right time, he'd ask her some questions. Starting with the incident in Russia. After a few minutes had passed in silence, he said, "You're not Katarina?"

"No. My name is Quinn. I was there on a CIA operation."

"Bullshit. I was on that op. You talked to one of our people. At length. As a secretary working for Dmitri, who knew nothing of his plans."

"So, let me get this straight. You're mad because I kept my cover? If you were on the op, that means you received a tip about Stanislav working with the Russians. That came from me. He was sloppy and called Dmitri while I was working for him. After some high-risk digging through his office, I fed the information back to Dan, who passed it to you." Stanislav, the leader of the camp that Cam had taken down on the operation, was doing the actual work to release the bioweapon. It wasn't until the end of the op that they realized he was working for Dmitri. And the CIA found out all of this from an intelligence source inside the country. He'd assumed the information came from a Russian asset the CIA was working, but Quinn's explanation was, unfortunately for him, plausible. And held a lot of detail for a highly classified operation very few knew about, even within the Agency. "Look, Cam, I understand we got off on the wrong foot."

Cam parked the truck outside of his condo. "Your foot wasn't the problem. Come inside. We're not done talking."

Quinn crossed her arms. "I haven't decided if I trust you yet."

"That's pretty rich considering I'm still bleeding. You have about a minute to decide if you trust me enough to have a conversation. Otherwise, I'm reporting you as unreliable and investigating this on my own."

"Excuse me? I'm unreliable? You thought I was a Russian spy because I'm good at my job."

"You also told me we started working the case next week."

"*We* do. I'm here early. When you came next week, *we* would start working the case. There is nothing more you can do right now. You're being unreasonable."

Cam set his mouth in a line and closed his eyes for a moment. He opened them and channeled his most reasonable voice. "Look, if you're half as good as the Director thinks you are, you need to get your shit together and tell me what's going on. Not in a week. Right now." There. He was the bigger person. He gave her a minute to decide. She was still grieving her friend, after all. Before exiting the truck, he changed his tactics. "Look, part of my job is to report if you're too invested in this. I get where you're coming from. If I was in your shoes, I'd want to be the person making things right. But you need to explain yourself, or I'm kicking you off the operation."

Quinn huffed out a breath. "Fine. Let's go inside."

He heard the passenger door open and shut as he walked towards his condo. The sound of measured footsteps followed him up to his front door. Cam flicked on the lights and Quinn adjusted her skirt before sitting on the couch. He raised an eyebrow. "You took your knife back, didn't you?"

She managed to look a little sheepish. "It's only a little one. Look, I'm sorry if I hurt you."

Cam laughed. "Please. I've been through BUD/S training and served in a war zone. I've dealt with worse."

Quinn raised an eyebrow. "You're a SEAL?"

"Was a SEAL. Now I spend my time chasing American operations officers on U.S. soil. Oh, and you should check your place to make sure you haven't had visitors. I swear I smelled bread baking this afternoon."

Quinn smiled. "Give me a second."

Moments later, she tapped on their shared door. Cam opened it and she entered, holding a plate with slices of bread and a few pats of butter. "Peace offering?"

"Fifteen minutes ago, you were going after me like a mixed martial arts fighter dying to get back in the ring. Now you're offering me baked goods?" He grinned and shook his head.

"What, I can't be a spy and a baker?"

Despite the circumstances, Cam barked out a laugh. "Alright, I'll take some bread. Since you didn't know I was coming, I'll assume you didn't have time to poison it." He reached for a slice and took a bite. It was good.

"Gee, thanks."

"Can you blame me for being concerned?" Cam held up a finger and then went to the kitchen to retrieve an ice pack for his face. The bruise on the top of his cheek would likely be a full-blown black eye by tomorrow morning, but ice would at least help with the swelling. "So, listen. Now that we got that all straightened out, we need to figure out how to get into IRT."

Quinn busied herself spreading some butter on a piece of the bread. "Quinn Givens starts Monday. That part was true. She's an expert in flight dynamics. So, I guess I'm a spy, a baker, and an aerospace engineer." She popped a piece of bread in her mouth.

Cam raised his eyebrows. "Just like that?"

"More or less. I have a background in nuclear engineering, and I'll fake the rest with a little help from our friends at NASA. Look, I didn't want to drag anyone else into this if there was still a lot of danger involved."

"Well, if you're going to insist on being in charge, at least you're good at it. In the future, though, why don't you ask me if I mind being put into a situation rather than making assumptions about my threshold for risk?"

"I'll do my best." Quinn put her bread on the plate and her hands on her knees. She let out a breath. "I know we didn't get off to the best start. But I need to be here."

"I get it. I really do. Now that we've got a plan, let's see if we can solve this thing."

"I appreciate that. Maybe you'll even like working with me."

"Can't get any worse. At least I got your knife before you had a chance to use it on me," Cam said with a grin.

5

KIARA HAMMOND BRACED ONE HAND ON THE SCAFFOLDING surrounding her satellite. She leaned in a little closer to check the next item on her list. Her baby would soon be placed on top of IRT's fancy new rocket, which was currently waiting for NASA's payload in the Vehicle Assembly Building at Kennedy Space Center. IRT was responsible for delivering the satellite into orbit, but her team at NASA was in charge of supervising its assembly and subsequent attachment to IRT's rocket. Soon, she would give the go-ahead for them to place the fairing over the satellite to get it ready for its trip to space. However, before they installed the satellite's protective cover, Kiara had to complete her final checks to make sure her girl was ready to fly. Fortunately, she'd spent most of the day working through the detailed list on her tablet without incident. When she reached the area where the satellite attached to the rocket, it became clear that something wasn't right.

Kiara squinted at a part that didn't belong in the assembly. "You've got to be kidding me," she said, even though there was no one close enough to hear her.

Her voice echoed back at her, slightly muffled by the mask she had over her face. The mask was the same bright white color as the protective gown and shoe covers she wore to keep particulate from damaging the satellite. While working in a cleanroom made her job a little harder, the last thing they needed was to get gunk into the satellite they couldn't clean off once it was in orbit. She was supposed to let a trained crew handle the work, but this time, she wanted to check in on the progress personally. Admittedly, she was micromanaging. Just a little bit. But then she'd found something, hadn't she? Before leaping to conclusions or hypothesizing about what might have gone wrong, Kiara pulled up the assembly prints on her tablet to verify that her memory was correct.

Kiara tapped on the back of the tablet with a finger, fighting the temptation not to just press the same button again in the hope that it would load faster. While she watched the little circle spin on the screen, she bit her lip. The likelihood that the extra part connected to her satellite was supposed to be there was next to nil. She'd reviewed every report and tolerance stack-up for this assembly personally. Slowly, the assembly drawings began to appear on the tablet.

The part that didn't belong was near the guidance systems – both the satellite and the rocket were loaded with GPS and several other sensors to keep it on target during ascent and once it was in orbit. Kiara scrolled to the image on the tablet that would confirm what she already knew – the small metal box shouldn't be there. It was sitting in the middle of what had been designed as an open space. She'd had to approve the inefficient use of space months ago – it was one of several to make sure the mass of the satellite and rocket were appropriately balanced. While something that size probably wouldn't meaningfully affect the flight path, someone at NASA wouldn't add bits and pieces to the satellite assembly without asking her team first. Kiara squinted at it, then lifted her tablet to take a picture. The camera on the tablet left much to be desired, but it would provide enough detail to explain to her boss that something had gone wrong. She tucked the tablet under her arm and resisted the urge to scratch her head through her hair cover.

Their head assembler, Frank, leaned against the base of the scaffolding with his arms crossed. He'd agreed to meet her earlier but had been patiently waiting for her to finish her inspection for more than half an hour. Bless him, he did an excellent job of not showing any signs of annoyance. She probably wouldn't be as forgiving of her own micromanagement if she were in his shoes. On the other hand, he was about thirty years her senior and had likely seen more than one engineer fuss over their baby in his time with NASA. She certainly wasn't the first and she probably wouldn't be the last. She looked down at him and he raised an eyebrow. "You happy up there, Ms. Hammond?"

"Not entirely. I need to check a few more things." Even though the part didn't belong, she wasn't willing to believe his team made a mistake just yet. Frank didn't miss much and he had more experience than she did. Not to mention, it was best not to bite the hand that assembled your projects.

"Shouldn't be any problems. I put that section together myself and it checks to the specifications."

Kiara sighed. Maybe she could let him come to his own conclusions so it didn't look like she was blaming his team. "I could be missing something. Can you come up and take a look?"

"Sure." Frank climbed up to the top of the scaffolding, printed copies of the assembly drawings in hand. He didn't have much patience for the electronic systems – they took too long and he was in the habit of scribbling notes on his drawings. In fairness to Frank, it was easier to work off of paper copies, but Kiara was checking everything and didn't want to lug a bunch of binders full of paperwork around. He remained nonplussed, confident in his years of experience. When Frank reached her, Kiara stepped out of his way and pointed at the offending component. Frank leaned in for a closer look. "Aha, you see, I didn't put that there. It's not on the print." He flipped through the pages until he got to the right section and pointed to the empty space where the small metal box sat. "Someone must have been working off the wrong drawings. I'll have to go back and check the paperwork again."

"Who else has been up here?"

"Besides the whole assembly crew? Inspectors, management, engineers on your team fussing over the details." He raised his eyebrows at her.

"Fair point. Let me ask around and I'll see if I can figure out what happened. This is the kind of stuff that gets missions scrubbed." Or blown up on the launchpad. Kiara's blood ran cold. If Frank didn't know about it, someone else had done this. Maybe even on purpose. There could be anything in that small cube. They had a protocol for this. A protocol she never expected to use, but here she was. She did her best to keep her voice even, hoping the mask would muffle any hint of the nerves lurking in her throat. "Frank, I'd rather you keep this between the two of us. Can you do that?" Frank nodded, once, knowingly. He'd worked at NASA his entire career. He had been hired to oversee the assembly of the military surveillance satellite to the rocket. Frank knew how to keep his mouth shut. Kiara needed to make a call to her supervisor. No, this one was an in-person discussion.

Half an hour later, Kiara was outside of her supervisor's office. She'd long admired Alan Smith. Alan was a retired colonel, a competent professional, and a good man. He'd hired her right out of college and had earned her complete loyalty within the first year of working for him. His door was open and she tapped on it.

"Come in." Alan reluctantly looked away from his work, locking his computer screen before greeting her with a curt nod. When he saw the look on her face, he crossed his arms. "Better spit it out. This doesn't have anything to do with you looking over the shoulders of the people assembling your baby, does it?"

"Not directly, no. Well, okay, yes it does. I found something." Kiara pulled up the image on her tablet. "Sir, this doesn't belong here. I don't know what it is."

Alan reached for her tablet and zoomed in on the details of her photo. He let out a breath. "You better let me handle this. And I'd like for you to take a few days off."

Kiara eyed him incredulously. "Excuse me, sir? We launch in less than three weeks. I don't have time for a day off."

"All the same. I think a few days would be a good idea."

"Did I do something wrong?"

Alan shook his head. "Not at all. You've done everything right. And it may be nothing. But I don't want you in the building when I start investigating this."

Kiara's stomach turned. "It's not nothing, is it?"

"It very well could be. But I can't be sure until I take a look. And I need to call a friend first." Alan crossed his arms as if there was nothing more to say, his version of a dismissal.

Kiara stood her ground. "Sir, it's my project."

"No, ma'am, it's NASA's project."

"Sir." She put her hands on her hips and waited for him to come around. Alan was firm, but he wasn't usually unmovable.

"Kiara, you're one of the best engineers on my team. I'm grateful you were paying attention. Now, I need you to forget you ever saw what you saw. And let me handle it."

"Frank saw it too. I already told him to keep it between us."

Alan's mouth set in a line. "Let me talk to him. Frank won't say anything."

"You need to tell me what's going on. We're supposed to be loading her on top of IRT's rocket in two weeks. I can't just disappear. There's work to be done and my team will have questions."

"If you won't take a few days off, I need you to at least lay low. Don't go back in the cleanroom to look at the satellite without someone with you. I'm an old man and I don't need the strain on my heart." Alan rubbed his chest. He wasn't a day over sixty and looked even younger. He'd never told her to stop working before. She'd found something ugly. It was just a little box. But the right little box, filled with the right material, could send a rocket wildly off its flight path, could destabilize it so that it crashed instead of sending its payload into orbit. Kiara crossed her arms. Alan sighed. "You really won't consider that time off, will you?"

"Not until I figure out who's trying to sabotage my satellite."

Alan went perfectly still. "Sabotage is a strong word to throw around, Kiara."

"Do you disagree?"

"I do not have enough evidence to make a conclusion either way. I do think whenever you suspect something like that, you need to be extremely cautious. Chances are, if you're right, we have an enemy close by. That box didn't get installed outside this building. People knew you were around, checking every last detail. Give me a couple of days to chase this down before you go back in. People expect me to be a pain in the ass. It'll raise fewer suspicions. And, for the sake of my heart, please call security if you feel worried about your safety. Even if it's nothing more than an uncomfortable feeling."

Kiara studied Alan. He met her eyes and waited, unmoved. She swallowed hard. "Okay. I'll lay low."

6

Morgan Grady stepped into the Director's office and closed the door behind her. Dan Floyd's office was bigger and more formal than hers, but it wasn't so stuffy it made him seem unapproachable. Well, he scared the new recruits a little, but that wasn't necessarily a bad thing for the Director of Special Operations. He had a reputation to uphold. Dan had been nothing but dependable since they'd met at the Farm a lifetime ago. While Dan was in his mid-forties and single, Morgan was married and had twin sons, now in college. It had been some time since either of them had worked undercover in the field, but it wasn't easy to shake the veil of secrecy and the burden of distrust in others' motivations.

Dan gestured for her to sit. "I heard Falcon met your man last night."

Morgan sat in the chair across from Dan and crossed her arms. "Yeah. It sounds like she misled him about the op. Cam was under the impression she would arrive next week. We're on the same team, Dan." Morgan didn't like games and wasn't going to let Dan off the hook that easily.

Dan crossed his arms. "Look, Falcon is still recovering from the loss of her partner. She said he came early and they bumped into each other in a bar. After some initial confusion, they figured it out." Morgan raised a skeptical eyebrow and Dan cringed. "Uh oh. How close to the truth was that explanation?"

"It sounds similar to Cam's version, although I expect there was more to it than that since he was pretty amped up about catching her until he found out she was CIA. I don't have all the details yet – he just sent me a short note saying she'd shown up unannounced and they'd had a near miss. I plan on asking him for the full story on our regular update call tomorrow. Is Falcon a liability?"

"She's trustworthy, just a little careful."

"You didn't answer my question."

"Falcon is used to operating independently. She threatened to go rogue unless we let her in on this. Trust me, she's the type you want working with you, not against you." Dan looked down at his notebook and tapped his pen against it.

"So, she strong-armed you. That's a first. And a concern."

"Mo, I trust her." Morgan narrowed her eyes at him. It'd been a long time since anyone besides her brother had called her that. Dan was either spooked or trying to charm her. Or both. "More than almost anyone. Her sense of right and wrong is absolute. Like someone else I know." He nodded at her.

"Flattery doesn't work on me, Dan."

"Regardless, I stand by my opinion."

Morgan crossed her arms. "My assessment of Cam is the same."

"Good. We've done what we can. Thanks for the update and let me know if you have any other problems. Let's continue to keep it compartmentalized, please. Only you, me, and the two operations officers, unless I say the word."

Morgan leaned forward. "This is the second time you've asked me to treat this like it was an inside job."

"I don't have any hard evidence to conclude it was an inside job."

"You can't charm me and bullshit me in the same meeting, Dan. You've already used up your quota."

Dan sighed. "I can't prove that it wasn't an inside job. I'm proceeding as if someone in the Agency was involved unless we hear otherwise. It's prudent and in line with our protocols. Nothing more, nothing less." Dan chose his words carefully. He was nervous.

"Let's meet on this. Regularly. So there aren't any more misunderstandings." Morgan rose from her chair and turned to leave.

Dan's phone rang and he studied the number. He held up a finger for her to stay and answered the call. "Alan! I was just planning on sending you some work for that little project we talked about. Oh. I see. Yes, of course. And you've checked it already? Let me see what I can do on my end and I'll get back to you soon." Dan listened for a few more moments before hanging up. "That was the contact at NASA I asked to help us with Falcon's paperwork. He's managing the satellite assembly for the next IRT launch. One of his people found a small device inside of the guts of the satellite that shouldn't be there."

"Is it going to blow up?"

"The satellite or the rocket?"

"Either one. You pick."

"Hopefully, neither. Our contact has checked the device and doesn't believe it's explosive. Regardless, he doesn't think it's big enough to do significant damage, and the payload is sitting in a cleanroom, away from major quantities of explosives. But it might play into this operation. We need someone to go down there and take a look at it until we can prove the two incidents aren't connected."

"Yeah, Cam is already dealing with the other end of this and his partner is on his honeymoon. How about your contact at NASA? Why can't he dig into it?"

"First, he doesn't know the full extent of the operation, and I'd like to keep it that way. Second, he thinks someone there did it and it's a safety issue. He's being cautious."

"Anyone else on your team you want to pull in?"

"No way. I want everyone except for Falcon out of this. She was in Russia when Rory was killed – totally out of contact. She's the only one on my team I can conclusively prove wasn't behind it."

"You want to get the FBI involved?" Morgan challenged. There was a mostly lighthearted rivalry between the two agencies, but for something like this, Dan would want to keep any undercover work in-house.

"Not unless you have someone you'd be willing to hire as a bodyguard for your grandma available..." Dan trailed off when Morgan grinned instead of commiserated with him.

"Actually, Cam's brother, Parker, is a special agent. He and his team gave us an assist on one of our other operations."

"Will Cam mind if we bring him in?"

"I don't think so. Parker's team is pretty tight-knit. We can assume he'll want to bring some of his people."

"He can bring one more, two at most. Vetted and approved by you personally. And let's wait to send them until Falcon starts her job. I'd like to have eyes on the ground at IRT watching for strange behavior if we're sending more of our own in."

"You got it, boss." Parker would probably want the big one, Mike Moretti, and the clever, spunky one, Alexis Thompson, to come along. But then again, the girlfriend and sometimes-consultant was a mechanical engineer who had the chops to help solve a rocket problem. It was time to call her contact in the Chicago FBI office for some backup.

7

Unit Chief Patrick Sandhill, or Sandy to those who knew him well, stared down at his phone, now ringing with the label "Private Number." He had loudly advocated for more cooperation between his Chicago branch of the FBI and their counterparts in the CIA. Which had taught him not to open his big mouth unless he was willing to face the consequences. His best team was now on speed dial whenever the CIA needed them. The last operation had been a few months ago, and the private number had better than even odds of being Morgan Grady. That woman could charm a snake into choking itself, and as soon as he answered, he would get talked into helping her with something. He'd bet good money that he would have to rearrange his team's workload before the day ended.

He sighed and answered, "Sandhill."

"Sandy, it's been too long. It's Morgan." He could hear the cheerful smile in her voice and rubbed his forehead. Not only did she need his help, but it was also probably going to be another doozy of an operation.

"What can I do for you today, Morgan?"

"We have a little situation in Florida I could use some help with. I was wondering if I could borrow your team for a few days. Parker and maybe one or two of his choosing?"

"If it's fieldwork, Alexis is benched. She's still in physical therapy for the bullet wound from the last CIA operation she worked on. Mike or Scarlett might be able to jump in. What's this about?"

"We have some questions about a rocket." Oh great. Someone was playing with something that could explode. He was definitely going to have to rearrange caseloads.

"You're going to want a scientist to go with them, aren't you?"

"We'd take an engineer. One that already has a relationship with the team, if possible." Morgan's tone made it sound like it was his decision, but she had someone in mind. An engineering professor turned FBI consultant who had already earned the trust of the CIA on a previous operation. All of their hand-chosen people would be approved by Morgan.

"Parker, Ree, and Mike, then?"

"If it isn't too much trouble." It was. But he'd do it anyway. Morgan wouldn't waste his time with anything less than a national security issue.

"It's a deal, if you do the paperwork. I'll have Parker reach out to Ree." A boyfriend/girlfriend team in the field was unusual, to say the least, but Sandy saw results from the two of them that his colleagues drooled over. Parker always got a little edgy putting Ree in the crosshairs, but she could handle herself, and it'd give him something to complain about. It was as good as settled.

"It's a deal. You're the best, Sandy. I owe you one."

"I'll hold you to that, Morgan." Sandy hung up the phone and rose from his desk to let his team know their day was going to take an unexpected turn.

PARKER MITCHELL EYED his empty coffee cup and considered a refill. He was wrapping up some paperwork for an investigation, but filling out forms didn't grab his attention like working in the field did. To keep things interesting, he and Mike had been taking turns pelting a small foam football into the back of each other's heads whenever the other one wasn't paying attention. The last successful throw had been two hours prior when poor Mikey had been accosted by a coworker asking if he could buy some of his wife's furniture. Scarlett Moretti was not only an accomplished profiler for the FBI, she was also quite good at repurposing furniture. Her stylish, reupholstered couches stood out from their ugly, distant relatives at the FBI office. Consequently, people often asked her if they could buy them, even if they were at work. This individual was obviously new to the Bureau and wasn't really aware that while Mike hated small talk, he particularly hated small talk about household furnishings. While Mike was staring after the man who caused his annoyance, Parker had exploited the opening with a perfect shot to the side of his neck. Mike had been holding the football since then, and it was only a matter of time before he made his move. Sandy was headed their way, giving Mike the opportunity to strike. Parker tried not to look over his shoulder at Mike as Sandy approached. He probably wouldn't throw it at Parker while their boss was approaching. Probably.

Parker had worked with Sandy for years, and the thin line between his eyebrows suggested they were in for an interesting new project. He stopped in the space between their desks and said, "You guys up for a special assignment?"

Parker raised an eyebrow. "Always, sir."

Mike crossed his arms and nodded his agreement. Sandy said, "This one's from Morgan."

"No problem, sir," Parker said.

"She wants you two and Dr. Ryland involved."

Parker cracked his neck. "Always a catch."

"Is that gonna be a problem, son?"

"That's Ree's call, not mine, sir."

Sandy nodded. "Smart man. You'll find yourself in a lot less hot water that way. You're going south for this one, so tell your girl we're finally sending her somewhere warm."

"Yeah, she'll appreciate that after our last job in Minnesota. And it'll be good for her to jump back into things. She's still a little embarrassed about the run-in she had with Dr. Fabian on the last trip." Ree had gone into a suspect's office to ask about one of his people. When he'd reached into a desk drawer, she'd drawn her weapon in self-defense. It turned out that Dr. Fabian had only been pulling a lab report out of his desk. They'd explained their way out of the situation without negative repercussions, but still, it rankled his perfectionist girlfriend that she had overreacted.

Sandy scratched his chin. "Look, our internal team ran through the footage, and while it wasn't optimal, her actions were defensible. She had no way of knowing that Dr. Fabian wasn't going to harm her. The team didn't see a need to pursue it further or ask her to stop working with us. Maybe let's have her go into this one unarmed so that she doesn't have to worry about it. You and Mike can watch her back."

"I'll let her know. She'll stew a bit, but she'll get it."

Mike crossed his arms. "Anything else we need to know before jumping in?"

Sandy nodded. "Probably. I get the feeling there's a lot of backstory even I don't know yet. Parker, find out how quickly you can get to D.C. for a briefing with Morgan. She'd like to meet with you in person as soon as Monday morning."

"Yes, sir."

Parker watched Sandy leave and rubbed his forehead. Not only was Ree on call when the FBI needed help, the CIA was starting to request her too. Whatever Morgan had planned was probably going to be just as dangerous as the last op – and Alexis came home from that one with a hole in her arm. A foam football nailed him on the back of the head. Yeah, that pretty much summed it up.

DR. REE RYLAND heaved a sigh and reread the same sentence for the third time. She was sitting at her desk at Indiana Polytechnic, working on her least favorite thing in the entire world – grant applications. In fairness to the grant applications, it was actually her second least favorite thing. Criminals trying to wreak havoc or kill her friends was generally worse. She retrieved a piece of chocolate out of her desk drawer and popped it in her mouth. One unexpected side benefit of moonlighting for the FBI was that it gave her a healthy dose of perspective. Thinking of her work with the FBI was a good reminder that she needed to check in with Alexis after work today. She had been in PT longer than expected. Alexis liked being benched about as much as she liked having fire ants in her shoes while running one of her half marathons. Maybe she should call Alexis now. Ree looked towards her cellphone and tapped a finger against her desk. Procrastination was tempting, but it wouldn't kill Ree to keep working on the applications. And the more time she spent on them now, the sooner she'd be done with them.

"Ree, if you sigh any louder, you're going scare away the undergrads," Dr. Matt Brown, her fellow professor and friend, quipped. Because of funding limitations, too common at a public university, Ree had been moved to the propulsion lab to work with Matt. Instead of the pissing match she'd expected, Matt had been nothing but nice to her. She'd come to enjoy the work almost as much as her previous job in automotive safety engineering. It didn't hurt that she genuinely loved learning new things, and her coworkers were great to work with. The professor who ran the lab was an old friend, and Matt was so welcoming, she'd fit in seamlessly within a few weeks. Neither would ever suspect she was moonlighting for the FBI. Or that her "writer" boyfriend was a special agent. They'd been so understanding about her family emergencies and last-minute conferences that she felt a little guilty her excuses to miss work were entirely fabricated.

"Really, Matt, they moved me to this lab because it made financial sense and now I have to ask for more money?"

"You're more likely to get grants approved here than in your last job. The logic still holds. It's just not that easy to get away from all of us. But nice try." Matt grinned and tapped his pencil against his desk.

Ree raised her eyebrows. "Your punishment, Dr. Brown, for not letting me wallow in peace is that you're going to review this proposal."

Matt laughed. "Seems fair. You're reviewing my next one, though."

Ree wrinkled her nose. She found the place where she'd left off just as her phone rang. Parker's picture flashed on the screen. He didn't call her during the workday unless it was important. "Saved by Parker." She wiggled it in the air and stepped into the hallway for some measure of privacy. Once she was alone, Ree answered. "Hey, babe."

"Hey." Parker's voice was clipped and just a little annoyed. It was definitely FBI business. "Look, Sandy wants to bring you in again."

"Even after…" Ree looked right, then left. The hallway was empty, but she still didn't want to verbalize it.

"Ree, you made a call. You were cleared. The only one that blames you is you."

"I love you, you know that?"

"I hope so. So the bad news is, we need you next week. Can you get away?" Ree closed her eyes to think. Her teaching schedule was light this summer, but her colleagues would still have questions. She tapped her finger against her lips. Parker mistook her processing the question for hesitation. "If it helps, we're going south this time. You might even get to see a beach."

"It helps a little. How long do you need me?" Ree checked the hallway one more time. She didn't see anyone else, but it still wasn't worth the risk of going into more detail.

"A week or so if you can swing it. Can you hop on a flight to D.C. Monday morning? We'll leave for Florida after meeting up with some friends. Like I said, our friends in Washington are eager to get us in place."

"Wow, you weren't kidding."

"Yeah, this one's big." Parker was prone to understatement, so this investigation promised to be interesting.

"I'll see if Matt can cover my classes next week, but I can probably make it work. Looking forward to helping you guys out."

"Yeah, I was afraid of that." Ree grinned at Parker's discomfort. Now she just had to try to focus on her grant proposal instead of thinking of all the reasons the government wanted to fly her to Florida.

8

Cam leaned against the countertop in his small kitchen. He sipped a cup of coffee from a plain ceramic mug and flipped through his surveillance plans, making notes where necessary. Quinn didn't start her new job until Monday, but he needed to have a strategy and the right equipment in place. The morning light had just begun peeking through the windows, and his new neighbor was already making noise next door. He opened the door that separated their two halves of the building and was pleasantly surprised to find her side open as well. Since she was extending an olive branch, he could do the same. Cam grabbed an extra mug from the cabinet and poured her a cup of coffee in the name of operational harmony. He knocked on the open door and found her on the couch, staring intently at an open three-ring binder with her brown hair pulled up in a messy bun. As he got closer, he saw the pages were filled with equations and diagrams. Once he was in front of her, Quinn looked up and blinked a few times. Her eyes brightened at the sight of the coffee. "Bless you." She looked at his face and grimaced. "Oh man, you still look terrible."

Cam raised an eyebrow. "Yeah, I had a misunderstanding with the wrong person. Remind me not to piss her off in the future." His lip was still a little swollen, and he'd noted that the bruise below his eye had turned a new shade of purple when he saw it in the mirror that morning. Quinn really packed a punch. Impressive, considering he had several inches and about fifty pounds on her.

"I'm really sorry about that. Well, I'm not sorry for defending myself. But I am sorry you got a black eye in the process."

"And a fat lip." Cam grinned and winced when he pulled his sore lip tight.

Quinn sniffed at the coffee. "Should I be worried this is laced with something? A tranquilizer, maybe?"

"Nah. I'm impressed. You've got a mean head butt."

Quinn took a sip of coffee and sighed in satisfaction. "Thanks. Really."

Before Cam could reply, his tablet started ringing. He placed his coffee on Quinn's kitchen table and jogged into his side of the condo to get it. He brought it back while the secure video feed connected. "Morgan, please tell me you have an update."

"Yes, but you're not going to like it. First, I want to hear what happened with Falcon. Your report was a little light on details, and Dan didn't know much more than I did." Morgan narrowed her eyes. "Whoa. I thought you said you only ran into Falcon. Did someone attack you both? You need to put this kind of thing in your updates, Cameron. I have to understand the situation on the ground to get you the help you need."

Cam cleared his throat and scratched his nose with his thumb. "Yeah. About that. As I said in my message, Falcon was working as Katarina on the Russia op. She was our source in Moscow. We had a small case of mistaken identity-"

"So, you said in your report. But how did you get a black eye?" She leaned into the screen. "And a split lip?"

"I misinterpreted some signals, cornered her, and Falcon acted in self-defense. We're fine now. No worries." Cam brought the tablet over to the couch where Quinn was sitting. Cam gestured to the tablet to make sure Quinn didn't mind showing her identity to Morgan. She gave a silent nod and he sat down next to her. She held her coffee mug in two hands and bobbed her head at Morgan, whose eyes had gone wide. "Really, Morgan. We just had a misunderstanding. She thought I was going to hurt her, so she acted accordingly. Then we shared baked goods while I iced my face. We're all squared away now."

Morgan's look was pure skepticism. "If you're sure…"

"Unequivocally. What news do you have for us?"

Morgan shook her head and refocused on the notes in front of her. "We got a call from our friend at NASA. They found a part in the satellite assembly that doesn't belong. They don't know what it is, but their eagle-eyed project manager spotted it. The assembly folks have no idea how it got there."

"Is it explosive? Do I need to go check it out?"

"No. I'm going to send someone else to look into it. That's the part I figured you wouldn't like."

"I thought we were keeping this thing locked down to just Falcon and me."

"We were. But I don't want her going into IRT without you there for backup. Although, it does appear she can handle herself…"

Cam rolled his eyes. Morgan was too focused on the job to give him a lot of hell about it, but she kept looking incredulously at his black eye. In all fairness, it hadn't happened very many times during their acquaintance. "Are you sending anyone I know?"

"Yeah, I thought you wouldn't mind if I reached out to our FBI friends in Chicago. I'll meet with them Monday and then send them down to Florida." Cam smiled. His brother and FBI agent, Parker Mitchell, was getting pulled in. It'd be nice to have another person he trusted on this with Tyler gone.

"You're right, I don't mind at all. Good call. Are they sending the engineer?" Cam referred to Ree Ryland, Parker's girlfriend, full-time science nerd and part-time sharpshooting badass.

"Yes. And the muscle." Mike Moretti was coming too. Good. If anyone had a chance of figuring out why a mysterious part appeared on the satellite, it was those three. Independently, they were impressive. Together, well, he wouldn't bet against them.

"Look, my contingency can jump in if needed." Cam had a buddy he trusted almost as much as his brother who would happily check things out. And he was qualified. Cam usually kept him in the wings, bringing him in as a consultant on sensitive jobs, keeping his name out of the paperwork. There was no such thing as too many contingency plans in his business.

"No need to bring in anyone else right now, Cam. Our Chicago friends have it covered. I'm sending you a picture of the unknown object now. Falcon, when you get into IRT, keep your eyes peeled for anything like this. We'll wait until you are settled in to investigate the component down at NASA Kennedy. That way, you have a fighting chance to see if there is any blowback at IRT. Let Dan or me know immediately if you see anything on the ground when you start work."

"Of course, ma'am."

"Oh, and Falcon?" Cam handed the tablet to Quinn and walked to the table to retrieve his coffee.

"Ma'am?"

"This better be the last time you punch one of my people in the face. You get exactly one chance to call it an accident."

"Yes, ma'am." Quinn's eyes went wide.

"For the record, it was a head butt," Cam yelled from across the room with a cheeky grin. He retrieved the tablet from Quinn. "We're all set here. Just get the FBI down to Florida to take a closer look at that part, and we'll go from there."

9

WHEN HER FIRST DAY AT WORK FINALLY ARRIVED, QUINN WOKE UP early. She communicated her plans to Cam, got all of the surveillance equipment he wanted her to wear in place, and drove to the expansive grounds of IRT. Cam would be close, but not on company property. It was no trouble for the communications equipment to reach that far, but the physical distance meant she was going in without help close by if there was a true emergency.

Quinn had passed the weekend buried under equations, neatly organized and translated into plain English in her thick three-ring binder. By Sunday evening, the pages had been folded over, marked up, and tabbed with small sticky notes. It was a wonder her highlighter hadn't run dry. However, each day gave her a little more confidence that she could make this work. While she wrote out long derivations of equations and solved practice problems on green engineering paper, Cam checked and double-checked their surveillance equipment and read through analyst reports. After a call to headquarters, he swapped out his oversized truck for a van that could house their video surveillance equipment. The tension of their early meeting hadn't broken completely, but their focus on preparing for Quinn's first day of work kept their weekend more low-key than expected. Cam's black eye had begun to fade from a purple-blue to more of a faint greenish-blue.

Quinn parked the car and scanned the horizon for threats, but saw only mountains. She ran a hand over her skirt. Given the security measures at the front door, Quinn had to resort to a non-metallic weapon the CIA had designed. It wasn't quite as sharp as a metal knife, but they'd used a neat composite material that could hold a sharp edge and would be a lot better than nothing in a pinch. Her loose skirt would give her easy access to the knife if she needed it in a hurry. Her shirt was a silky button-up that she'd complimented with a white pearl necklace and trendy glasses. Quinn adjusted her large purse on her arm. It was outfitted with a surveillance camera and filled with all of the things she supposed women typically took to work. She smiled politely at her new colleagues as she entered.

"Quinn! So good to see you again." Ben met her at the door with a hearty handshake. "I'm so glad you could start with us so quickly. All of our experienced folks are working on the next launch, and we'll take all the help we can get. Let's get you introduced to the team, and then you can get started."

Quinn stared at Ben's back on the way into the building. His eyes seemed kind, but spies were chosen for their professions because they were good at playing a role. Ben had been with the company for five years. Even a sociopath would struggle to hide their true nature for that length of time. She would find out soon enough what his people thought of him.

Ben directed her to an area of cubicles, and the men and women sitting in them turned to greet her. After introductions were made, he led her to a desk with a stack of paper nearly eight inches high. She eyed it incredulously.

"Sorry, Quinn, but your computer login isn't quite ready yet. Since we got you in the door so quickly, we're waiting on security to approve your access to our systems. In the meantime, we'll have you focus on our training materials. As you can see, this should keep you busy for the next few days." Ben apologized for the brevity of the introduction and left for his next meeting.

Quinn turned to make small talk with her new colleagues, but they were already back to work, staring intently at their computer screens. While the lobby had been all pleasantries and futuristic décor, the tension was palpable in the cube farm. She considered asking what was going on, but it was too soon. She sighed and pulled the first training document off the top of the pile.

SHORTLY AFTER BEN HALL left his eager new recruit to her mountain of paperwork, he settled into his seat in the IRT auditorium for a managers-only counterespionage training. He scratched the back of his left hand with his right while he waited for the presenter to begin. While a counterespionage training wasn't particularly unusual in a business that routinely sent top-secret government projects into orbit, this was the second one in six months, with new content. His management hadn't told him anything specific, which meant whatever was happening probably didn't involve his team. Still, he had to attend the trainings that told him to keep doing what he always did. So, that was helpful. He managed not to roll his eyes before they got started.

In addition to whatever corporate was dealing with, his team had really been under the gun lately. While the IRT failure investigation team had publicly announced that a bad part was responsible for the rocket that had exploded, they hadn't been able to fully rule out the flight path chosen by the real-time launch control software. His team's software. And one of his best people had goofed up the part of the code that sent error messages during launch.

Since the failure investigation report came out, everyone had been pulling long hours, reviewing the calculations and code they'd developed from scratch as if they'd never seen it before. Just in case they had a bigger problem than the error messages. Ben rolled his neck. His newest employee, Quinn, seemed competent and excited about the future, qualities his team desperately needed right now. He'd called her references the hour after she'd left her interview. They'd heaped praises upon her skillset and attitude. He offered her the job before someone else snapped her up. Hopefully, her positive attitude would be as contagious as the frustration and disappointment that had permeated his team since they'd lost the last rocket.

The presenter tapped the microphone and cleared her throat. She flipped through a bunch of PowerPoint slides and sounded only slightly less bored than he was. The training was nothing new – just the typical "if you see something, say something" crap. When the training ended, Ben followed the swarm of his coworkers out into the hallway. Well, that was an hour of his life he'd never get back.

Once outside the training room, Ben waffled between checking on Quinn and reviewing the reports that demanded his attention. Most of his people were probably hunkered down in their cubicles, working through the intricacies of all possible launch windows and flight paths. Of course, the rocket would only launch if the internal failure investigation team felt like there was no risk of another issue. While IRT was insured for their financial losses, the company didn't need the reputational loss of losing two rockets in a row. You couldn't just order up another satellite if a launch went sideways. Ben rubbed his neck and stared into space until he felt an elbow nudge his arm.

Most of his team kept to themselves. Only one person would figuratively and literally nudge him into action. "Hey, Hannah," he said without turning to face her.

"Ben, you know that creeps me out." He could hear the smile in her voice. "You step in a puddle of glue? You haven't moved since I spotted you at the end of the hallway."

"No, I was just thinking through a problem and my brain froze. You know how it goes." He turned to greet her.

"I probably wouldn't." Hannah grinned. She was their librarian, technical writer, all-in-one jargon-to-English translator. She regularly sold herself short but was always willing to lend a hand, even if it was something as simple as scanning a document.

"I doubt that. Regardless, you're used to us getting hung up on our own problems."

"Listen, you guys are going to come out of this okay. I'm sure of it. In any case, I hope you get unstuck."

Inspiration struck and Ben gestured for Hannah to move to the side of the hallway. "Hey, Hannah?"

"Hey, Ben?" Hannah raised an eyebrow. It wasn't that they weren't friendly, but Ben was usually so busy with his work he wasn't known for chit-chat.

"I've got a new employee that started today. I wonder if you wouldn't mind showing her the ropes a little?"

"Sure, I'd be happy to show her around."

"You're so good at connecting with people, Hannah. We appreciate having you here."

"Don't oversell it, Ben. I said I'd do it."

"You're the best, Hannah." She gave him a small salute. Hannah was the perfect person to make Quinn feel at home. And Ben wouldn't have to deal with all the touchy-feely stuff so he could focus on getting the government's newest satellite into orbit, on time and in one piece. Two birds, one stone.

AFTER A WEEKEND of playing nice with his new teammate, Cam got to spend his first day of real operations work sitting on his butt in the back of a van. Every few minutes, he'd get up and do some squats or push-ups to pass the time and to keep his legs from getting stiff. So far, Quinn's job consisted of reading training materials at her cube while generally being ignored by the other engineers. For the last three hours. Cam rubbed a hand down his face. Well, when the CIA had created an elaborate lie to get her into the job, no one expected an instant payoff. That only happened in the movies. Still, just in case things moved quickly, he kept a close eye on her surroundings, thanks to one camera in her glasses and another in the handbag she'd carefully positioned next to her desk. Quinn had made the requisite effort of small talk at the coffee pot shortly after arriving, but her fellow employees were hyper-focused on the next launch. This team was responsible for the software that would determine the path the rocket would take, from the time it left the launchpad to the moment the satellite was delivered into the correct orbit. The team's fear of failure was evident from their body language when they talked to her or one another. Tense shoulders, very little casual conversation. Their behavior was odd at best – he'd thought it was a bad part that made the last rocket explode.

"Hey, Falcon. See if you can figure out why they're all so upset. I thought this team was just the GPS."

The video feed on her glasses moved up, then down. She'd heard him. Cam tapped his finger against his leg and cracked his neck. Working in the surveillance van was so much worse than slipping into an alias and getting the job done personally. He saw a few more people milling around behind her and wrote down their names and the time, matching them to a list of employee photos Morgan had provided. It probably wouldn't accomplish much, but it made him feel moderately useful. An hour later, he realized Quinn was skimming her finger along words, blocking out certain letters in order to make a sentence: "Having fun?"

Cam chuckled. "Oh, yes. This is what I said in my CIA application. Please, Uncle Sam, let me watch someone else read training documents. It's all I've ever dreamed of." The feed jiggled a little as Quinn snickered. A woman approached Quinn from about ten yards behind her. "You have company."

Once the woman got close and tapped on Quinn's cube wall, Quinn turned to greet her. Cam checked his notes and confirmed that it was Hannah Jenkins, the technical writer. Trendy outfit, smart glasses, friendly smile. According to Rory's notes, Hannah was the self-appointed head of social activities for their team. They'd spoken several times at trivia night.

"Hi, you must be the new engineer. I'm Hannah. I'm a technical writer and I help support your team." Hannah stuck out a hand and Quinn shook it.

"Hi, Hannah! It's great to meet you. I'm Quinn Givens. I'm so excited to be here." The tone of Quinn's voice was pure sunshine and light. It was different enough from their interactions that he had to bite back a laugh. Well, at least she didn't feel like she needed to put on an act around him.

"Wait, I think I've seen you before. You were at trivia night last week, right?" Shit. Cam tensed. She'd seen him, too. He leaned closer to the monitor.

"I was. I came for a drink after my interview – I didn't realize there would be so many IRT employees there! It's a good thing I didn't embarrass myself."

Hannah leaned forward, conspiratorially, "You met Chris from accounting. He was totally smitten with you. He came to hang out with us after he struck out and you left with someone. And I didn't know you'd be working with us! I would have introduced myself."

The video feed went perfectly still, but only for a moment. "Oh, dear. I was just being friendly. I hope he understands."

"Of course. You were just being nice. He was hoping for more, hence the reason he came over to our table to mope. But if he starts coming down to chat and you don't want him to, I'll let him know you have a boyfriend."

"Thanks, but Cam's not my boyfriend. He's an old friend from college and we left to catch up. It was too loud to talk in the bar."

Hannah winked. "If that's what the kids are calling it these days."

"No, really. Cam and I would never work. Most of the time, I don't know whether to hug him or kill him." Cam laughed out loud, hoping it'd release the tension Quinn was probably feeling. That part of her explanation could very likely be genuine.

"Well, let's not have you killing anyone your first week. Pretty sure that'll get you fired. Maybe that part of the training is somewhere towards the bottom of the pile?" Hannah grinned. "How about I show you around? My guess is your overachieving coworkers are hunkered down, hoping if they study hard enough, they'll pass the next test. They probably forgot all about making the new kid feel welcome."

"I completely understand. And I'd love a tour, if you're offering." Quinn rose to follow Hannah, and Cam got his first look into the IRT facility.

10

AFTER MAKING ARRANGEMENTS FOR HER IMPROMPTU VACATION FROM her real job, Ree took a quick flight into Washington Dulles late Monday morning. The boys would be meeting her in D.C., which let her squeeze in some grading before she left. She'd even managed to edit a couple of research papers on the flight so she could enjoy her time with Parker, whenever they weren't doing work for the FBI. Once the plane landed, Ree hoisted her carry-on bag onto her shoulder and walked up the jet bridge. She passed through the door that led to the terminal and spied Parker leaning casually against a wall. Mike stood just past him, arms crossed, watching his surroundings. Parker spotted her and his eyes lit up. Ree grinned and made a beeline for the two men. She shook Mike's hand and greeted Parker with a hug, pulling him close. She took a moment to appreciate his warmth and breathed in the smell of his cologne. Since they had an audience, she reluctantly left it at a hug and the three sometimes-partners walked to the car.

Parker sat in the backseat with Ree and she reached for his hand. "Where are we going?"

"Langley."

Ree turned to face him. "What are we doing for the CIA?"

Parker shrugged. "Don't know yet. Sandy's explanation was pretty light on details. We'll find out when we get there." Ree settled back against her seat. She had just seen Cam at a family dinner a few weeks prior, and he'd given no indication he needed their help. It was odd that he'd bring them all the way to D.C. to talk. For the rest of the trip, they made small talk, but a part of Ree's brain kept speculating about what Cam would be asking of them. What would require a separate flight to meet at the CIA building instead of a phone call?

They reached the gates and showed ID. Mike parked the car and the team entered the building. Ree placed her purse on the scanner and once again provided her ID. While her work for the FBI had been unusual thus far, walking over the large, granite CIA seal embedded into the floor tile in the lobby felt like something else entirely. After they passed through security, they were escorted by an armed guard through a number of hallways to a small waiting area. There was a nameplate outside the office that read "Morgan Grady." Ree raised an eyebrow. "Is Cam…okay?"

Before Parker could answer, the door to the office opened. A compact woman with short hair and a no-nonsense expression waved them in. Once they were inside, she closed the door and handshakes were exchanged. "Hi, I'm Morgan." She looked up at Mike's towering frame, "You must be Mike. Don't worry, I know you're more than just the muscle. And Parker, we're going to need your quick thinking for the undercover bit of this. Dr. Ryland, thank you for coming – we appreciate you lending your expertise on this one. Also, please allow me to thank you all for the assist on our last operation. It's very nice to finally meet everyone in person."

Morgan gestured for them to take a seat. Her office was neat and purpose-built. The furniture was a long way from fussy. Ree sat and began to tap her thumb on her knee. "Ma'am, I'm happy to do what I can, but don't you have a whole building full of people more prepared than I am to help? What's going on?"

Morgan folded her hands on her desk. "Great question, Dr. Ryland. We've had an unfortunate incident, and we're being very careful about who we bring onto this operation."

Mike narrowed his eyes and rested his elbows on his knees. "Define unfortunate."

"An operations officer was killed on American soil, Agent Moretti. Cam and a fellow operations officer are investigating the incident at an up-and-coming rocket design company in Victoria, Washington."

"They're at IRT?" Ree leaned forward. IRT's rockets were cutting edge and many of her students drooled at the mere idea of working for them. They'd been wildly successful, particularly in light of the number of critics who believed that what they were doing couldn't be done.

Morgan nodded approvingly. "Yes. Although I'd appreciate if you treat that information as top secret. One of their rockets blew up shortly after liftoff recently. We sent an operations officer to investigate because some things weren't adding up. The house she was staying in exploded. Cam and his partner are trying to figure out why."

"Holy shit." Mike leaned back in his chair. "What do you need from us?"

Morgan handed them each a file. "Someone at NASA found an extra part on the satellite that an IRT rocket will be launching very soon. Under the circumstances, I'd like for you to get a closer look at it. Our source doesn't believe it's explosive, but we'll give you some equipment to confirm that assessment."

Parker crossed his arms. "And you reached out to the FBI. Which means you think someone in the Agency blew your officer's cover."

Morgan nodded. "I'm hoping to be proven wrong, Agent Mitchell. Certainly, she could have been made without internal help. However, I've been forced to consider the possibility that our operations officer walked into some sort of trap. Cam is aware of the risks. Until we find our killer, I want a team whose loyalty is unquestioned. And a team that knows what they're getting into."

Parker narrowed his eyes. "You didn't just want FBI. You wanted Cam's brother and his team."

"I won't lie. It was a factor. It helps that you guys are excellent. I'd be hard-pressed to find people more equipped for the job. If you want out, let me know. I'll walk you out, ask you not to share this information with anyone, and you can go on to your next investigation. However, if you're willing to help, I'd like to debrief you further."

Ree raised an eyebrow. "Just so I'm clear, you are asking me to fly with these guys to Kennedy Space Center, look inside a rocket and troubleshoot what might go wrong?"

"Very likely, yes, Dr. Ryland. We'll start you on the satellite, but it could also involve IRT's equipment. I understand you are a civilian and you aren't–"

"I'm in. When do we leave?"

Parker laughed. "Ree, she said you have to get debriefed first."

"So, tonight? I mean, how long does it take to get debriefed?" Ree grinned. "IRT is the company version of a celebrity in my world. And, I get to help make sure their next rocket launches without issue? Come on. That's awesome."

Mike looked at Morgan. "I think what Ree's saying is, we're in."

Morgan smiled and gestured for them to open their folders. An 8x10 photo of a neat, well-ordered assembly was inside. Without knowing what it was supposed to look like, it was hard to tell why they had a problem. A box was circled on the photo, but that didn't tell her much. Ree looked up from the photo at Morgan. "Do you have any additional explanation of what I'm looking at? It's hard to tell what the box could do to the satellite, just from the picture."

"I'm going to have you meet with Alan Smith. He'll be able to answer any questions you have. Then, we'll need you to assess what the box might contain before they remove it. We have some tools you can use to test the contents."

Mike grinned. "You're gonna let us play with CIA toys? You *are* worried."

"You could say that. I'm not sure what this is or if it could even take down a rocket. That's what I need you guys to find out." She handed them a full backpack. "Everything else you need is in here, along with the secure tablet you'll use to get in touch with me. And Cam."

"You got it, ma'am. We'll do what we can." Parker pulled the backpack off the desk.

"Stay safe out there. Sandy will kill me if one of you gets hurt again."

. . .

THREE HOURS LATER, Parker and his team were on an evening flight to Orlando, and Ree was practically bouncing in her seat. Mike was out cold and Parker opened one eye to look at the woman he loved. "You need to get some sleep."

Ree reached for his hand. "I know." She leaned closer and whispered, "But, do you realize, I get to see everything I never get to see, up close. Do my part to make it work? This is a dream come true."

Parker raised an eyebrow. "Don't you do stuff like this every day?"

"I usually only get to play with small scale experiments. This is the real deal. There are some...drawbacks to this assignment, but how often to you get to look under the hood of something like this? Oh man, it's a good thing we can't tell Alexis what's going on. She would be so jealous." Despite the late hour, Ree's eyes were bright.

Parker gave her a kiss on the cheek, squeezed her hand. Alexis was always up for fieldwork, but it was hard to imagine her being more enthusiastic than Ree about this one. He'd let her hang onto her excitement a little longer. While her engineer brain was likely imagining the design of the rocket and satellite components that she'd get to see up close, he was working through how he would counteract the potential danger. Unlike her last investigation, Ree actually worked in the propulsion field and might be recognized. He pulled Morgan aside after their debrief to mention it, and they'd scheduled a phone call for tomorrow morning to work out a plan. Going in without one wasn't an option. Worse, if this was in any way connected to the officer's death that Cam was investigating, getting caught in a lie would be an even bigger problem than usual.

11

After a less than fruitful first day at IRT, Quinn returned to her condo to retrieve her running clothes out of her temporary dresser. Before she met with Cam for their evening meeting, she needed to burn off some energy. While these types of operations usually took time – months, or even years, if it was really ugly – it didn't make it any easier to deal with the strain of waiting until the right moment to dig for the truth. Their condo complex had a small gym, which would give her some alone time to process her day before regrouping with her new partner. Ideally, she'd set up some workout equipment in the spare room in her place, but she hadn't gotten around to it yet. And she still had enough optimism to hope that it wouldn't be necessary to settle in for the long term. Quinn jogged to the gym and spotted the treadmills. Fortunately, they faced the door, and she could work out some of the stress that had taken up residence in her neck without checking over her shoulder every ten seconds.

There had been no hint of a specific issue with the upcoming launch around the watercooler today, but there had been a lot of unspoken tension. Her coworkers either didn't trust her enough to tell her, or they didn't know that NASA found a problem with the satellite. While the part Morgan had called them about could be a simple case of an employee making a mistake, under the circumstances, it was more likely that someone was trying to sabotage IRT's next launch. And if there was a saboteur involved, there was a non-zero possibility that they had done something to the last one too. But what was the motive? Competitors had a vested interest in making sure IRT's rocket didn't fly. Another country was a strong contender as well, since a government satellite was going for a ride on this thing, and that was where NASA found the mystery box.

As tempting as it was to get on a plane to Florida to help investigate the new lead, someone at the IRT facility was involved in this, or Rory wouldn't have been caught in the middle. It would just take time for Quinn to build trust with her new coworkers. The engineering profession attracted a fair number of introverts, and the only way to get to know an introvert was one sentence at a time. The next launch would go up in a couple of weeks. She had been assigned to review her coworkers' calculations so she'd be ready to help with the following launch, a more advanced test flight of the rocket that would send astronauts into space. She could do the job, thanks to her background and prep work, which helped pass the time. The pre-launch preparation stage of a project was a tough time to make small talk.

The door to the gym opened, and Cam looked briefly surprised to see her before nodding at her and getting on the treadmill next to hers. He set his pace to a half a mile an hour faster than hers, and she narrowed her eyes before upping her speed to match his. He had the nerve to laugh and the game was on. Over an hour later, neither had stopped running and Quinn's legs were burning. She'd done a strength workout the day before and shouldn't be pushing herself so hard, but she wasn't going to be the one to quit first. Mercifully, Cam began his cool down and Quinn slowed down to 0.1 miles an hour faster than him. She hadn't come to the gym to get in a competition, but she wasn't about to lose one.

A few minutes later, Cam got off the treadmill and pulled his foot up behind him in a quad stretch. When she stopped her treadmill and joined him, he raised an eyebrow. "How much longer would you have run?"

Quinn flicked a bead of sweat off of her nose with her thumb and put her hands on her hips. "As long as it took."

Cam barked out a laugh. "I have a feeling you are going to be an interesting partner, Q." Before Quinn could retort, he raised a hand. "Give me half an hour to shower and meet me at my place. I'll order a pizza. After that run, I think we'll both need it."

CAM GOT into the shower and let the water flow through his hair. He hadn't planned on running so far tonight, but Quinn had surprised him. She was competitive. The look on her face when he went a little faster than her was priceless. Like him, she preferred to keep others out of her operations until she had a firm handle on how they needed to be run. Really, they were more alike than they were different. He chuckled. Learning to be adaptable would be good for them both.

Cam flicked off the shower and pulled on some comfortable pants. He dried his leg well and reattached his prosthetic. While it was technically waterproof, it felt nice to pull it off every now and again. It was more comfortable than the first one he'd been given, that was for sure. When Morgan recruited him to the CIA, he'd worked with a design team to make a custom prosthetic that could stand up to the rigors of his job. And it was flexible enough to use every day, even when he wanted to go for a run. They'd broken a few before they'd gotten the design right, but the technology he'd helped develop could now be used to help other wounded servicemen and women.

The doorbell rang and Cam paid for their pizza. He dropped the pizza on the kitchen table, pulled a couple of light beers out of the fridge and an ice pack out of the freezer. He propped his foot up on the coffee table and dropped the ice pack on the spot under his knee where the artificial limb attached to his leg. The cold felt good and would also minimize the chance of swelling. Shortly after he took his first bite of pizza, Quinn slipped through their shared door with two bowls of salad in hand. She was wearing athletic clothes and her wet hair was up in a ponytail. She thanked him for the pizza and beer. Cam accepted the salad gratefully and took a bite. Once he swallowed, he said, "Thanks for this. So, what's are your first impressions?"

"Well, you saw what I saw. A lot of formality and people keeping to themselves. A lot of tension I didn't fully understand. I wanted to attribute it to the failed launch, but this team just determines the flight path – they don't choose the mechanical components. I didn't want to overplay my hand, so I waited for people to talk. No one brought up anything that raised any red flags. Maybe because I was the new kid."

"Did you think anyone was overly friendly or overly hostile?"

"No hostility, but I think Ben asked Hannah – she's the technical writer that Rory met – to keep an eye on me. She was around a lot today. I get the impression that she's the designated trainer for new hires. She knows just about every scientist and engineer that even walks by our department. She would be a good source of information if I can gain her trust."

"Technical writer? What does that even mean?"

"She's in charge of translating all of the technical jargon into government-approved reports."

"Oh? So she has a lot of access, then?"

"Yeah. I'm going to mention her in my email to Dan, but I'm sure she's already undergone a pretty thorough background check. With her level of access, she's got to be in a government system somewhere. Dan also mentioned the CIA has a few contacts on the inside. It's possible she's one of them."

"But he doesn't want you to know who they are?"

"No." Quinn's voice was tight. She didn't agree with the call. Interesting. Cam decided to push.

"Why?"

"He said it was compartmentalized 'for a reason.'"

"And you didn't question that?"

Quinn's nostrils flared and she set her mouth in a line. "No. I didn't have to. Dan thinks this might have been an inside job. I think he's afraid I'll act differently if I meet one of them."

"Didn't realize Dan had already jumped there." Cam rubbed the back of his neck. He and Morgan harbored suspicions, but finding out the Director did too didn't help. This was why the CIA was so careful about the spread of information. You never knew the motives of the person receiving it.

"Yeah. Why do you think I didn't want you involved?"

"Because you're a control freak?" Cam grinned and Quinn laughed.

"That may be true. But I also didn't want a target on anyone else's back."

"It wouldn't be the first time I had a target on my back." Cam lifted his pant leg, showing Quinn the prosthetic attached to his leg. It had been covered by the long pants he wore to the gym. "I appreciate you trying to protect everyone else around you. Here's the thing, though. I lost everything under the knee in Iraq, Quinn. Could have lost my life. I'm lucky I didn't. My buddy dragged me to safety and almost got killed in the process. I figure I'm living on borrowed time. I plan to make the most of it."

Quinn's mouth dropped open. It wasn't the first time someone had been surprised by his leg, but her disbelief was especially understandable, since he'd met her step for step on the treadmill. Yes, he had to endure pain, but he'd also put in a lot of hard work developing the new limb. It was more versatile than its off-the-shelf counterpart and almost as good as his real leg. He was proud of what he'd accomplished. She swallowed hard. "Understood."

"I'm on your team, Quinn."

"I know, Cam." Cam reached towards Quinn's back and she had the decency to look embarrassed. She leaned forward, pulled the sheathed knife out of the small of her back, and placed it on the table. Quinn raised both hands in the air. "Look, I'm used to being cautious."

Cam raised an eyebrow. Nice to know his instincts hadn't been dulled by sitting in a surveillance van all day. The knife had likely been digging into her back for the last five minutes. She'd probably brought it in the other times, but she'd worn skirts then. A knife was a lot more comfortable strapped to your leg.

Quinn cleared her throat. "So, if our bosses are worried about this being an inside job, who are the FBI folks she called in from Chicago?"

"Some people we know well. I did some work with them a few months ago."

"You trust them?"

"With my life. For reasons I'd rather not get into right now." Just because Quinn was softening up didn't mean she needed to know his family was involved. She wasn't the only one who protected what mattered.

"Okay. Well, I'll keep trying to win over the engineers, and we'll see what your friends in the FBI come up with. Then once we figure out where we guessed wrong, we'll adapt."

"Sounds like a plan."

12

Ree watched the palm trees through the car window as Mike drove the team to Kennedy Space Center. She had to bite her lip to keep the smile off of her face. Particularly once she found out they'd be working in the historic and gigantic Vehicle Assembly Building. Giddy excitement overshadowed her nerves – the rockets that sent men to the moon had been assembled in that building. Of course, there was an element of danger. Parker and Mike had already mentioned it over breakfast this morning. She didn't need the reminder, any more than she needed to hit her thumb with a hammer to know that it would hurt. She didn't go into FBI investigations thinking it was as safe as watching a movie on her couch. However, her team had always had her back. Parker spent fifteen minutes talking with Morgan about security before they'd even left the hotel room.

Morgan and Parker had concluded it'd be best for Ree to go in as herself under false pretenses, and she agreed. It was a solid plan. It was infinitely better than lying about who she was and getting caught by people who ran around in the same professional circles she did. She wouldn't broadcast her presence, and if any of her coworkers found out she was at NASA, she'd claim she was there assisting on a research project. Which meant she could ask real questions instead of playing dumb around the area of her expertise.

Ree's heart began to pound when they took the turn labeled for employees instead of the road that led to the large visitor's complex and museum. It was really happening. After they showed ID to the guard and passed through the security gate, Ree's phone rang.

When she saw Alexis's name on the screen, Ree answered on speaker. "Alex! How are you?"

"Good. Hey, I heard from Sandy that you guys are out working on something for Morgan. I wanted to let you know Jordan and I are on call if you need anything. Just say the word."

Jordan Sykes was their local computer expert, and if something needed to be found online, no one would find it faster than him. Even better, if someone needed access to a locked system, he usually found a way to make that happen too.

"Thanks. Are you cleared for that?"

"No," Mike answered from the driver's seat. "Aren't you supposed to be doing PT this morning, Agent Thompson?"

"I already went this morning, Moretti. I think my physical therapist was a drill sergeant in her past life. I just wanted to let you know I'm here if you need me." Her voice was a little flatter than usual. She didn't handle being benched well.

"I appreciate it, Alex. How's the arm?"

Alexis sighed. "Getting better. Slower than I'd like, but my doctor doesn't think the damage will be permanent. I'm in PT three days a week still, though. It isn't pretty, but they think I'll be back up to speed in a few months."

Ree took the call off speaker. "Hey, it's just me now. Are you okay? I mean, really, okay?" Alexis was great at taking care of everyone else, but like a lot of people good at taking care of others, she tended to put herself last.

"Honestly, I'm struggling. Jordan suggested I go spend some time with the canine unit. Apparently, they need some help training new pups. I think he's just tired of me hanging around his desk complaining about being stuck doing paperwork. He's trying to cheer me up. He spends a lot of time on the internet. Cute animals are his go-to."

"Yeah, but how long have you talked about wanting a dog? I'm with Jordan on this one. Hanging out with a bunch of puppies in training is exactly what you need. So much adorable you won't even think about us. Otherwise, you're going to check in to see if you can help like once a day. And unless Morgan allows it, you know we're not going to be able to tell you anything. I'm onto you, friend. You don't idle well."

Alexis laughed. "Guilty as charged. Alright, I'll give it a try. But seriously-"

"I know, I know. If we need help, you're the first person we'll call."

"Perfect. Hey, Ree. I know you're excited, but be careful. Sandy said you didn't need us to send the normal documents for your alias. I don't know what you're doing, but I'm not 100 percent comfortable with you going somewhere you might be recognized."

"Thanks, Alex. I've got Parker and Mike with me. They'll watch my back. We're here. I have to go. Go teach some police puppies. And I'm going to need pictures. Especially if they are wearing little doggy police vests. But please, wait to send them until the evening. I can't afford the distraction during the day."

"It's a deal. Go get 'em, you guys."

Parker pulled the car into a space outside the massive building. Large enough to house a fully-built rocket right side up, the human-sized entry doors were tiny compared to the rest of the building. He gave each of them a badge attached to a lanyard. "Our first stop is Alan Smith's office. He reported the incident – we'll get what we need directly from him."

Ree raised an eyebrow. "And he knows we're FBI?"

"Officially, no. He's former military – a retired colonel. He made the call to Dan, so he might figure out we're not what we seem. He just won't know the details. Morgan wants to keep that way. What happened back in Washington was pretty nasty, and right now, they're compartmentalizing this pretty hard."

"So, who does he think we are?"

"Alan has been told that we're from NASA's safety investigation team, employing an outside expert to understand why the installation didn't meet specification. Practically, you don't rise to Alan's level unless you're sharp. We're counting on him understanding we're on his side without asking too many questions. We will actually need you to write up a report, by the way."

"I just got finished writing grant applications and I'm writing reports on my days off? Man, I need to negotiate my working conditions a little better. Last time, it was budgets, this time, a safety report."

Mike shrugged. "You're the one who wanted to look at rockets. You didn't ask if there would be homework."

Ree grinned. "I'll make sure I ask next time. In fairness to the CIA, I'm a professor. I should know better than to sign up for a class without checking the syllabus."

With that, two FBI agents and one engineering professor placed their lanyards over their necks and entered the building to pay a visit to Alan Smith. After explaining their purpose to a few curious individuals along the way, they finally found his office. The door was cracked a fraction and a heated argument was happening behind it. Parker raised a hand to stop them before they entered.

A woman's voice said, "Alan, you've got to let me help."

"I called it in, Kiara. We've got three folks from the safety investigation team arriving today to take a look at it. They'll help us figure out what to do next."

"A safety team? They've never seen our satellite. What can they do that I can't? What if that part is damaging the ones next to it while we wait?"

"Kiara. It's metal. It's just sitting there. Unless it's going to explode, your parts will be fine." A silence followed. "It's not going to explode, Kiara."

"We could solve this more quickly if I met with them. I helped design some of these components. I can help."

Parker pulled Ree to the side. "Whoever he's talking to seems worked up. Do you want us to go in first? Deescalate the situation?"

Ree crossed her arms. "Have you ever met a design engineer? Someone messed with her baby. I didn't sound too different when I found out someone was sending missile parts to my lab. C'mon. Let's get in there before she leaves. I think I like her already."

Parker knocked softly on the door, then entered. The woman, Kiara, presumably, spun on a heel to greet them. She was probably in her early thirties. Her black hair was twisted up into a clip and she clutched oversized pieces of paper tightly against her chest.

"Are we interrupting anything?" Parker asked.

Alan waved them in. "No, I was just talking with my project manager, Kiara, about a few technical details. She's in charge of the satellite assembly and attachment to IRT's rocket. She was just leaving." Alan gestured for them to sit and gave Kiara a look. She nodded politely at them, took a moment to appraise them, and left the room.

Once the door closed, Parker crossed the room to shake hands with Alan. "It's nice to meet you, Colonel. I'm Parker Landon, with the safety investigation team. This is my associate, Mike Riley. We've asked Dr. Ree Ryland to help us with our investigation as well. She's a professor at Indiana Polytechnic with expertise in this area."

"This work is considered top secret. Is Dr. Ryland cleared for this?"

"She is. We have a small set of outside experts with clearance, although we don't advertise who they are, and we only bring them in when absolutely necessary. For the obvious reasons. Any time there is a potential safety issue, we bring in someone from the outside for an objective point of view. Standard protocol." Parker's tone was confident, but he managed to look a little bored – one benefit of working for the government was his fluency in bureaucratic-speak. Parker pulled out a notebook. "So, can you tell us what you know? Have you figured out who installed the box? And why?"

Alan shook his head. "I haven't. We're still trying to determine where the breach of protocol occurred. Here are some close-up images I was able to get after most of the crew had left for the day." Alan gave them a set of photos.

"Do you know what might be in the box?" Ree tapped one of the images.

"I'm not sure. It looks like it might be welded to one of the brackets. It's coming straight up off the other parts."

Mike said, "Have you tested it for explosives?"

Alan studied Mike for a moment, then shook his head. "Unofficially, I don't think it's explosive. Technically, I don't have the equipment I would need for a formal evaluation. I checked it with a thermal imaging camera, since I had one in the lab, and nothing lit up. Not surprising. However, when I was getting the images, I found a small wire leading into the communication systems. I disconnected it as a precaution."

Parker nodded. "That's helpful. Thank you. Is it possible the box was placed there on accident?"

"It's possible. We just haven't figured out why someone would think to put it there. They'd have to be doing pretty sloppy work." Alan swallowed hard. "I can get you in the building this evening to take a closer look if you'd like."

"That works." Mike patted his backpack. "We have the tools we need to get some additional information. We'll let you know what we find. And please keep our presence here confidential."

Alan found a spot on the wall to study. "I will ask my people not to mention it. However, I assumed your visit was typical for a situation like this and told my people you were coming. You all seem to have… some additional interests."

Parker crossed his arms. "Let's start by figuring out what's in the thing. Then, we'll see if it's a big deal that everyone knows we're here. We will take you up on your offer to get us in tonight."

Alan nodded. "Of course."

Parker stood and shook Alan's hand. Mike and Ree followed suit and left his office. Ree paused outside the door when Parker didn't follow them. She leaned a little closer to the door to hear their conversation.

Parker said in a low voice, "Colonel, you seem to understand that Mike and I may not be everything we seem. However, Dr. Ryland is a civilian who believes we are only here to investigate the breach of safety protocols on IRT's rocket. Please keep this between us."

"Of course. Understood. Come back at 8 PM this evening, and I'll get you in when there aren't as many people around to ask questions."

13

In his office at IRT, Ben rubbed his temples and resisted the temptation to bang his head against his desk. He was almost ready to leave for the day when an engineer he worked with down at Kennedy Space Center emailed him as a courtesy. A safety team was there today to look at the satellite. Unbelievable that NASA wouldn't at least let him know his launch window could be delayed. Actually, some poor schmuck had probably written a memo that was still making its way through sixteen layers of management before it would ever get to him. He'd have to send one of his people to keep the peace and make sure that the inspector didn't derail his team's progress. He considered sending Chuck since he had the most experience. However, Chuck also had no filter and the cynicism that came from seeing it all before. While he wouldn't trade Chuck for any other engineer to get the job done, he didn't want to start a power struggle with a NASA committee. The last thing they needed was to be in bureaucratic purgatory for so long that they delayed the launch indefinitely. He'd put buffer in the schedule, but government committees ate buffer for breakfast, lunch, and dinner.

Ben closed his eyes for a moment but opened them when he heard someone clearing their throat. Hannah was standing at his desk with

Quinn in tow. "Hey, Ben. I showed the newbie the ropes yesterday and walked her around a little more today. Anything else you want us to cover?"

Ben smiled. Suddenly, he had the answer to his problem. And it didn't even require pulling his experienced people away from their work. "Thanks, Hannah. Really appreciate you making her feel welcome. Nothing comes to mind on that topic, but before you go, I have a favor to ask."

"Of me, or Quinn?"

"Actually, both of you. NASA found a problem on the part of the satellite that attaches to the rocket. Somewhere along the way, someone screwed up. Good news, one of their people spotted it. Bad news, they've called in a committee."

Quinn took a step closer. "That could be a big delay, right?"

"Exactly. Glad you catch on quick. Listen, the last thing my team needs right now is a distraction. But since you're just getting started, what if you went down there for your first project? You have the technical chops to learn as you go, even though it's a little early. I need you to do the shake and howdy with the committee and try and get a sense of what they're looking for. You can report back to me and I'll help direct you if you need it. We really just need to have one of our people show up to let them know we're available for questions, we care, etc. Hannah knows a lot of the people down there. She could go with you, so you aren't totally on your own."

Quinn nodded. "Sure. I could do that."

Hannah threw an arm around Quinn. "And I'll help her find her way around. No problem, boss."

"Thank you. You're both lifesavers."

Quinn smiled. "We're just happy to help."

AFTER MOST OF the crew had left for the day, Ree and her team followed Alan's instructions and suited up to enter the clean environment. They were covered head to toe in protective gear. The getup was actually pretty similar to what she'd worn in Dani's lab the last time she'd moonlighted for the FBI. However, this time, it was to protect the satellite from their lint and dirt instead of protecting them from the bugs in Dani's lab. Ree shivered at the memory. She didn't miss the ominous red biohazard signs that had been ubiquitous at VacTech.

After rereading the instructions from Alan about what they could and could not touch, they entered the cleanroom without him. He was planning on leaving for the evening while they worked – Ree wasn't sure if fear or strategy drove his decision. Her money was on strategy. Alan was a smart man and had already figured out someone on his team was likely involved. He'd called in for backup before anyone got hurt, including him.

Ree entered the cleanroom and swallowed hard when she got close to the satellite sitting in the center of the room. It was gorgeous. The pristine white fairing was close by and ready to install, but was not yet covering it. The satellite was larger than she'd expected and was surrounded by scaffolding and stairs on wheels. It'd be an even more incredible sight once it was attached to the rocket. The rocket itself was larger than the job required, considering it was only sending a satellite into low Earth orbit. However, it was more than the delivery vehicle for whatever secret satellite the U.S. military wanted to deploy – it would also be proof that IRT could safely transport people to the International Space Station or back to the moon someday. Even before jumping in on the investigation, she'd been eagerly following IRT's progress online. It was one more reason Ree was happy to help the FBI troubleshoot – if they fixed it and the launch went well, she would get to be a small part of history.

When they reached the section of the scaffolding near where the satellite would connect to the rocket, they climbed one of the rolling staircases to get a better view. Ree peeked into the assembly and directed their attention to the box she'd seen in Alan's photos. Mike raised a small piece of equipment and pointed it at it. He grunted. Ree peeked over his shoulder at the image displayed on the small screen. "Translation for the rest of us, Mikey?"

"Inconclusive." Mike pulled out a long, thin swab with a bit of foam on the end. He wiped it along the surface of the metal and Ree cringed. Kiara the engineer would have kittens if she saw Mike poking at her equipment with a stick. Even a stick with a soft end. Mike placed the swab inside of a reader and Ree's heart began to pound. They were the only ones in the quiet room. The realization sent an eerie feeling tickling up her back. A heavy metal door slammed and Ree whirled to see where it came from. Parker stepped in front of her, placing himself between her and the source of the noise. The footsteps got louder and Mike's reader beeped. The footsteps stopped cold, then resumed and faded away.

Ree's palms began to sweat underneath her blue gloves. When all was quiet again, she whispered, "Are they gone?"

Parker nodded and Mike held up the reader. "Alan was right. There's no trace of explosives on this. Morgan's equipment is showing there's a circuit board inside with a battery attached to it. What the hell is it supposed to do if it doesn't go boom?"

Ree leaned into the inner workings of the equipment, praying she didn't fall. She didn't need to become infamous for being the professor who smashed part of a multimillion-dollar, top-secret satellite to bits. "Can you hand me the camera?" Ree carefully slid the strap around her arm and took pictures past where the wire was dangling near the box. Mike offered a knee while Parker held her waist so she could lever the camera straight out from her body, facing down into the assembly. Alan had been in a hurry, and the detail on his photos didn't show everything. Since it took three of them to get the camera at the right angle, it was easy to see why he didn't get a good shot.

When she pulled back the camera, she hopped off of Mike's knee and looked at her photos. "Good news, it's not welded. It's clamped on in the back with a bolt. Easy to take off with the right tools. Bad news, since that wire was connected to the communication systems, it's definitely supposed to do something. But what?"

"If you're stumped, I'm stumped." Mike eyed the picture.

Parker studied the photo. "Maybe they're hitching a ride on the main board to do something? Or they could be capturing measurement data? Sending it somewhere?"

Ree tapped her finger against the photo displayed on the back of the camera. "There's no way to know unless we ask Alan." Ree sighed. "I can knock out a fancy report with our findings. If Mike says it won't explode, let's recommend that Alan's team removes it. We can study it at my lab or back at the Chicago office once it's off this thing. I'd pull it off myself, but it's around a bunch of delicate equipment. I'd rather let the overprotective project manager do it so we don't hurt anything else while we're in there. I really don't want to be the one that screws something up."

Parker nodded. "Sounds good. How long will it take you to put the report together?"

"Couple of hours, tops. Let's meet with Alan again tomorrow. We'll get this project back on track in another day or two – or however long it takes his people to fix it. And Mike, you're going to figure out who came in while we were here, right?"

"Yeah. I'll go through the footage. They didn't get close enough to see us, but I'd like to know who turned tail and ran when they realized they weren't in here alone."

Ree smiled. "And we have a plan. That's why I like working with you guys. We'll be on our way back home before you know it."

14

Despite falling asleep at a reasonable time, Quinn snapped awake while her room was still pitch black. She opened one eye to check her phone and winced at the harsh light of the screen. It was only 2 AM. Quinn flopped over onto her side and burrowed deeper into the covers. When sleep didn't come, her brain took the opportunity to start planning her next steps. While it was convenient to be sent to Kennedy Space Center, going with an IRT employee was a complication. Not just any IRT employee, but the one who had suspicions about her and Cam. Despite their rocky start, Quinn was going to have to find a way to bring Cam along for backup. Going alone with an unknown wasn't worth the risk/benefit. If Hannah had seen them their first night on the town, they could go as a couple or at least as an "it's complicated." Quinn rubbed her face. She might be able to bring him in as a consultant…but why would they listen to a new employee about which consultant to hire?

Quinn stared into the blackness of her room, attempting to clear her mind so she could go back to sleep. She really should bounce her ideas off of Cam. But since he wasn't awake at dark o'clock, it would have to wait. When it became clear that her body wasn't going to go back to sleep any time soon, Quinn grumbled and threw the heavy blanket off.

Instead of working through more worst-case scenarios, she padded into the kitchen to inventory the contents of the fridge. Heavy cream, eggs, butter. She could work with that. Everything else she needed for éclairs was in the cabinet.

Quinn pulled a small saucepan out of the cabinet and combined the butter, water, and salt. Before long, she was incorporating flour and eggs into a Pâté à Choux dough that even the hosts of her favorite baking show would approve of. She held the spatula sideways and watched the dough form a neat "V". She efficiently transferred the dough to a freezer bag, cut off a corner of the bag and piped the dough into oblong shapes. She turned on some music and placed the éclairs in the oven to bake. Quinn brought together a chocolate pastry cream filling to the sound of her favorite band, humming as she stirred. As the oven timer beeped, there was a knock on the door that separated her place from Cam's. She licked some stray chocolate off her finger, dripping a bit onto her shirt in the process. She shouted, "One minute!" before pulling her éclairs out of the oven and walking over to their shared doors.

She opened her side of the condo to an amused Cam. His hair was mussed from sleep and he ran a hand through it. "Do I smell chocolate?"

Quinn grinned. "Guilty as charged."

"You know it's the middle of the night, right?"

"I couldn't sleep. Sorry if I woke you."

"No, it wasn't you." Cam looked around her into the small kitchen. "Are you sharing?"

Quinn turned down the volume on her music. "I could probably arrange that."

"You know, you could have come after me with baked goods instead of a knife the night we met. Attracting more flies with chocolate than beating the crap out of the flies, or something like that."

"Be nice or I'll put laxatives in your éclairs."

Cam barked out a laugh and Quinn gestured for him to join her in the kitchen. She tapped a finger on the bottom of the pastries. They weren't quite cool enough to fill. Still, she wasn't totally prepared to make conversation with her new partner in the middle of the night. Rory had always slept through Quinn's strange habit of night baking when she couldn't sleep. Just to get a rise out of him, she pulled a knife out of the drawer. He eyed her and she flipped the handle end towards him. "Why don't you cut the éclairs, so I don't scare you. And for the record, you'd boxed me in against your truck, and I thought you were going to hurt me. You're a lot bigger than I am."

Cam accepted the knife. "Glad you trust me enough to arm me. Sorry about that. In my defense, I thought you were the threat. Your Russian is impeccable."

"Why, thank you." Quinn did a little curtsy. "It's one of many weapons in my arsenal."

He eyed her critically. "You don't have another knife tucked into your pajama pants, do you?"

"Keep your eyes on the éclairs, Watchman. I wasn't expecting company, so I'm not armed. You're safe." Cam rubbed lightly at his almost faded black eye as if he didn't mean to, but the small smirk forming at the corner of his mouth gave him away. She threw a dish towel at him, and he ducked, laughing. Quinn poured the chocolate cream into a flat dish to cool and popped it in the fridge to speed the process. Cam sawed at the éclairs, handling the first few like they were munitions. His early attempts were pretty ugly, but he kept modifying his approach until they looked almost as good as hers. She cleaned the kitchen while he finished up. Once the last pot was clean, she hopped up on the kitchen counter. The cream still needed time to cool. "If I didn't wake you up, why weren't you sleeping?"

"I don't, sometimes."

Quinn quirked an eyebrow. "Thinking too much?"

Cam crossed his arms. "You could say that. If someone isn't actively trying to kill me, I usually sleep like a baby. But every now and again, I wake up. I hit the gym or do some pull-ups for a little while and I'm usually good. But I don't usually wake up and smell baked goods. My stomach insisted on the detour." He gestured to the somewhat mangled pastries. "Since I've done my part, do I get to try them when they're done?"

"Of course." She gentled her tone. "Why don't you sleep?"

"Quinn, I've lost friends I considered brothers. It happens sometimes."

Quinn's throat got tight and she turned away to hide the tears welling up in her eyes without her permission. She choked them back and jumped off the counter to dry the pots and pans. Without turning to look at him, she asked, "Did you ever feel responsible? Like you should have done something to prevent it, even if you couldn't?"

"All the time. Even when it didn't make sense. Especially when it didn't make sense." He waited for her to turn around and make eye contact. "You want to talk about it?"

"I'll be fine." Quinn busied herself checking the pastry cream in the fridge, even though it needed a little more time.

"Tell me about Rory. What did she think about your baking?"

"She said I was nuts but always appreciated the results. Rory slept through everything, but she was always better than I was about sleeping. About trusting the systems we had in place, in general, really. I never sleep well on an op. I don't trust any system." Cam raised an eyebrow. "And it might take me a little while to trust people as well. This is getting dangerously close to feeling like therapy. I'm not going there."

Cam shrugged. "Why not? It helps to get it on the table."

Quinn took a step back. "Really? You're this big tough guy and you're the one talking to me about my feelings?"

"You think I'm tough?" Cam crossed his arms so his biceps bumped up, and she rolled her eyes at him and looked for another dish towel to throw. Cam dodged behind a post in the kitchen. "It doesn't make you less tough to admit you're grieving. In fact, it's probably a lot harder than stuffing your feelings down and hoping they'll go away. The Navy set me up with someone to talk to after the explosion. I thought it would be a waste of time, but I'm glad I went."

Quinn looked around for something else to clean, but the kitchen was already spotless. "This has been a very unexpected conversation. But thanks. I think." Quinn turned to pull the pastry cream out of the fridge – it was close enough. She poured the cooled filling into another homemade piping bag and began filling the éclairs.

Cam popped one in his mouth and his eyes went wide. "Holy shit. This is good," he said around the dessert.

"Thanks. I mean, if you're comparing it to doing pull-ups because you can't sleep, it's not really a tough competition."

"I don't mind pull-ups. Where'd you learn to do this?"

"A lot of downtime on operations. I don't sit still well."

"No kidding."

Quinn spied another dish towel and grabbed it. Cam raised his hands in self-defense and she eyed him before setting it back on the counter. "And I have a bit of a sweet tooth." Quinn took a bite. Yes, that definitely took the edge off of getting up early. "Next time, we can do pull-ups. For now, éclairs." She raised her treat in the air in a toast. "So, I've been thinking about how we play this."

"Yeah, me too."

"I want you there."

Cam cocked an eyebrow, and she took a bite to buy time to finish forming her thought. "Because I'm tough?"

Quinn rolled her eyes. "You aren't going to let that go, are you?"

Cam shook his head. "No way. But you were saying?"

"Hannah saw us the first night we were in town and knows we know each other. I've got a bunch of half-baked ideas on how we could bring you along, but I spent most of my time baking poking holes in them. That said, I've thought of sixteen different ways to disarm Hannah in the unlikely event she is our mastermind."

"You never can tell with people. It's definitely too soon to cross anyone off the list. Speaking of, what are your impressions of Ben? He keeps popping up a lot of places."

"He seems nice enough. Pretty busy, but takes time to check in on me every once in a while. Mostly he just seems like he has more stuff to do than he has time to do it."

"Don't you think it's odd that he found out our people were sniffing around NASA-Kennedy? He was left out of the loop for a reason."

"Yeah. It's possible he's our criminal, but it's also possible he's just got some friends down at Kennedy watching his back. We can find out more about that once we're in Florida. The real challenge is how to bring you with us." Quinn rubbed a spot between her eyebrows and reached for another éclair.

"I could pose as an employee in another department. It's a big enough company that Hannah wouldn't necessarily know I just jumped in. We'll say someone at NASA to called me in to help. Materials research, maybe? Since they've been having trouble with bad parts?"

Quinn nodded. "That might actually work. I'll call Dan and make it happen. What if Hannah looks you up in the company directory?"

"We'll have one of Dan's people put me in the system. If they can't do it, I've got a friend in the FBI who can help. Dude can hack any system and he can do it a lot faster if you can sneak him in."

Quinn nodded. "That's no problem. Just let me know what he needs. So, who are these people the FBI is sending and how well do you know them?"

Cam laughed. "Better than you think. I've known one of them for years and the other one I trust completely. We'll probably run into them while we're down there, so I'll get you pictures and their aliases for this operation."

"Good. If Morgan approved of them, I'm guessing they're more than a little good at their job. Nice work, Cam."

Cam smiled. "You know, you're really nice when you forget to hate me."

"I don't hate you, Cam."

"I kind of figured. I mean, you had every chance to poison me and didn't. Unless it takes time for the poison to kick in." Cam grabbed his throat and acted like he was choking.

Quinn snorted. "Look, I'm not always such a hard ass." She ran a hand through her hair. She probably looked a mess with a smudge of chocolate on her shirt and red, sleepy eyes.

"I know." Cam leaned in. "You and I, we're not built to wallow. Rory would be proud of you, you know. It takes strength to hunt down a murderer with a smile on your face. Looking everyone in the eye like they're your best friend when one of them is your worst enemy." Quinn swallowed hard, nodded. Cam crossed his arms. "Will you head butt me again if I give you a hug?"

Quinn laughed. "You're never going to let me live that down."

"You're correct." Quinn took a step closer to him and Cam hugged her. "If you need to bake 400 éclairs to feel better, bake 400 éclairs. Just don't pretend like it didn't happen. That's when it bites you in the ass. Oh, and keep sharing what you stress-bake. These are good." Cam leaned around her to grab another éclair.

"Sage advice."

"Good night, Q. Thanks for the treats." Cam patted his stomach. "Next time, we're doing pull-ups first."

15

In his well-appointed office in a Moscow government building, Dmitri glowered at the large, sealed envelope his newest assistant had placed on his desk. His last assistant had lasted only a few months after leaving due to health issues. It was too bad. She had been competent. Of course, he never kept them too long. He didn't need the security issues. A cursory glance at the inner materials of the envelope confirmed Dmitri's fears. His country's intelligence service had suspicions about what had happened in Romania. They wanted to ask him some questions. Dmitri swallowed hard. He'd worked hard to keep his plans under the radar for this reason. He just needed to keep them off his back long enough to execute the plan that would make up for his failed operation.

Dmitri still had plausible deniability about his involvement in the Romanian operation. It was plain bad luck that the World Health Organization had recognized that his men had the measles before they could run the vaccination clinic and spread the contagion. Several of the men had been quarantined and later jailed, which was unfortunate but unpreventable. However, the man he needed most had managed to escape quarantine to join him back in Russia. Despite the suspicions of his country's intelligence services, it would be difficult for them to prove his responsibility. The camp had been disbanded and no hint of Russian involvement remained in the Carpathian Mountains. The fact that the American woman still lived was inconvenient, yes, but not worth the risk of cleanup. The only thing she could point to now was a camp that no longer existed. It was too bad his operation had failed, but Dmitri hadn't made it this far without a backup plan. In fact, his little outbreak experiment had been good practice for his more ambitious mission, Operation Vostok.

Operation Vostok had been planned for a long time. Too long, in fact. His efforts had been hampered by the members of his own government who valued their cooperation with the Americans. His government would appreciate his efforts, but only if he was successful. If he was not, they didn't even need to know of his attempt. His colleagues remained unaware that he'd quietly recruited a small group of allies who would suit his purposes. Few spies had the patience for long-duration, low-intensity overseas missions and Dmitri had rewarded them both monetarily and with a sense of purpose missing from their own lives. Their contact was necessarily limited and meticulously planned.

His most trusted contact had been steadily delivering results, but was notoriously paranoid, only risking contact every few months. He checked the calendar. Their plans should be moving forward, but he would need to confirm they had been set into motion. It was time to reach out to his network once again.

CAM WOKE up a little later than usual due to his unexpected middle of the night talk with Quinn. He chuckled before he raised his head from the pillow. She could probably kill a bad guy with her little finger if she wanted to, and she was awake…baking éclairs. Well, if the CIA ever started an employee bake-off, she'd win hands-down. And she'd finally opened up to him. A little. While he hadn't intended to drag her emotions out of her, she needed to get them out there and deal with them. They both needed a clear head. With any luck, the CIA would be able to overnight him a fake badge by tomorrow, and they could both get a closer look at whatever was happening at NASA-Kennedy. Only one more day of watching her work and he could get to the fun part.

Cam got himself ready for the day and then knocked on their shared door. He wasn't sure if their night meeting was a one-off or would set the tone for an improving partnership. She opened the door and met him with an éclair. "Breakfast?"

"Great idea. What's a donut but a fried cake with frosting? This is even baked." He sniffed at it suspiciously.

"Really? You still doubt me?"

"How many times last night did you threaten to lace it with something? You've had time this time."

Quinn rolled her eyes, took a bite and handed it back to him. "Only once. And doubting me just cost you half an éclair."

"Hey, you're the one with a weird laxative obsession. Don't blame this on me."

"You did not just say I have a weird laxative obsession."

"I did." He batted his eyelashes. "You ready for another day at the office, dear?"

Quinn bounced on the balls of her feet like a boxer. "I was born ready. Let's see how quickly I can book a flight to Florida. I've always wanted to spend some time at Cocoa Beach."

WHEN QUINN ARRIVED at the office, she successfully made a little small talk with her new coworkers. She'd brought some of the least mangled éclairs to share and the pastries did most of the work for her. By approaching them at their own desks, she managed to get a peek at the information displayed on their computers while they chatted about their work and their backgrounds. Most were obsessing over the software that would control the trajectory of the next rocket launch. The path of the rocket was automated based on data received in real-time through software they'd created in-house. Most of the team was concentrating on double-checking the entirety of the code, one line at a time. To her, it seemed a little short notice to be fixing anything, but no one offered additional explanation. Once she ran out of questions she could reasonably ask without suspicion, she dropped off her things at her desk and went to the breakroom for coffee. Chuck, a senior aerospace engineer on the team, was pouring himself a cup and Quinn tensed. She had barely spoken with him over the past few days, deliberately. His name had come up frequently in Rory's notes, alongside Hannah and another engineer who was no longer with the company. She'd slowed her approach to him on purpose, not wanting to appear too eager to get to know him.

"Hey...Chuck?" Quinn lowered her shoulders slightly to make herself appear as non-threatening as possible. It wasn't just the face that could give an operative away.

"Hi – Quinn, right? How are you settling in?" Chuck was middle-aged, with salt and pepper hair. His shirt was a little wrinkled at the bottom, and he had missed a few spots shaving underneath his chin.

"Really well. Everyone has been so friendly! I just hope that I can keep up with you guys."

"Well, I don't think Ben would have hired you if you couldn't. We just have a little more experience, that's all."

"How long have you worked here?"

"About five years. I worked for a government contractor before I came here, designing parts for the military. But this was where all the fun was happening." Chuck smiled and raised the coffee pot to pour her a cup. Quinn accepted and he leaned back against the countertop of the coffee station. Good, he wanted to talk.

"So, Chuck. Do you mind if I ask you a few newbie questions?"

"Of course not. That's what I'm here for. If I don't mentor other engineers, they'll put me in management as punishment." Quinn raised an eyebrow and Chuck took a sip of coffee before explaining. "There are two tracks to advancing here – a technical path and a management path. If you want to avoid management, you go the technical route. But you have to teach the new kids when they come in. So really, you'd be doing me a favor."

Quinn smiled. Chuck was easy to talk to. No wonder Rory had been sucked into his orbit. She'd have to tread carefully. She leaned in, conspiratorially. "Why is everyone so freaked out about this next launch? I mean, I get that they want it to be successful, but is it always like this?"

Chuck shook his head. "No, it isn't. In fact, this is pretty uncharacteristic of this team. We were all as enthusiastic as you, until we lost that rocket."

"Wasn't that due to a bad part or something? I remember reading that in the news."

"That's what the news said," Chuck said, knowingly. Quinn's heart began to race. She wrapped a hand around her warm mug and forced herself to look merely curious instead of desperate for the rest of the story. "Our internal report concluded the most likely cause of failure was a bad part. But here's the thing. The rocket went off its intended flight path. If it goes too far off and puts the people near the launch site at risk, the software onboard the rocket will terminate the flight."

"I'm sorry, are you saying the rocket blew itself up?"

Chuck looked around before answering. "We're not sure. The data we received were inconclusive. However, the rocket started going off course before any large forces were detected by our sensors. And the internal investigation couldn't completely rule out the flight path chosen by our software."

"Large forces, like what?"

"Like the force of something major breaking. Or a small explosion that might indicate a fuel leak. You'd think we'd see something unusual in the data. But we didn't. The rocket went off course, then came the boom."

"What does that mean?" Quinn took a sip of coffee.

"It means that our team has some work to do to prove we weren't at fault. Ben isn't sure if our software has a bug in it. The computer decides where the rocket goes based on conditions and input data in real-time, but someone has to program it, right? That's all on us."

"But you don't think there is a problem with the code?"

"I'm skeptical. The sequence of events doesn't match up with a bad part, but we can't find any errors in the flight path code. So, it was most likely a bad part." Chuck looked into his mug. "And I don't want to badmouth anyone – but let's just say that sometimes, mistakes happen. So no one wants to get overconfident either."

Quinn swallowed hard and heard Cam let out a low whistle in her earpiece. "Good job, Q. Keep working him, but don't overplay it. You've already earned your paycheck today."

Quinn wrapped both hands around her mug. "Why didn't Ben tell me?"

Chuck shrugged. "He's been trying to keep the peace around here. We've already lost an engineer over it. Ben is trying to keep morale high."

"So, are you doing the same thing as everyone else, then? Working through the code?"

Chuck nodded. "Yeah – that's what the team wants me to do. Except I've combed through every line we've written in the last five years. The code is solid. It doesn't make sense that all of the others would launch successfully while only one went off course."

"Wow, thanks for letting me know. Ben asked me to go to Florida, go see the latest rocket myself. Would you mind if I call you if I have any questions? I mean, I want to help you stay out of management and all of that. It's all about you."

Chuck smiled. "Of course. Thanks for doing me a solid." He raised a hand for a fist bump and she met him in the middle.

Quinn went back to her desk and turned on her computer. She blew out a breath. Rory must have sensed something was up, but did she know about all of this? Even Ben hadn't given her the full story and she worked here. Quinn began to review the contents of the code with a new purpose and enthusiasm. The code itself didn't make much sense, but buried within it were the equations she'd spent the last couple of weeks studying. She at least knew what they were supposed to look like. Accelerometer, GPS, and gyroscope data provided the real-time information needed to direct the rocket engines. Quinn began to imagine the tilt of the rocket and the compensating thrust in the context of infinite possibilities and foul play. She took a sip of her coffee and leaned into her computer until she heard a noise behind her. She turned around and smiled when she saw Hannah at her desk, holding a folder.

"Hey, newbie! I just booked our flights – can you pack a bag to leave this afternoon?"

Quinn took one last look at the code on her monitor, then turned toward Hannah with a smile on her face. It would have to wait.

"Absolutely. Do I need to book a hotel or anything?"

"Nope. I have it all handled." Hannah gave her the bright red folder, filled with every travel document she needed, neatly color-coded. "I hope you don't mind travelling with me."

"Not at all, Hannah. You've been so welcoming." Quinn gestured to the folder. "And organized. I really appreciate it."

Hannah adjusted her scarf and gave her a small smile. "Just happy to help."

In her earpiece, Cam said, "Flip it open to the flight information so I can see it. I'll get a ticket. Dan got me in the system this morning. I'll see if I can get my badge sent to Florida. It's not ideal, but we'll have to run into each other at the airport and then improvise."

16

THE SUN SHONE THROUGH THE HOTEL CURTAINS AND REE STRETCHED awake. It took her a moment to remember she was still in Florida. They would debrief Alan today. But first, she needed to finish her official report. Parker was still asleep and she planted a soft kiss on his cheek before rolling out of bed to brew some standard-issue hotel coffee. She padded over the tiny coffee machine and pushed a few buttons to make them both a cup. The previous night had been a little more exciting than they'd expected. She'd had a hard time falling asleep. Before they left the NASA facility, Mike had acquired the footage of their unexpected guest and sent it to Morgan for facial analysis. Ree was a bit skeptical they would get everything they needed, since the cleanroom attire made it difficult to ID someone, even when she knew who it was supposed to be. However, the CIA had a lot of tools at their disposal. Maybe they'd pull a rabbit out of their hat.

Ree turned on her laptop and put the finishing touches on the report, detailing potential safety issues along with her professional opinion on how to fix them. She looked through it again to carefully edit out any language that sounded like it could come from someone working for the FBI. No mention of potential sabotage, just the reminder that safety procedures were there for a reason, and more training was required so that mistakes like this weren't made in the future. This memo would be hand-delivered to Alan, along with any information Mike could glean from the surveillance footage. She could be back in Indiana as soon as tomorrow. Someone from Alan's team would have to remove the offending component and retest literally everything in a pretty short amount of time. It was theoretically possible, but they'd be cutting it close. The coffee maker beeped and she retrieved her cup, eyeing the powdered creamer packet before deciding to go without.

Half an hour later, and due in no small part to the smell of coffee filling their hotel room, Parker came up behind Ree at the small desk and began rubbing her shoulders. "Once you're done, want to go for a walk on the beach?"

Ree smiled. "Of course."

After Ree was happy with her report, she sent a copy to Morgan. Cam and his partner would be able to read it as soon as this afternoon. She stretched her back and they left to go for a walk. As soon as they reached the sand, Ree removed her shoes and Parker followed suit. Shoes in one hand, she reached for Parker and he pulled her close. The sun flashed off the water and kids splashed in the waves. It was summer and the morning was already hot and humid. Ree sank her toes into the wet sand and looked out at the ocean. Parker and Ree watched the waves come in in silence. They didn't get to do this often enough. Ree still hadn't gotten used to the feeling of peace that washed over her when Parker was around. She wasn't naïve enough to believe they wouldn't ever argue over things like dirty socks on the floor or whose family they would visit on a holiday, but she was just hopeful enough to think she might have found her forever in him. She rested her head on his shoulder. "I'm nuts about you, you know that?"

"You'd have to be. Think of all the messes I've dragged you into already." He nudged her shoulder with his.

"As I recall, I volunteered for most of them."

"True. I'm impressed by both your tenacity and your heart." Parker put a hand in his pocket and took a deep breath, ready to say something else, but his phone buzzed. He sighed and withdrew his hand. "Unfortunately for us, it's time to go. Mike's going to meet us in a few minutes. Let's go break the news to Alan."

Fifteen minutes later, they were on their way to Kennedy Space Center. Once Mike started the car, he began his update without preamble. "We cleaned up the footage of our unexpected guest from last night. Even with the CIA's help, I can't figure out who joined us. It's impossible to tell under all that gear, and our friend was avoiding the cameras. Probably on purpose."

"Aren't there a bunch in that area?" Ree scrunched her nose as if she had tasted something bitter.

"You'd think. But no, just a couple around the entrance. The government doesn't want to generate live footage of how we build our satellites."

Parker nodded. "Yeah, it'd just be one more thing that could get hacked. I assume you already checked the keycard records?"

"Yes. According to the records, one of the janitorial staff badged in while we were there. The only problem is, the badge is registered to someone who quit a few months ago. Their badge was deactivated the day they left and reactivated a few weeks ago."

Parker raised an eyebrow. "Shit. Do we tell NASA to deactivate the badge, or will that tip off our guy?"

Mike shrugged. "We can have them send out a BS HR email about making sure that old employees aren't active in the system and have them do a mass update without raising suspicions. But P, we have a problem. It was used again an hour after we left. We didn't get the hole plugged in time."

Ree rubbed her face. "That complicates things."

Parker looked out the window. "It's not ideal, but we'll handle it. Let's get in there one more time to see if our guy messed with the equipment or if he was just checking on the part he added. We'll bring Alan with us this time. We'll do another check for explosives, then we'll have his team inspect everything else that our guy might have easy access to. Cam and his partner should be headed this way soon. We'll stick around until we can meet with them, exchange information, and then get the heck out of here."

An hour later, they were once again outside of Alan's office, right before their meeting with him began. His project manager, Kiara, had also been invited, so they could see her face when they broke the news. They entered through the open door, and Alan directed them to a small conference table. Ree held the folder with her findings against her chest, watching Alan carefully. While he had suspicions about Parker and Mike, she needed to come out of this appearing at least somewhat ignorant of their connections to his friend at the CIA.

Once everyone had exchanged greetings, Ree passed out copies of her report. "Hi, everyone. If you can just take a look here, you'll see some additional images of the component that was mistakenly added to the assembly. The only piece of good news is that it appears to have been bolted on, not welded, as you had originally suspected."

Alan pulled at his tie and studied the cover page. Ree had added zoomed-in, high-resolution photos of where the box was attached. "That's helpful. I wasn't able to capture it at this angle. What do you recommend?"

"In my report, I recommended you revisit your procedures and shore up your documentation, since we have no idea who might have added this component. I haven't seen earlier revisions of your instructions, but I would check to see if someone was told to add this at some point."

Kiara narrowed her eyes at the picture. "Nothing like this has ever been on any of the plans or instructions I've signed off on."

Alan sighed. "Do you believe someone did this deliberately?"

Ree gave her most doe-eyed look to Alan. "That's not really my area of expertise. I was just here to provide an objective opinion on the safety of the satellite. In my professional opinion, if that part doesn't belong there and we don't know what it does, it could certainly impact safety and should be removed."

Parker cleared his throat. "My associate, Mike Riley, and I have incorporated Dr. Ryland's feedback into a broader analysis that addresses your question. I'll send that to you separately. We recommend that you or your team remove the part immediately. We've scanned it for explosive material." He directed his gaze to Kiara. "We didn't find anything that would explode. Given that there is no danger to the person removing the part, I think we should get rid of it today."

Kiara raised an eyebrow. "Thank you. I agree with your assessment. Alan, can I go take it off my satellite now?" She placed her hands on the arms of her chair, ready to push herself up.

Mike held up a finger. "We have one small problem. While we were investigating the part, someone entered the cleanroom. We retrieved the security logs and found that the individual used an old badge to get in. I'd recommend updating your systems so that can't happen in the future."

Kiara's eyes went wide. "Did you see who it was?"

Mike shook his head. "We weren't able to tell from the security footage. They were careful about how they passed the hallway cameras as well. I'd be happy to show the video to you, if you think you might recognize them."

Alan nodded. "Yes, we'd appreciate that."

Mike pulled up the footage on his phone, but even after several loops through the video, Alan and Kiara remained silent. Ree rubbed the back of her neck. "Maybe you guys can think about it, and we can go get that satellite back up to snuff?"

Kiara nodded. "That is a plan I can get behind."

Ree raised a hand. "Kiara, after we leave, I'd recommend you check every exposed component. Top to bottom. Full inspection."

"I suspected. Even with most of it ready to go, that usually takes two weeks."

"Can you squeeze it in?"

Kiara let out a low breath. "Someone is trying to sabotage my satellite. Yeah, we'll make it work."

Alan nodded. "I agree. And we need to limit access to that room. We'll cut off the access on all keycards and keep a close eye on who goes in."

"Easy does it." Mike tapped on the report. "If this is intentional, you don't want to tip off the guy or gal doing this. I know a guy who can help install a camera or two, just in case they come back. We'll make sure security knows to keep an eye out so they can intervene quickly."

Alan closed his eyes. "Someone is going to have to tell IRT that we found a problem. I just got word their people are coming in this evening."

Ree nodded. "Of course. I'd be happy to walk them through what happened and help you develop a plan that will help prevent this from happening in the future."

"Thank you, Dr. Ryland. Why don't you come in with me and Kiara when we disconnect the component? We'll make sure it's just the three of us, so we don't raise the alarm."

Parker's jaw tightened, but his voice was pure reason. "I'm not sure it'll make a lot of difference at this point. People already know we're here. Why don't we all go in? You can let Kiara's team know we found something after we take care of it." Parker cleared his throat. "And we'll need to confirm yesterday's visitor didn't add anything dangerous or explosive to the box while they were in the room."

Kiara raised an eyebrow at Parker. "Who do you work for, again?"

"NASA's safety investigation team."

Alan steepled his fingers. "Let's go take care of the problem. Then, I'll help you get your baby ready. Deal?"

Kiara nodded and they all left to take a closer look at the tiny component presenting a big problem.

It was a full half-hour later before Ree followed the NASA team into the controlled area to change into cleanroom gear. They'd decided to go in at shift change to keep the number of witnesses as low as possible. While they were getting gowned up to go inside, a man who was just leaving took off his protective garments and eyed them warily. Kiara nodded at him and he grunted a hello. Mike turned to watch him leave. Once he was gone, Kiara said in a low voice, "That's Tim. He's on my team. Don't take his attitude personally. He must have figured out you're with the safety team. No offense, but my team thinks you guys are trying to impress someone at NASA by finding problems that don't exist."

"Really?" Ree pulled a head covering over her hair, tucking in stray strands.

"Well, I didn't tell them what I found. If you didn't know we'd found something, wouldn't you think NASA was overreacting?"

Ree zipped up her pristine white gown. "Oh. Definitely. Shew, I'm glad it doesn't get this intense in my lab." When Kiara wasn't looking, Parker gave her a wink. Okay, maybe it did get this intense in her lab. Just not all the time. She wouldn't be here at all if a criminal hadn't smuggled missile guidance system components into her lab, drawing the attention of the FBI.

Once the large room was as empty as it was going to get, the team of engineers and FBI agents went to disassemble the offending component from the satellite. Alan plucked a few wrenches out of the cleanest workbench Ree had ever seen as they passed it. As the designated safety expert on their team, Ree led the way. She was the first to realize the box was gone. Her chest tightened. She grabbed Parker by the elbow and pointed to the now-empty space.

Parker's eyes narrowed. "Alan, we may have a problem. Did one of your people remove the box already?"

Alan shook his head and Mike moved to the other side of Ree, protecting her exposed side. Mike said, "The guy that came in last night must have realized we knew it was there."

Alan rubbed his forehead. "What's next?"

Mike gestured to the door they'd come through a few moments prior. "The plan holds. You inspect the satellite again. We keep an eye on the place like someone is trying to blow this thing up. I'll set up some live surveillance and talk to security." Mike seemed relaxed, which meant he would be functioning as at least one part of the surveillance team. Nothing made Mike happier than watching four cameras at once and figuring out the key detail to catch the criminal.

Alan swallowed. "That sounds...reasonable."

Parker nodded. "Great. And let's keep everyone out of here at night. Kiara, will that delay your launch schedule?"

Kiara shook her head. "I think we can make it. Just barely. If Alan can help, we can power through it."

Ree eyed Kiara. "Do you usually do a final check?"

Kiara nodded. "There is a formal check completed by the inspectors. My check isn't on the schedule or anything. I just wanted to make sure everything went right."

Ree patted Kiara on the back. "Well, it's a good thing you did."

Mike narrowed his eyes at Ree. "Dr. Ryland, we'd appreciate it if you didn't mention any of this when you get back to the university. I know we brought you in for a safety issue, but this is worse than we expected. Do you think you could stick around for a few more days?"

Ree nodded. Mike was so good at this, it was scary. You'd never guess from his formal demeanor that she'd played poker with him and his wife at their home in Chicago the weekend prior. Technically, she'd been getting her butt kicked by him and his wife in poker the week prior. Scarlett was a profiler, Mike observed people for a living, and Ree was out of her depth in their house. "Sure. I can stay if you need my help. I don't mind."

Mike shrugged. "If you have the time, we'd appreciate it."

"Of course. Why don't we let Kiara and Alan complete their inspections and we'll regroup tomorrow with the team from IRT?"

"Sounds like a plan." The team exited quietly and Mike retrieved his surveillance equipment from the car. In a few short hours, hallways were cleared and additional cameras were quietly installed, none of them visible to the naked eye.

17

"Hmm. That's odd." Hannah stared into her cell phone. Quinn tapped an impatient toe while she waited for Hannah to finish her thought. They'd just passed through airport security and were gathering their bags, jackets, and shoes as each item popped out of the end of the security scanner. Hannah slipped her feet back into her high heels, still reading the message. "Ben said the safety team found a bigger problem than we expected on the satellite, and they want to talk to us about it tomorrow. Looks like we'll be doing more than just reassuring the team everything is going to be fine. Hm. And the company is going to send someone else along with us, apparently. Ben doesn't know him, but a manager in the materials department got the same call and wanted to send someone to check it out. Makes sense, since a bad part blew up the last one." Hannah's normally cheerful demeanor went blank before her eyes brightened again. She shrugged. "Well, we won't be bored."

Quinn followed Hannah to their gate, ducking around fellow travelers while guiding her carry-on suitcase through the crowd. While hers was utilitarian, black, and nearly indistinguishable from those around it, Hannah's was bright purple and matched the flecks of color in her scarf and the gems in her earrings. With Hannah, no detail was overlooked. Not a bad quality to have in a technical writer.

Quinn watched for danger in her surroundings and tried not to make it obvious that she was also keeping an ear out for Cam. In addition to the announcements on the intercom around her, she heard a different set of crowd noises through her earpiece. He, like her, was navigating the airport but wasn't in the same general area yet. Despite the extra mental burden of processing two separate streams of noise, she didn't want to turn the earpiece off until they met up. Since she hadn't seen Cam since he found out they were leaving today, she could only assume he'd been doing cartwheels in the condo as he packed his things. She could hardly blame him. Sitting in a van watching surveillance footage sounded as appealing as watching someone clip their toenails all day.

When they reached their gate, Quinn heard the announcements overhead echoed in her ear. A woman in front of her stepped to the side and Cam came into view. In her ear, she heard, "Showtime."

He walked towards them and Hannah whispered into her ear, "*Who is that?*" Hannah looked Cam up and down, then began fanning herself.

Quinn managed to keep herself from rolling her eyes when Cam's lips quirked. He heard that. Like he needed more confidence. "My old friend. From the bar? Ben told you a materials guy was coming along, right? His name wasn't Cam, by any chance, was it?"

Hannah checked her phone. "It was."

Quinn sighed. "Well, this should be interesting. Cam is my 'it's complicated.'"

"Well, hello, Mr. Complicated," Hannah said, dragging out the words.

Cam approached them and gave Quinn a friendly hug. "Quinn! I didn't know you were coming! So, you got the job?" Quinn nodded and Cam reached out a hand to Hannah, who shook it. "I'm Cam Wilson. I'm with the materials department."

"Hannah Jenkins. It's very nice to meet you."

Cam nudged Quinn with his shoulder. He lowered his voice, but not so low Hannah wouldn't hear him. "I hope you don't mind me jumping into all of this."

"Why would I mind? You're the right guy for the job." Quinn gave him a shrug then looked away.

Hannah raised her eyebrows at Quinn. All of the time Cam spent watching Hannah had been well spent. His strategy for the office busybody was spot on. Hannah was always looking for a story to share and their awkward interaction would give her a thread to pull on. A thread that would keep her away from the ones they didn't want her going after. Hannah looked at Cam. "So, Cam, do you know what's going on?"

"I don't. But after the last mishap, they want to rule out anything materials related."

"Well, I'm glad you're coming along, then." They passed the next several minutes with small talk and the occasional awkward pause until the airline called for passengers to start boarding.

Mercifully, the three didn't have to sit together, so instead of worrying about every detail of her interactions with Cam while her new coworker looked on, Quinn was able to relax and plan her next steps on the flight. Before takeoff, her phone buzzed with a message from Dan. She was in the window seat and her middle seat neighbor was already snoring. She covered her phone with one hand and checked the message. Not only did they have a problem, they had an active problem. Shit. This was going to complicate things. It would be another several hours before their flight landed. They'd be too late to jump into the fray today. She'd have to coordinate with Cam tonight to put a plan together. Preferably away from Hannah's curious gaze.

By the time they landed and were standing in line at the rental car counter, Quinn and Hannah were chatting like old friends while Cam looked on. Hannah had reached out to some of her contacts at NASA-Kennedy for more information, and the rumor mill there was actively churning. Hannah read aloud from her latest text message. "Alan brought a team in to look at where the satellite attaches to our rocket. Looks like bad news. There was a part on the assembly that didn't belong, and they removed it."

Quinn raised an eyebrow. Hannah's version of what happened was different from Dan's. The FBI team was likely planting semi-truths.

That might help her find Hannah's source. "What does that mean? Someone screwed up?"

Hannah shrugged. "Gosh, I don't know. NASA designs the satellite to mate with our rocket, but they tend to keep their stuff pretty secretive. I wish I knew more." Hannah looked around her, then leaned in. "Good thing Ben sent us in case they blame us for a miscommunication. We should probably get in there and do some damage control."

"Maybe we can meet with…who was it again?" Quinn rubbed her neck. "Alan? What does he do?"

"Alan Smith. He runs the whole show. He's a retired colonel and runs a tight ship, so to speak. Ben arranged for us to meet with him tomorrow. Maybe we can talk him into inviting whatever safety committee they pulled on board too. Rumor has it, it's a bunch of consultants. Heaven help us if they aren't in a hurry. We'll never get this thing launched on time." Hannah gave a dramatic shudder. They reached the front of the line and went quiet as Hannah ticked all the boxes for their rental car. She jangled the keys. "Let's go get settled in and tomorrow we can figure out what's going on."

Later that evening, Quinn heard a light knock on the door shared with the hotel room next to hers. She grinned and opened the adjoining door. "I thought I was going to get some time off from you, Cam. They didn't even ask me if I minded sharing a door with you this time."

He smiled. "Blame Dan. His people picked the rooms."

"Do you think Hannah will get suspicious about us?"

"Well, she already has suspicions, for all the wrong reasons. That should keep her from digging too deep." Cam brushed imaginary dirt off his shoulder.

"Yeah, don't gloat too hard, Watchman."

"Hey, I've just been watching you read training material. I'm proud I can contribute to the op without getting a black eye."

"Ha. So, I've been thinking about our strategy for tomorrow. Did Morgan tell you that the satellite's extra part disappeared just as mysteriously as it had appeared? Alan's team didn't pull it off, like Hannah's friend suggested."

"Yeah. I heard. Also, I spoke with my contact in the FBI. Their team is still here."

"I thought they were leaving when we showed up."

Cam crossed his arms. "Under the circumstances, they offered to stick around for a few extra days. See if we can work together to smoke out our bad guy."

Quinn retrieved a freezer bag from her suitcase, and Cam grinned when she handed over one of two well-traveled, smooshed éclairs. She'd frozen them so they would survive the journey, and they had, but just barely. She sat cross-legged on the end of the bed in the small room. She patted the spot beside her and Cam joined her. "Anyone skip town since they've been on the ground?"

"Not yet. We're watching, though. One of the FBI guys has security footage, but even NASA couldn't tell which one of their people removed the device. They used a decoy badge to get into the room to conceal their identity. Suggests a whole hell of a lot of intent."

"Do we know what the part was supposed to do?"

"Negative. We only know it wasn't rigged to explode. It had a computer chip, a battery, and a connection to the brains of the rocket."

Quinn took a bite of éclair and considered. "Would they be measuring anything during liftoff? Maybe someone is interested in the navigation data."

Cam frowned. "That's one theory. Do you believe it?"

"Not really. Seems like a lot of effort for a flight path. Even though it was on NASA's end, with everything else we know, it seems like it'd have to be related to IRT. But I don't have anything solid. I've just been staring at data and calculations for the last few days. There's a lot more to IRT's software than I originally thought. From what I understand, they've been able to automate quite a bit more than their competition. It's possible someone would want detailed data so they could replicate IRT's systems. Take away their competitive advantage. Did the part leave the building?"

"We don't know. The part is pretty small – easy enough to tuck into a bag when no one is looking. However, it's possible it's still in the building. Even if they hid it away somewhere, we can't search the place from top to bottom." Cam tapped a finger against his lips. "But we could put a scanner over the exit and scan for metal that shape and size. Morgan or Dan could get us set up. Oh, and you should know, the

FBI team will be at our meeting with Alan. Their names are Mike and Parker. They're posing as a safety investigation team, and have brought in a college professor to complete the ruse. They know I'm CIA and will likely figure out you are too."

"And you said you trust these guys?"

"Absolutely. They've asked me to let you know they are keeping the professor in the dark about what's going on. Her name is Dr. Ree Ryland. She'll be at our meeting with Alan as well."

"Well, we'll have to do our jobs right, so we can get Dr. Ryland home safely, and soon."

18

The following morning, Quinn met Hannah and Cam in the lobby. Hannah had a smile on her face and coffees in hand. She gave them each one and led them to the car with all the confidence of a tour guide leading a large group of easily distracted tourists using only a large red umbrella. "Our first meeting is with Alan and the safety investigation team. I've already spoken to Ben. He wants us to make small talk with Alan's team to get a sense for what's going on. Don't worry, I'll handle updating Ben, so you guys can focus on keeping Alan happy."

"Thank you for that." Quinn took a sip of her coffee. "And for this."

"Of course. It's what I'm here for! Now, let's get you guys to that meeting."

An hour later, the small team from IRT was escorted to Alan's office, where several others were waiting. The big guy, Mike, was built like a linebacker but shook her hand gently, giving no indication he knew they she was CIA. Parker's eyes sparkled with intelligence and he shook her hand firmly. There was something familiar about him. She didn't recall seeing him on previous operations, but he might have been on one of them. In the background, most likely, since her brain couldn't articulate how she knew him. He too, didn't give away anything. Finally, the professor greeted them both warmly. She was friendly, but focused. The makeup beneath her eyes had a slightly yellow tint to it – she hadn't been sleeping well and was trying to cover up the purple underneath them. Quinn might not have noticed if she didn't regularly use makeup to conceal her identity or manipulate the perception of others. The right eye drops could cause red eyes and a little purple shadow worked wonders to create a look of worry underneath the eye. To cover a bruise often required a layer of white shoe polish under makeup, but she rarely got those on her face. Fortunately, Cam's black eye had faded and she hadn't needed to help him camouflage it today.

After they'd met to their allies in the FBI, Alan Smith introduced himself. He was average in height but wore his expectations of others in his shoulders and direct gaze. If he wasn't smiling, she might consider him formidable. Quinn liked him immediately. Finally, a woman stopped tapping her pen against her notebook long enough to greet them. This was Kiara, the project manager. Her eyes darted between her notebook and the room, and she shifted uncomfortably in her seat. Understandable, considering what had happened. Quinn would need to get her alone to be sure she wasn't a part of the sabotage, but that was easily done. Hannah stayed in front of Quinn to ease every introduction, exchanging pleasantries with Alan and Kiara and explaining her role to the safety investigation team. Her ability to work a room almost rivaled Rory's. Ben's logic for sending her along was becoming increasingly apparent.

When they finally settled down around a large conference table in Alan's office, Quinn did her best to appear as if she hadn't already heard the explanation that someone had removed the offending parts without the team's knowledge. She looked shocked at the right moments and concerned at others. Before she could offer a plan, Hannah looked up from writing her notes. "Thank you so much for filling us in. While the satellite is not technically our assembly, I'd be happy to help coordinate a secondary inspection near the rocket/satellite interface."

Alan gave a sigh of relief. "That would be very much appreciated.

And your associates can help you?" Alan looked pointedly at Quinn and Cam.

"Absolutely." Hannah's look was sympathetic, yet professional. "I'm assuming you are going to limit access to the room until the inspections are complete?"

Alan nodded. "Yes, that's our plan. Here are the badges you'll need to enter the room. We ask that you don't go in without me or Kiara." Alan slid over three badges and Quinn forced herself not to gape. His trust was appreciated but, as of yet, totally unearned. Perhaps the FBI had a tighter watch on the place than she thought, and they wanted to make it easy to let people in. They'd probably loaded up the room with hidden cameras, hoping someone would tamper with the parts. She made a mental note to make sure the FBI counterparts Cam trusted so much had a solid plan for surveillance when she met with them later.

Quinn slid a badge over her neck. "Kiara, would you mind giving me a tour? I'm new to IRT and I'd like to get a closer look at everything."

Kiara nodded. "Sure, I'd be happy to. Hannah, you've seen it all before. If you want to focus on anything else, I can show Quinn and Cam around before we kick off the inspections."

Hannah smiled a bright smile. "Of course! I have a lot of people I'd like to say hello to while you guys work on the hard stuff." She gathered her things and gave a friendly wave as she left.

Kiara led Quinn and Cam down a hallway into a small room, leaving the FBI contingent behind with Alan. Kiara gave them instructions on how to put on cleanroom gear. Once everyone was ready, they entered the expansive room. While the satellite would soon be covered by a protective outer skin, the satellite and attachment point to the rocket were still very much exposed. Kiara pointed to the base of the assembly. "That's where we'll need you guys to concentrate your inspection. I'll take care of the satellite. Given the nature of the payload, NASA wants to make sure you stick to the interfaces critical for connecting the satellite to IRT's rocket. With someone from my team in the room."

Quinn nodded and turned to get a closer look at the attachment point. She nearly ran into a man, dressed like her, with only his eyes visible. He stuck out a hand.

"Hey, I'm Tim. I work on Kiki's team." Kiara turned and her eyes narrowed a bit. Interesting. Quinn shook his hand. When she tried to pull away, he held it a bit longer than she wanted him to. She fought the instinct to twist his hand around and drop him to the ground. Instead, she let him have his moment. Unfortunately, he immediately got the wrong impression. Without letting go of her hand, he lowered his voice, "I haven't seen you around here before."

Okay. That was enough of that. Quinn pulled her hand free. "I'm new to IRT. I heard you guys had some trouble and came down to help."

"That's what I'm here for too." Tim let his eyes linger on hers for a moment. He winked and turned to face Kiara. Cam leaned over to inspect a part, putting himself between Quinn and Tim. "Kiki, I ran the tests. Everything seems fine to me. I'll leave the reports with the raw data on your desk." He turned to face Quinn. "You guys have nothing to worry about. We're checking everything, top to bottom. But let me know if I can help you with anything else."

Since Tim seemed interested in her, albeit oblivious to social cues, Quinn took a moment to plant an idea. "Thank you so much, Tim. Hopefully, we can chat again soon. About your work here?" Tim seemed to have a lot of romantic energy. If he couldn't take no for an answer, she didn't want to put him in a position where she'd have to drop him or break his nose.

Tim's eyes lit up. "Oh yeah. I can make that happen."

Quinn managed not to wrinkle her nose. He probably considered himself a proficient flirt. Tim sauntered off and Quinn turned to face Kiara. "Is he always like that?"

Kiara looked away. "Like what?"

"A little over the top."

"He's very… familiar. But he's never done anything against policy, so there isn't much we can do about it. Unless he breaks the rules. Which he hasn't," Kiara said, with an air of finality. It sounded like she was parroting back something someone had said to her. Interesting.

"Okay. Let's go check out that satellite."

Kiara dutifully showed them the section where the mysterious part had been attached, and Quinn took pictures to send back to Ben. Ben had a good reputation, and Quinn didn't believe he was involved. His problem was that he had two people's worth of work to do and he was only one person. He was so focused on the minutiae of the flight paths and software, it was unlikely that he missed an important technical detail. The truth had to be more complicated than that.

After Kiara was finished, they left the room as a group. As they were de-gowning, Quinn asked, "How much of a delay is this for you guys?"

"Well, thanks to some automated tests Tim developed, we'll get her back on track without a delay to the launch. Usually, our inspection takes longer, but there are no signs of tampering on the outside of the satellite and no problems we could detect on the inside of the satellite. I think we'll be able to put the fairing on soon and get her loaded onto your rocket. Did everything seem okay on the attachment end to you?"

Quinn nodded, with more authority and confidence than she actually felt. "It did. It doesn't look like anything was damaged. I took some pictures to send to Ben. If he has anything he wants me to double-check, we'll do that. But from our end, I think you're going to be alright."

Kiara breathed a sigh of relief. "Good. Actually, great. That's the best news I've heard this week."

A few minutes later, Kiara led them to the office area where the rest of her team sat. Tim had gone back to his desk and was now talking to Hannah. He seemed to have a different demeanor around Hannah than he did with Kiara and Quinn, but before Quinn could put her finger on it, Hannah put a hand on his shoulder. "Okay, Tim. Thanks for all of your help. It's always good to see you."

Tim looked Quinn up, then down. Without the gown to cover her features, he took his time this time. Lovely. "And hello again. It was nice to meet you, Quinn. And...what was it again?"

"Cam."

"Yes, and Cam. It was great to meet you both."

Quinn led Cam and Hannah away from Tim's desk before her

suspicions about him became obvious. Once they were away from the offices, Hannah asked, "How did it go in there, newbie?"

Quinn sighed. "It was okay. I'm just so new to all of this. How much do you know about all that stuff?"

Hannah shrugged. "Just what I see in the reports. I wish I could teach you more, but I don't have the background you guys do. I spent some time with the team while you were checking out the satellite. I spread some goodwill, found out the safety team doesn't blame IRT for the issue, especially since it happened on NASA's end. So I'm not sure Ben needs to be as worried as he is. Cam, did you get a chance to check any of the materials, or whatever it is you do?"

"Not as much I was hoping to. I'm really interested in what they found on the satellite, but there was no sign of it. You didn't happen to see the box lying around anywhere, did you?"

Hannah shook her head. "I wish I had, but no. I'll let you know if I hear anything, though."

Half an hour later, they were back at the hotel. Hannah parked the car and yawned. "Well, I think I'm going to get a quick dinner and call it a night. You two stay out of trouble, Quinn and her 'it's complicated.'" Hannah waggled her eyebrows.

Quinn managed to look sheepish and Hannah waved as they parted ways.

When they returned to their rooms, Cam sent a message to the FBI team. Parker and Mike knocked on Cam's door a few minutes later. Parker asked for a moment alone with Cam, and Quinn went to her room with the big one, Mike. She nodded at him and he eyed her critically. "So how long have you been working with Cam?"

Quinn thought for a moment. "About a week."

"Who do you think is behind this?" Mike crossed his arms and raised an eyebrow.

"Too soon to say."

"Yeah, what's your gut feel?"

Quinn recognized the questions for the test that they were. Mike didn't seem like the type to suffer fools. She straightened her back. "Gut feel? I think we have two people involved. One here, one at IRT. There is no way one person could manage all of this without leaving more of a trail. I met a guy named Tim today. I'd like to keep a close eye on him. His personality was off-putting, and he was sniffing around while Kiara was giving us a tour."

"That's the guy in charge of testing. He has access and knowledge. You want to search his lab?"

Quinn considered the question, then nodded. "Yeah. I guess I do. But we can't just barge in. I'm planning on approaching him at his desk tomorrow to talk about his role in the project. I'll take a closer look at his desk. Then we can go check out his lab."

Mike nodded. "I can run point in the surveillance van while you guys go in. I've already got scanners set up at the exit, checking for the part we found on the rocket. Cam said you were asking about it."

Quinn grinned. "Ah, Morgan hooked you up. I was wondering why Alan was so free with the badges."

Mike smiled. "Yeah, I'm going to start working with the CIA more often. You have all the cool toys. I don't know if I'm sending them back."

The door between their shared rooms opened and the two men returned. They were similar in build and look, but mostly it was their intense focus that made them seem like a pair. Parker reached out a hand. "Quinn. It's nice to meet you without pretense. Cam says you're good people." Quinn raised an eyebrow at Cam and he shrugged. A knock sounded on the door and Parker walked over to open it.

Dr. Ree Ryland, the professor caught in the middle of everything, bounded in. She gave Parker a quick kiss on the cheek. "Hey, Quinn."

Quinn laughed. "Wow. You're good. I thought you were clueless."

Ree smiled. "Thank you. That was the point."

"You're an FBI agent?"

"Not an agent. I just consult on occasion."

Parker crossed his arms. "Quinn, we've got Ree using her real name on this one. I don't like it, but we couldn't keep it under our hat since she works in a propulsion lab for a living. Unfortunately, what made her the right woman for the job also put her at some risk. Please keep the fact that we occasionally engage Dr. Ryland for our work between us."

Quinn raised an eyebrow. "Do you often kiss your coworkers? I think you need to kiss Cam next if that's the case. Then Mike here doesn't want to get left out."

Parker laughed. "Cam said you were a handful. Ree is also my girlfriend. It's a long story. Just assume I have a vested interest in keeping her safe."

Quinn nodded and made room for Ree to stand in their group. "Understood, Parker. Okay, Professor, in your professional opinion, what the hell is going on?"

Ree pulled a notebook from her purse. "I made some notes, but in short, they attached the mystery part in a way that was designed not to make noise and was hard to see. If Kiara hadn't been running her checks, which were not on the schedule, no one would have noticed it. More importantly, our criminal had some knowledge of the dimensions of the part they attached it to. You can't just go around bolting parts on satellites. This part was made with a high degree of precision for a very specific purpose. Which means it's probably one of the assemblers with access to the engineering drawings, or someone on Kiara's team. I don't know if they are hitching a ride on the spy satellite to gather data or trying to sabotage it."

"The last rocket blew up. Could it be related?" Quinn crossed her arms.

Ree closed the notebook. "NASA said that IRT claims the explosion was the result of a bad part and they have no reason to doubt the story. I disagree with their assessment. This is the same team that worked on the last launch. How could they not be related? Particularly since IRT is using one of the high bays at NASA's Vehicle Assembly Building. I think we have the same saboteur for both rockets, even if the methods of sabotage are different."

"Why do you say that?" Quinn agreed with the professor but wanted to see if they'd come to the same conclusions for the same reasons.

"The odds of a part like this accidentally getting installed are low enough to be practically impossible. Also, if you have someone who might get caught at any moment, why wouldn't they sabotage as many launches as they can before they get caught? What if something in a different box blew up the last launch? They could have stuffed the last one with explosives and attached it the same way. Or the box we found could somehow take down the rocket and we don't fully understand how yet. If we could open it up and take a look at it, it would help. But that ship has sailed."

"Do you think the parts already walked out of the building?"

Ree sighed. "Probably. But it looked like it was made from a lightweight specialty alloy, which isn't that easy to replace on short notice. Also, if the board was custom, it's pretty difficult to order a new one on a tight timeline. So, if the part is valuable and hard to duplicate, our criminal might have pulled it and kept it close so they could use it somewhere else."

Parker crossed his arms. "What do you think about Kiara? She keeps coming up."

Quinn and Ree shook their heads at the same time. Ree frowned. "No. But my money is on one of her people. That's why I think we need to talk to them."

Quinn nodded. "Tim's first on my list."

"Yeah. He sends up some red flags."

Mike said, "Ree, you got a red flag from a passing grunt when you saw him?"

Ree smiled. "I figure out what you want when you grunt questions from the surveillance van." Mike shook his head. "But seriously, I got it from the grunt and from talking to Kiara. Tim has been pulling late hours to run all of his tests before the launch date. Convenient if he's our guy. We need to go check things out, see what he knows."

Quinn sighed. "I agree. Plus, he acted pretty weird around me."

Cam raised an eyebrow. "He was hitting on you, Quinn."

Quinn felt her cheeks flush. "That might be true, but the way he was going about it was weird. Kiara acted like it wasn't the first time he'd done that. And I wasn't into it. He didn't seem to pick up on that. Isn't that a little unprofessional? On the other hand, if he's our guy, don't you think he'd be laying low, not hitting on visiting engineers?"

Cam shrugged. "You'd think. But you never can tell with people. Some have more self-control than others. And if they're working for someone pulling the strings, masterminds can't always afford to be picky about who they bring in to do their dirty work. Let's see what we can find out about Tim tomorrow."

"Agreed. But we need to shake Hannah. She'll try and come with us to make introductions. She's friendly enough, but I don't know her. I mean, I barely trust Cam enough to bring him along." Quinn nudged him a little with her shoulder.

Cam laughed. "Coming from someone who was still armed when she visited me to share her baked goods."

Quinn shrugged. "Well, I was checking to see if your black eye was better. Who knows? You could have been mad."

Ree's eyes went wide. "Um…I thought you guys were okay? I mean, you seem okay-"

Cam laughed. "We are. We just had a little misunderstanding when we first met."

Quinn and Cam exchanged a look, and Quinn explained. "I was cornered. I apologized. And I fed you afterward."

"I appreciated that." He winked at her and looked at Ree. "That's why we had to tell Quinn about you, Ree. She's got a mean head butt if she thinks you're the bad guy." Quinn threw a light elbow at Cam and he dodged it easily, laughing. "See what I mean?" She shook her head and they began to plan the next day in earnest.

19

THE FOLLOWING MORNING, REE AND PARKER WERE THE FIRST TO arrive at the Vehicle Assembly Building. They waited close to the entrance at a small sitting area, ready to ambush Hannah when she arrived. While they waited, Ree sipped her coffee and tried to find her calm. Even though this was the third time she'd worked with the FBI team, she still couldn't wrap her mind around the fact she was working in the iconic NASA building instead of just taking the bus tour past it. Every time she got close to the big rocket, now upright in the center of one of the high bays, her heart nearly burst with awe. Parker squeezed her hand and she smiled at him. In her earpiece, Ree heard Mike's voice. "You're up. The IRT crew will reach you in thirty seconds." Ree rose from her chair in concert with Parker. They began walking towards the entrance, so their contact would appear incidental. They had rehearsed their lines over breakfast in their room and Ree began to speak when Parker winked at her.

"Parker, we have to tell IRT. They need to know."

"Dr. Ryland, your job is to assess the safety of the satellite. Which you have done exceedingly well. But it's not your call. IRT will be informed per the normal protocols when it's the right – ahem. Hello, folks."

Hannah raised an eyebrow. Her fun-loving personality evaporated for a fraction of a second before a coy smile replaced her concern. "What are you two up to? And weren't there three of you before?"

Ree forced herself to appear sheepish and looked expectantly at Parker, who cleared his throat. "Um, we were just…talking about some issues we found. Mike came down with a bad case of the stomach flu, so he's unfortunately stuck in his hotel room."

"I'm sorry to hear that. I've been with IRT for a number of years now. If there's an issue, I've probably seen it before. I could get you in touch with the right people to solve it." Hannah shrugged as if she had all the time in the world to talk about it, but there was an edge to her easy indifference.

Ree spoke in a low whisper. "Maybe we could run the non-top secret items past these guys. So they know. I think IRT would really appreciate having this information." She shot a look at Parker.

Cam checked his watch. "Thanks, guys, but we're supposed to meet with Kiara in a few minutes. Maybe in a few hours?"

Hannah looked between them. "Why don't I meet with Dr. Ryland and Parker, gather the information, and we can talk about it as a team over lunch? I wasn't going to do anything other than take notes anyway. And then Dr. Ryland and her associate won't be kept waiting."

QUINN SMILED. "You're the best, Hannah. Thank you." It was a good thing Ree and Parker were on her team. The two of them were a well-oiled machine, and poor, sweet Hannah didn't stand a chance.

Hannah pulled her bag up to her shoulder. "Just doing my job. It's nothing." She followed Ree and Parker away and Quinn managed not to give Cam a fist-bump when they turned the corner. Their counterparts in the FBI would give Hannah enough red herrings to keep her busy for the morning. At last, they were free to investigate their most promising leads without a nosy civilian looking over their shoulder.

Mike's voice crackled into her earpiece. "Okay, Parker and Ree, I'm switching over to Cam and Quinn's channel. Sound the alarm if you have a problem, otherwise, we'll record you and look over the footage later." A couple of gentle taps were Parker's answer and their line went quiet. "Okay, guys, let's go find us a saboteur."

Quinn led the way to Kiara's office. Meeting in Alan's office had been a great neutralizer, but Quinn wanted to watch Kiara's interactions with her team on her own turf. There was a feel to team dynamics that you could never truly understand unless you were there in person. If she hadn't had coffee with Chuck, the senior engineer at IRT, she'd still believe IRT's explanation that the last rocket exploded because of a bad part.

When they entered Kiara's area, a few curious faces stared back at them. Tim looked up from his work with a sly smile and walked over to greet them. "Hey Quinn, it's nice to see you back so soon. NASA won't let you close to the satellite without supervision, huh?"

Quinn laughed. "No way. Kiara asked us to do some additional inspections today. On the rocket only. With one of you guys around. I think NASA is going to put a big piece of red tape around the top of the rocket to make sure we don't do anything to mess up the satellite attachment."

Tim laughed, resting his hand on her arm. Quinn moved it away and Cam's jaw clenched, but only for a moment. "Have you seen Kiara?"

Kiara popped her head out of her office. Her eyes looked tired and her hair was pulled back into a bun. "Present. Be with you in a minute."

Tim rested his elbow on the top of a short cubicle wall. "So, let me know if you guys find anything, okay? We really can't afford any more problems on this one. If that satellite gets blown up, NASA will go ballistic. We're all on the same team."

Quinn nodded. "Thanks, Tim. We appreciate it. What do you do for Kiara, again?"

Tim shrugged. "I design the tests we use to make sure everything is safe to go up."

Cam raised an eyebrow. "Like the equipment?"

Tim nodded. "The equipment, sometimes, but a lot of the time, I'm just using off-the-shelf equipment to test everything and make sure she's ready to fly. I design tests that make it easy for the inspectors to plug in the electrical parts and make sure they're working without having to test each component individually."

Quinn leaned forward. "So, were you the one who discovered the part that NASA is freaking out about?"

Tim's eyes went wide. "That's what all the additional inspections are for?"

Quinn heard Mike's voice in her ear. "He's playing you, Quinn. Kiara said he already knows."

Quinn put a hand over her mouth. "I'm sorry. Please forget I said that. I thought they told everyone. Ben will kill me if he finds out I told someone who didn't know." She lowered her voice to a whisper. "Ben sent us down when he heard NASA found something. We're supposed to figure out if the rocket launch is still on schedule."

Tim crossed his arms. "I won't say anything. Tell him you have it on good authority everything is going to plan. I tested everything personally. She's ready to fly. It's just a matter of Kiara double-checking my work."

Quinn smiled. "Thanks, Tim. I owe you one."

Kiara came out of her office, notebook in hand. "Ready to go, guys?"

Quinn nodded and gave Tim a small wave as they left. When they rounded the corner, she let Kiara get ahead of them a bit. She leaned into Cam. "Did that seem weird to you?"

"Very. Let's get into his lab today and rifle through the drawers."

Kiara looked back at them, gave them a funny look. "You guys coming?" It was too bad they couldn't ask her point-blank if she suspected her coworkers of sabotage without blowing their covers. At best, that was Parker and Mike's job. However, today, she'd offered to accompany them while they worked through the inspections on the rocket, currently waiting for the satellite in the high bay. Ben had sent a list of things for Quinn and Cam to check. Kiara would supervise and help where needed. It would give them some valuable time to see if they could learn anything else from the busy project manager while they worked.

Several minutes later, Quinn had uploaded the checklist Ben had provided to a NASA-approved tablet. While nearly everything had been covered by the skin of the rocket when it was brought to the Vehicle Assembly Building, a few panels could be opened for final checks. They started with the first one and Cam dutifully took pictures while Quinn checked off the items on Ben's list. All of the pieces matched the ones in the images Ben sent her. Quinn placed the electronic test equipment up to the right checkpoints and all the readings came back normal. She repeated this on each section, and once she gave her approval, the final panels were installed and sealed. They could be removed if someone at IRT thought she missed something, but broken seals would tell them if someone got into it. It would provide at least a small deterrent to their saboteur.

Regardless, Mike had installed cameras in the large high bay, and anyone would be hard-pressed to come up with an excuse for mucking about with their rocket after IRT had blessed it. Kiara had been close by, but had been mostly quiet, silently observing Quinn's work over her shoulder. As the assemblers put the last panel into position, Quinn patted Kiara on the shoulder. "Thanks for keeping a close eye on things here when we can't." Kiara smiled, but her eyes were a little sad. Quinn let the silence settle between them but didn't break eye contact. "Why don't you seem happier about getting this done?"

"I'm just wondering what else I could have missed."

"We inspected everything on our end. If you do the same on yours, that's all we can do."

Kiara rubbed her forehead. "I agree. Thanks so much for your help. Let's get you guys out of here. I need to see if the safety committee needs anything else and then I can finish up my reports for the day." Kiara walked them to the exit. "I'll let you see your own way out, unless you have any other meetings before you go?"

Quinn checked her watch. "No, I think we're all set. I might pop in and say goodbye to Alan before we leave."

"Sounds good. Thanks again." Kiara walked down a hallway, rubbing the back of her neck as she left. After she turned a corner, Cam turned to face Quinn. "Next stop, Tim's lab?"

"You read my mind. Mike, we clear?"

"For now. His lab is locked, but your badges will work on all doors. We'll delete your entry records as soon as you enter. Morgan hooked me up with a tech guy who works quick. Walk towards Alan's office and take a hard right at the third hallway. Second door on the left after that."

"Do you have eyes on the hallway?"

"Exactly one, so I need you to work quickly. You'll have about twenty seconds to clear the area if I see someone coming. Check the hallways and make sure no one is following you. I can get Ree and Parker in to help in a pinch, but let's only hit that big red button if you're in danger."

The hallway was completely empty. "No one is around. We'll improvise if someone walks in and we can't get out."

"Okay. I'll let you know if you have company."

"You're the best." Quinn grinned. Cam was right – the FBI team wasn't messing around.

A few moments later, Quinn approached Tim's lab with Cam close behind, looking up and down the hallway one last time before entering. Satisfied no one was around, Quinn ran her badge over the scanner and the door clicked open. When they entered, they separated and each took a side of the lab to make sure it was empty. No one was there. Cam shut the door gently behind them and Quinn felt her pulse kick up a notch. There was no way they could explain their presence behind a locked door easily at this point. But after their discussion with Tim, they had to take the risk. He had no reason to lie to them unless he was hiding something.

Not so long ago, Quinn was rifling through her old boss's drawers in Moscow, worried he would walk in at any moment. This wasn't her first rodeo. There was a trick to searching a space without getting caught. She pulled a wand out of her bag to scan for bugs in each section, then gently pulled open each drawer, looking for pieces of tape or anything else that a spy might use to figure out someone had been snooping. There was no obvious spycraft at work, so she methodically kept searching through the drawers. Halfway through a cabinet, she pulled a drawer to full open, but a divider in the back of the drawer made it stop a little bit short of its neighbors. "Cam, get over here."

Cam came over, noiselessly, and she wiggled the drawer a bit to get the cover off the false back. Two boxes, identical to the one in Ree's pictures, sat in the uncovered space, with a coated wire sticking out of each box like an antenna. Quinn ran the bug sweeper over the top again, but nothing triggered the alarm. The devices weren't actively collecting data right now. Interesting. "What do you do?" she whispered to the boxes. She considered taking one with her but thought better of it. If they removed the boxes, they might never find out who put them on the satellite in the first place. A small camera would make prosecuting the right person that much easier when they came back for their parts. She pulled an adhesive camera out of her bag and attached it to the underside of the drawer. She flicked it on and the bug sweeper sounded a beep. The camera was working, but could also be detected. It was a risk they'd just have to take.

"Guys, Tim's coming. Get out of there now." Mike's voice in her ear made Quinn jump.

Quinn looked at the door. They could get out in time, but not if she put the drawer back in order. "No time."

"I'm coming in for backup."

20

Quinn replaced the false back of the drawer and closed it, moving slower than she would like, but as fast as she was willing to risk. Cam ran a hand over the drawer, making sure nothing was amiss. Quinn checked her watch. Twenty seconds had passed. They didn't have enough time to get out without being spotted. Cam grabbed her by the hand and pulled her to a closet. They stuffed themselves into a narrow space between the boxes and closed the door as quietly as possible.

"You didn't ignore the rules and bring your gun, did you?" Cam whispered.

Quinn shook her head, her heart pounding. "No. And I had to wear pants to be around the rocket. No knife." There was barely enough space to stand in the tiny closet and her front was pressed against Cam's back. The heavy door to the lab space opened and closed with a thud and click. Would Tim go straight for the drawer? Were they even his parts? How was she going to explain why she and Cam were stuffed in a closet if he checked it? If Tim was their guy and he found them in a closet, they'd be sitting ducks.

The sound of footsteps approaching the closet stopped her short. She rolled her eyes. Damn it. She'd never had to do this before and always promised herself it'd be World War III before she used her feminine wiles to influence an op. She didn't need to be a stereotype. But Rory had died and she could too if she didn't do something drastic. Quinn flipped Cam around and grabbed him by the front of his shirt. His eyes went wide. Quinn whispered, "We need a reason to be in here."

Quinn leaned in and he wrapped his arms around her. His lips pressed against hers and she slid her hands around Cam's back. Her knees buckled against her will. The door handle creaked and she frantically pulled his shirt out of his pants. They needed to look like they'd lost control – and Quinn wouldn't completely have to fake it. But she didn't have time to think about that right now.

The door opened and light flooded the closet. Cam startled and winked at her before he turned, blocking her with one hand. Quinn leaned around him, making her eyes wide and frightened. By the height Tim's eyebrows achieved, Cam did a great job of acting like he was affected. Quinn did her best to look flushed and embarrassed, which required very little acting on her part. She reached a hand out to Cam's waist to steady herself and he placed a hand over hers.

Cam pulled on her hand. "Um, we'll just be going. Hey man, I'd appreciate it if you didn't say anything. We're not really allowed to date. Work rules, and all."

Tim eyed them. He nodded knowingly and smiled. "Yeah, I get it. No problem. Just one question. How'd you get into the lab?"

Cam squeezed her hand. "The door was cracked open. Was it not supposed to be open?"

Tim shook his head. "No – it's a controlled lab."

"Oh, man. I'm sorry. I just…you understand."

"Yeah, I do. Listen, I'm not going to rat you out. Maybe you can do me a favor too?"

Cam nodded, started tucking in his shirt. "Yeah, man, anything. I owe you one."

"Can you keep the safety committee off my back? I'm just trying to get this thing off the ground and I need them off my case to do my job. I'm going to miss a date and get fired if they keep breathing down my neck."

"Yeah, absolutely. I'll talk to them. I think I can get them to back off." Cam pulled Quinn out from behind him. He kept her in front of him until they left Tim's lab. Once they were in the hallway, they ran into Mike, who had barely broken a sweat, but made it to them inside of about three minutes.

"You guys okay? It sounded like someone was panicking."

And...Mike had heard heavy breathing. Well, that made things less humiliating. Quinn decided he didn't need to know the full extent of what had actually happened, even if he'd already guessed. Quinn shrugged. "We were a little worried, but we improvised. Thanks for the heads up. It's him. I'm 99 percent sure."

"Why don't you have him in handcuffs?" Mike raised an eyebrow.

"The other 1 percent. I planted a camera. It should be streaming as we speak."

Mike pulled up the feed on his phone and then gave them a small salute. "Nice work. I'll get back to the van and keep an eye on it. I'm supposed to be sick with the stomach flu."

Quinn nodded, her hands on her hips. Her heart was racing like she'd just run a marathon. Cam looked at her with a mischievous grin. "Didn't know you were into me, Q."

Quinn rolled her eyes. "Please. It was kiss you or get caught."

Cam shrugged. "If you say so."

"It was better than getting shot. That's all I'm going to say." Quinn tried to saunter off but stumbled. She took a deep breath and went to go find their FBI allies.

Minutes later, Mike was in their ear again. "Tim pulled the components from the drawer and is on the move. You spooked him. He's headed towards the high bay."

"That was fast. Let's go," Quinn said, and turned a corner to cut Tim off before he could reach the high bay.

Cam held a hand on her arm. "Give him a head start. Let's see what he's going to do with them. Mike, you have cameras in there?"

"Affirmative, Cam. We've got eyes on. Parker and Ree are in there with Kiara now, watching her back while she goes through NASA's checkboxes. Hannah went back to talk with someone on Kiara's team."

Quinn took a deep breath. "Okay. Let us know when he gets in there, Mike."

Several minutes later, Mike's voice buzzed in Quinn's ear. "He's in with the rocket. Parts were hidden under his jacket."

"Any sign of a weapon?" Cam started walking towards the high bay and Quinn followed.

"Negative. Doesn't mean he doesn't have one. Do you want security involved?"

Quinn scratched the back of her neck. "No. We still don't know if he's working alone. We need to get him out of there without a scuffle and see who gets upset he's gone missing."

A few minutes later, Quinn and Cam reached the doors to the high bay to get to the man sabotaging IRT's rocket. Hopefully, no bloodletting would be involved. Kiara would kill her.

"Hey, Quinn!" Hannah's bright voice made Quinn jump. "Hey, Mr. It's Complicated." Cam smiled a tight smile. "Aw, come on. Don't think I haven't noticed what you guys are up to. The secret looks. The smiles."

Quinn placed a hand on the door to the high bays and tried her best to look mysterious. "I can neither confirm nor deny. Hey, sorry, Hannah, but Kiara needs us to answer some questions. We'll see you in a little bit, okay?"

Hannah smiled and gave them a small salute. "You got it."

Mike's voice crackled in their ear. "Parker and Ree know you're coming, you guys. They've got Kiara tucked in behind the rocket. Get in there and get Tim out as quick as you can."

When they entered, they only saw feet at the bottom of the rocket, on a scaffold near the engines. There was a control panel in that area, but not much else. Quinn and Cam approached Tim slowly, spreading out to close him in. When he lowered himself from the engine, he waved at them. "Hey, lovebirds."

"Hey, Tim. Do you mind showing me what you're working on?" Quinn took a few steps closer, but he raised a hand to head her off.

"I'm sorry, Quinn. But this work is classified. You can't see it."

"That's not NASA's end of the rocket, Tim." Quinn moved her hand to her side but remembered her knife was in the hotel room.

Tim's voice faltered a bit. "I didn't want to tell you, but I found another problem." Tim began reaching for something in his pocket and Cam closed the distance between them. Tim changed tactics and tried to punch Cam. Cam dodged it, easily, swept his leg, and pinned him to the floor. He pulled the knife from Tim's pocket and slid it to Quinn.

"Don't move. You're coming with me." Tim tried to bite Cam, but he twisted Tim's wrist around, pressing his thumb into the back of Tim's hand. Tim whimpered. "We can do this the easy way or the hard way. I would suggest you go quietly if you don't want me to do that again." Tim stilled and the two escorted him away. Quinn dropped back. She whispered, "Mike, make sure Parker and Ree check this spot. Tim was under the rocket when we saw him."

Cam led Tim back to his lab and badged in. Mike was inside, waiting with a pair of handcuffs. He snapped them on Tim. "Care to explain what you were doing under the rocket?"

Sweat began to form at Tim's temples. "I was just running some tests."

Cam narrowed his eyes at Tim and he shrank back. "Nice try. Who are you working for?"

Tim looked at the floor. "I don't know."

Quinn crossed her arms. "Bullshit."

Mike flipped his FBI badge out. "I'd appreciate it if you'd answer my friends' questions. If you cooperate with us, we'll do what we can to lower your sentence."

Adrenaline pumped through Quinn's body, but she managed to keep her voice even and reasonable. "You're going to need our help, Tim. We just caught you sabotaging a rocket. That's a lot of jail time, right, Mike?"

Mike nodded and Tim's eyes darted between Quinn and Mike. "I didn't sabotage anything. The boxes just take measurements."

Quinn shook her head. "Listen, Mike, if he's not going to tell us the truth, just get him out of here."

Mike took a step towards Tim. Tim flinched. "It's true. Someone offered me a side job. They wanted flight path data."

"And you decided to give it to them? Just like that?"

Tim shrugged. "If they were smart, they could get most of what they asked me to measure off of video footage of the launches or through publicly available data. I figured if they couldn't figure it out on their own, I could relieve them of some of their money."

Quinn narrowed her eyes. "Okay. Who did you relieve of their money?"

Tim met her eyes, then began to study the floor. Quinn let the silence sit for a moment. Tim was going to turn on whoever hired him – he wasn't going down with the ship. She just needed to give him enough time to get there. He looked up. "I really don't know. They called me once. I didn't recognize the voice. Everything else went through an email address. The email address changes every week. Someone shipped the parts to my house and I put them on the satellites."

"Okay, if the parts just measure flight paths, why did the last launch explode?"

"IRT thinks it was a bad part. There are a thousand reasons a rocket could fail. Measurement equipment isn't even on the list."

Quinn studied Tim. Unfortunately for her, he believed the story he was telling. "And what about Rory?"

"I don't know who that is." Quinn started towards Tim, but Cam caught her arm. Tim shrunk back.

Quinn crossed her arms. "What *do* you know, Tim?"

"That's all. I'll give you everything I have. Take my phone, everything is on there. I just don't want to go to jail."

Quinn swallowed back her anger. Yes, he folded easily, but he was also a pawn. The trail could end with him. "I think that ship has sailed. But we appreciate your help and will do our part to lower your sentence if we can. Mike, why don't you take it from here?" Mike nodded. Quinn left to go find Hannah with Cam following silently behind. As she walked away with a neutral expression, blood still pounded in her ears. Criminals often missed the obvious in order to justify their actions. Of course, the boxes took down the rockets, but Tim ignored the possibility to make a quick buck. And he didn't know anything about Rory.

After checking a few of the office spaces, Quinn found Hannah chatting up Kiara in the cleanroom. Quinn knocked on the window and both women came out. When Quinn told Kiara that Tim had been walked out by Alan and security, her shoulders sagged – either with relief or disappointment. Hannah patted her on the shoulder before leaving with the rest of the team. "Sorry to hear one of your guys got let go. Honestly, he was always a little weird. Let me know if you need any help, or just someone to talk to, okay?"

Kiara gave her a weak smile. "Thanks, Hannah. I'll let you know."

By the end of the day, their FBI colleagues had confirmed that Tim had both boxes on the scaffold but hadn't had time to install them. Cam retrieved the parts and would be sending them back to Morgan for a more thorough analysis. Once they were back in the hotel room, the FBI team met Quinn and Cam for a debrief.

After everyone was inside, Ree shut the door to the room. "Good job, guys. Kiara had no idea you arrested her employee while she was in the same room."

Quinn smiled. "In her defense, the room is big enough to hold a rocket. It's easy to miss something like that."

"Are you going to tell her?"

Quinn shrugged. "We'll tell her a version of the truth. I think we'll say he made a careless mistake and was fired on the spot. Don't worry about us, though. We'll figure it out."

Ree crossed her arms. "Did you get anything from Tim?"

"No. He confessed immediately, but whoever he was working with was smart enough to limit what he knew and lie to him about what he was doing. Probably because they knew if he got caught, he wouldn't keep his mouth shut. He even had pictures of the rocket engines and inner components on his cell phone. The email addresses he used are now defunct. We'll try to track the payments and shipments of the parts, but I suspect we're going to run into a lot of dead ends."

Ree rubbed her forehead. "Well, at least you took care of the problem here."

Quinn exchanged a look with Cam. "Yeah. I hope."

Parker looked at his watch. "Sorry to cut this short, but it's time for us to get out of here. Nice working with you both." They said their goodbyes and the FBI team left to catch their flight.

At Alan's insistence, the IRT team returned to Seattle the following morning, since their inspections were now complete. Practically, it was time to get out of Kennedy Space Center before the gossip started, and Hannah started to get suspicious. They'd successfully removed their criminal at KSC. They needed to get back to the IRT facility to see if anyone there was upset about it. They'd managed to keep Hannah blissfully unaware of their activities even as she'd provided daily updates to Ben. Despite the lack of information from Tim, they'd at least put him out of play and found out what he knew. It was hard to imagine how their trip could have gone better under the circumstances.

21

Ree returned to her desk at Indiana Polytechnic and booted up her computer. After a busy week out of the office catching bad guys, a fair amount of emails had piled up. At least it was summer. Leaving during the fall or spring semester would have been so much worse. Matt had generously covered her classes, but she still had homework to grade. The emails would have to wait until later. She needed to get the pile of graded homework back to her students this afternoon. She flipped through the assignments with her pen in hand, providing feedback and correcting free body diagrams as she graded. After a half-hour had passed, she looked up from the papers and rubbed her eyes.

Ree pulled a chocolate from her drawer and her mind began to drift back to Florida. Her part of the investigation was over. Kiara remained in the dark about the true nature of Tim's arrest, believing that Alan had fired Tim for making a mistake. Cam and Quinn would return to IRT to see if they could ferret out anyone else that might be involved. There was no sign of any more offending components. The satellite could be placed on top of the rocket soon in preparation for the launch. Alan had even invited them to come back to see it, an invitation Ree planned to take full advantage of, since the launch was on a Saturday. While launches were frequently rescheduled, she'd always wanted to see one in person and would take the risk of an extra flight to Florida in hopes of catching it on its scheduled day.

The chocolate melted and she took a sip of coffee. Arresting Tim had been almost too easy. A quick arrest should be a good thing. Still, something bothered her. A CIA operations officer had been killed at IRT and Quinn thought two people were in on this. Quinn had tried to get information out of Hannah about Tim, but she'd been pleasantly unhelpful. Ree took another sip of coffee. Her discomfort turned into a bitter taste in her mouth when she realized the problem. The office gossip would care about Tim. Would speculate about Tim. Instead, Quinn said Hannah had waved away his actions as trivial. Hannah's work was detailed, thorough, and there wasn't so much as a punctuation mark out of place. She must know more than she was letting on. Was she protecting someone?

Ree pulled out her phone to text Parker. It took her a moment to articulate her concerns, but once she'd sent the message, she could finally focus on grading her papers. Once they were complete, she answered her urgent emails and went back to help Matt in the lab. They were working on a project that would require her to set up a new piece of test equipment. FBI or no FBI work, she still had research to finish. She badged into the secure lab and the door unlocked with a beep and a click. Because they often worked on experiments that required rocket fuel, the precaution was a necessary one, even on a college campus. Matt greeted her when she entered and Ree used the time assembling the equipment to try and process what else she might be missing. Her phone buzzed in her pocket and she checked it, careful not to let Matt see the screen. Parker had passed her concerns onto Cam and Quinn and thanked her for the lead. Now she just had to be patient enough to let Quinn find the answer and not think about it too much. It was easier said than done.

When Ree walked home from work that evening, she couldn't quite push the problem of Hannah to the back of her mind. After she entered the house and locked the door, her phone rang with an unknown number. "Hello?"

"Hi Ree, it's Quinn. Do you have a minute?"

"Of course. What's up?"

"I need an opinion."

Ree put her keys on a hook by the door and went to pour a glass of wine. This might be a long conversation. "I'm always happy to give one. Have you found anything new?"

"Not new, per se. I've been staring at the code they use to guide the rockets today."

"Um, that sounds amazing. Can I see it?"

Quinn chuckled. "I forget how much you like this stuff. I don't think so. I barely convinced them to let me look at it. But I have a question for you. I know you're a mechanical engineer, but do you know anything about control systems?"

"Yeah. It's not my favorite subject, but I had to take a few classes in them. What's your question?"

"Would it be possible to manipulate the inputs into a software? I mean, it isn't my area of expertise, but I like equations. And the code looks perfect. But here's the thing – if the code is perfect…"

"The inputs could be bad. Shew. Wouldn't they know that by now?"

"That's the thing. I found out from one of the engineers here that they aren't sure if the last rocket self-destructed. They're programmed to do that when they go off course."

"How could they not know?"

"Apparently, they started getting weird readings, but they never received the signal the rocket was going to explode. Then the rocket went boom. IRT assumed it was a bad part. Some folks on my team have their doubts."

Ree took a sip of wine. "So you're saying they don't actually know why their last multimillion dollar rocket blew up?"

"That's exactly what I'm saying. The whole 'bad part' theory is exactly that – a theory. And I'm looking at the code, and wondering if it's possible to manipulate the inputs. What's your professional opinion?"

"I mean, it's possible, but you'd catch it on inspections. NASA has a very rigorous process. I went through it all with Kiara. They plug in a standard set of inputs to the electronic systems and then…oh no. That's it."

"What's it?"

"The testing NASA developed is a pre-decided, standard set of inputs. If you figure out what they are, you can beat them. You program your device to act normal during testing and then start sabotaging the rocket once the data is real. Kiara might still have a problem. Tell her to check anything that connects with the brains of the rocket. Using a different set of test parameters than they've ever used before."

"I'll call her and let her know. Thanks, Ree. I owe you one."

"You got it. And hey, I don't know what's going on with you and Cam, but he's one of the best people I know. You could do a lot worse."

"Um…thanks. But the whole closet thing was just a show for Tim."

"What closet thing?"

"Cam didn't mention anything?"

"No, he left that part out." Ree laughed and took a sip of wine. "What were you two doing in a closet?"

Quinn cleared her throat. "We just got cornered and had to fabricate some backstory. It was no big deal."

Ree bit her lip to keep from laughing again. "If you say so. Let me know if you need anything else."

"Thanks, Ree. I'll let you know how things turn out. With the rocket."

QUINN OPENED the door to leave the small conference room she'd slipped into to call Ree. She kept her walk slow and easy when she went to meet Cam in the work cafeteria. He'd heard her conversation with Ree in his earpiece and, aside from the embarrassing bit at the end, it'd been a useful time-saver. They both got a coffee and sat close to one another at a table.

"I sent Morgan a message. Dan is going to call Alan so he or Kiara can run the tests," Cam said, into his coffee. "We should know how it all works out soon. The rocket will get transported to the launchpad tomorrow if we pass."

"Good. Thank you. Do we need to go down there again?"

"I don't think so. But I think you need to take a close look at your team. Ree is on to something. Hannah knows more than she's letting on. Rory thought the Flight Navigation team knew something. Any other candidates?"

Quinn took a sip of coffee and looked slowly around the cafeteria, making sure everyone around was out of earshot. "Chuck knows a ton about the software, but truthfully, everyone has touched it. And the programming looks good. I don't think you need someone manipulating the software if they can send it the wrong inputs. It might just be someone who understands the code."

"Like Ben?"

"I didn't think so at first, but he knows more than anyone else about how it works."

"Anyone particularly talkative about the technology?"

"I mean, there's Hannah, but she's usually just asking about my day or about you, not the technology. She's really nosy, but she seems to be mostly focused on superficial things or people. Ben is everywhere all at once. Chuck, for me, is a no. I'll keep an eye on him but he seems like a genuinely good person. If we get you closer to Hannah, maybe you can help figure out what she's hiding. Or who she's protecting."

Cam finished up his coffee and stood. "Okay. Let's think about the best way to approach her and talk about it after work. Keep doing your thing, but I think we're getting closer."

"I know. Be careful, Cam."

That evening, Quinn went to Cam's "house" for their nightly meeting. His condo smelled fantastic. He was still in the kitchen, so she said loud enough for him to hear, "I'm not sure this is fair. I have a frozen meal planned for dinner and this smells way better."

Cam walked out of his small kitchen holding two plates heaped with food. "Correction. If you're up for it, you can have real food instead of a frozen meal. I owe you for all the desserts you've been making. Hope you like your steak medium. I don't know how to cook it any other way. It's not up to my usual standard, though. I had to make it in a pan and not on a grill. But it'll do."

"You made me a steak dinner?"

"Yeah, some of us take people out to dinner before they accost them in a closet." Cam gave her a mischievous grin and she nudged him in the stomach. He jumped back, keeping the plates in the air. "Hey, I don't want any trouble. My black eye is finally gone."

Quinn followed Cam to his small kitchen table. She raised an eyebrow. "Number one – making out with you in a closet kept Tim from realizing what we were up to. Number two – you didn't seem to think it was a bad idea at the time. Number three – why don't you tell me what's put you in such a good mood?"

Cam joined her at the table and cut into his steak. Before lifting the piece to his mouth, he said, "I heard from Morgan. After Dan passed along the idea from you and Ree, Kiara and Alan found another device on the rocket. A tiny little circuit board and battery nested under some other equipment, hidden from inspection by a small panel. It's an exact replica of the ones we found in Tim's lab. That part came from IRT. Gives more credence to the theory he has an accomplice up here."

"Hot damn."

"Exactly. Only one input failed the test and it was the one that provided orientation data for the rocket. It fits your theory perfectly. Bad data gets sent to the launch control software, the rocket goes boom because it thinks it's going off course."

"And now we know how to prevent it on future launches." Quinn raised her hand in a fist bump and Cam met her in the middle. "Is that all?"

"Nope. it gets better." Quinn placed her silverware on the table. "The analysts disassembled the parts we gave them and traced them to their source. The circuit board is from a small factory in Moscow."

Quinn raised a hand to her mouth. "Holy shit. It's Russian?"

Cam nodded. "Oh yeah. And the NSA traced the call to Tim back to the same number our friends in Romania were using to get in touch with Dmitri. What are the odds Dmitri is behind this? On the one hand, it's totally unrelated to releasing a bioweapon. On the other, he seems to have some level of comfort with operating a team over here. Do you remember seeing anything while you were there that could be related?"

Quinn closed her eyes, visualizing his office. Before she'd left, she'd rifled through all of his files, looking for something, anything that could explain what he was up to in Romania. Her memory was good but fell short of photographic. She'd been looking for evidence that would point her to why he was making biological weapons, so nothing came to mind immediately. She imagined herself walking over to the file cabinets and running her finger along the tops of his file folders. Then it hit her. Her eyes popped open. "Vostok. Dmitri had a folder labeled Vostok. There was a piece of paper with a series of numbers on it. Nothing else, though. So that doesn't do us much good."

"Vostok is Russian for east. What does that mean? Is that a code for an operation?"

"Oh yeah, it does mean 'east'. I forget you're a polyglot. But it's not the literal translation. The Vostok rockets launched the first Russian satellites and later took people up into space. Dmitri is meddling in the space program. Why would he mess with a U.S. company? It's not even NASA."

"No, it isn't. But we are launching a spy satellite...oh no. It's bigger than that. What's the next launch for IRT? After this one?"

"The test launch to prepare to put people into space. Which won't fly if another rocket explodes. Which means we'll still need the Russians to give us a ride to the space station. Shit."

Cam paused for a moment. "Do you think his bosses know what he's up to?"

Quinn sighed. "I highly doubt it. Dmitri is all about jockeying for position. Which means if he's planning something this big, he doesn't tell anyone about it. If he loses, no one is the wiser. That way, he always wins. No way his bosses know about this. Can you imagine the embarrassment if the news got ahold of the story that Russia supported the sabotage of U.S. rockets? Even if they wanted to, they wouldn't risk it. Dmitri is definitely acting alone. But they give him a long leash and he's got a lot of resources at his disposal, so that doesn't make it any easier for us to catch him. Especially if he has multiple people working for him over here."

"Agree with that. Tim is the second person we've found working for Dmitri. It's like finding mice in your house – where there's one, there are usually two. Where there's two, well, you're going to need a lot of mousetraps."

"Do we tip off Tim that we know he's working for the Russians?"

"No way. First of all, I don't think he knows he's working for the Russians. If he's a good liar and working with a network, we don't know what he could communicate from jail. We need him to think he's won. So, we have until the launch before his allies realize they have a problem. Then we can try and shake down Tim again. We can't do much about Dmitri from here, but if we get enough information, we can put Dmitri out of play. If we can prove what he's up to, his bosses will have to take him out of circulation."

"I like it. We have a plan." Quinn dug into her meal in earnest. "This is good, Cam. I might have to keep you around."

"Keep me around? If it was a different era, after what you did, you might have to marry me." Cam grinned.

Quinn rolled her eyes. "Dan didn't warn me you latched on to things like this. That needs to go in your file. I might even put that in my next email." She pretended to pull up an email on her phone and drew out the words. "Has trouble letting things go."

Cam cracked a smile at her and she looked away. "Any ideas on how to figure out what Hannah knows about any of this?"

Quinn shrugged. "Why don't you stop by the office tomorrow and see if Hannah tells you anything she hasn't told me? Then, we can try to figure out more at trivia night. There's another one tomorrow. We could warm her up while we're there. Or at least see who she's spending time with socially."

"Sounds like a plan." Cam looked into a space past Quinn.

"What is it?"

"Have you ever noticed something funny about the way she talks?"

"What do you mean? Besides the fact that she's super enthusiastic about everything?"

Cam frowned. "No. It's not that. It's the inflection in her voice. It's something I do when I'm trying to get a dialect just right. I focus, not on the words themselves, but how people say them. If you're struggling with a dialect, sometimes it's easier to try and tune yourself into a mood, then you can nail the dialect. Almost like you're acting out a character. I can't quite put my finger on if she's doing that, though. Listen tomorrow, tell me what you think."

"I'll keep an ear out for anything funny. I'm pretty good with a few languages, but if half of what Dan says about you is true, you're out of my league on the mechanics of language. I've just had a ton of practice on a few of them. Could she be covering up for her nerves?"

"Absolutely. Let's see what we can figure out tomorrow. The launch happens this weekend and it'd be nice to button things up here before that."

Quinn rose to take her empty plate to the kitchen and Cam followed behind her with his. Before returning to her condo, she leaned against a wall. "Thanks for dinner. It was spectacular."

"You're welcome."

"Listen, I have a question for you. Actually, more of a statement. I'm sorry if the whole making out in a closet thing made you uncomfortable. I made a call, but I didn't intend to upset you. I hope I didn't misread your willingness or overstep professional boundaries. I've never done that on an operation. Ever. And I don't want it to be a problem. But if it is, I'll do what I can to make it right."

Cam raised an eyebrow. "You think it bothered me?"

"You've mentioned it a few times and it was an impulsive decision. I just want you to see me as a fellow professional."

"I do." Cam crossed his arms and got an inscrutable look on his face.

"And I don't want you to think less of me because I resorted to a honey trap."

"Don't think that's what it's called if you're on the same team."

"You're killing me, Cam. I'm trying to apologize."

Cam leaned against the wall across from her. "Quinn, if someone bothers me, I don't stew about it and I definitely don't unleash a bunch of passive-aggressive BS on someone. I just tell them. You made a call that kept us out of hot water. Frankly, it was the right call since we're both alive and Tim's in custody. So, good work. And don't sweat it. And if you have to do it again, I'll take one for the team. But warn a guy next time. I'm not sure that was my best work."

Quinn narrowed her eyes at him. "Um. Thanks. I think."

"That said, I will continue to give you a hard time about it."

"It seems to be how you communicate."

"Only with people I like, Quinn. And if it really bothers you, I'll stop. Just say the word. I'm a smartass, not a jerk." Cam grinned. Quinn's stomach tightened and she bit her lip. Oh, this was not good. She'd only brought it up for the sake of operational harmony. She let out a deep breath.

"Goodnight, Cam."

"Night, Quinn."

22

Despite the nice meal, potential breakthrough on the investigation, and what should have been some measure of stress relief, Quinn once again found herself awake at 2 AM. Going to trivia night tonight was minor compared to the adventure they'd just been on, but also where Rory had gotten herself into trouble. Quinn's stomach burned at the realization. A few tears formed in her eyes. They fell down her cheeks and she let the grief soak into her pillow. Cam was right, she needed to feel it, not push it away. Several minutes later with her eyes burning, she thought through some opening lines for her new IRT friends at trivia night. Issues processed, she should have been able to go back to sleep, but instead, her body began to wake up. Quinn sighed, flipped over, and closed her eyes tight.

Several minutes later and no closer to falling asleep, Quinn rose to check the contents of the kitchen. She had some leftover oatmeal, some chocolate chips and cranberries. By the time she added all the butter needed for the recipe she knew by heart, they wouldn't necessarily be the healthiest oatmeal bars, but they would definitely be the best tasting. She turned on the oven and quickly combined the ingredients, working the spoon through the dense dough. She scooped the thick mixture into a small baking dish and set a timer. A knock at her door made her jump, then smile. She chided herself and pushed it away. When she'd first met Cam, he seemed like the quintessential CIA tough guy. Her stereotypes were further reinforced when she found out he used to be a SEAL. And he was still both of those people. But he was quickly evolving into someone she trusted when trust didn't come easily or naturally in her job. She scratched the back of her neck. "Come in."

Cam entered wearing pajama pants and a Navy t-shirt. He smiled a sleepy smile. "Are the cookies ready yet?"

"Do you always think with your stomach? And I hope you won't be disappointed to find out they're oatmeal bars."

He rubbed his stomach. "I can be flexible. You okay?"

Quinn wrapped her arms around her middle. "I will be. Just working through some stuff. Like a friend of mine recommended."

"Your friend sounds really smart. Anything I can help with?"

Quinn shrugged and Cam walked over to give her a hug. She leaned into him, wrapping her arms around his waist. "You're making it very hard for me to dislike you, Cam."

"I'm not sure that's a bad thing since we're working on the same team." Cam didn't pull back from the hug and she didn't exactly mind. "Is that a problem?"

Quinn nodded and swallowed hard. "I don't get attached to people." But she didn't let go and he still didn't move away.

Cam tucked a loose hair behind her ear. "I understand that. Would you like me to be a bigger jerk? I generally try not to be an asshole but I can work on it."

Quinn laughed but didn't pull away just yet. "That won't be necessary."

"You know there are no bad guys waiting to catch us, no one watching us right now. Curtains are closed."

Quinn raised an eyebrow. "I'm aware of that. Any reason you're pointing that out?"

"Because…I'd like to kiss you again, and I want to be clear that it's not for the operation. It isn't because there is someone waiting outside we need to fool. Is that okay with you? I don't want another black eye." His tone was teasing, but it was the hint of vulnerability that did her in.

Quinn nodded and he kissed her softly. She felt her knees buckle and he lifted her to the counter so they would be eye to eye. This needed to stop, or it was going to get way out of hand. Quinn closed her eyes and took a deep breath. A shrill beep snapped her out of her fog. Cam stepped out of the way and Quinn jumped off the counter to get her oatmeal bars out of the oven. She pulled on an oven mitt and her hand shook slightly as she pulled them out. She took off the mitt and used it to fan her face. "This isn't something I usually do. Have ever done. I...I'm interested. But I think we need to take operational hanky-panky off the table."

"Operational hanky-panky?" The corner of Cam's mouth twitched.

"You know, like a summer camp fling. I don't want to be the most convenient girl around. I don't want you to be the most convenient guy around. And I don't trust myself right now."

Cam grinned and she whacked him with the oven mitt. He pulled her close one more time and she sunk into him, just a little bit. It wasn't her fault, really. There was something electric between them. "Okay. No summer camp flings. But, after this is all over, I'd like to take you on a date. Even if Dan makes me fill out paperwork first."

Quinn bit her lip. "This is going to be dicey."

"Yeah, I know. But I would have cut and run after our first meeting if I was afraid of things getting dicey." Quinn rested her head on his shoulder and Cam ran a hand down her back. "I am going to take a raincheck on the baked goods. I need to get back to work. I'm told I have a date waiting for me on the other side of this operation."

Quinn threaded her hand through Cam's. "That sounds good, Cam. Really good."

CAM WOKE up to the faint smell of oatmeal bars and grinned. He wouldn't quite have believed what had happened the night before if he didn't have some evidence he hadn't imagined it. It wasn't as if he didn't date on occasion, but he'd never met anyone quite like Quinn. She was a total badass but also good to the core. In fact, he hadn't considered he had a chance with her until she grabbed him in the closet. So he kept it professional and maintained his distance. Then her knees buckled under her and all bets were off. While he never liked to play that close to the line of fire on an op, their proximity to danger at least came with some side benefits. Cam ran a hand down his face. He should be focused on finding out more about Hannah right now, not thinking about what had happened between them. This was why it would be a good idea to avoid – what did Quinn call it? Operational hanky-panky. He chuckled, threw the sheets off the bed, and began to prepare himself for the day ahead.

After their usual morning meeting, Cam and Quinn left in separate vehicles. Cam parked the van in a new spot on the other side of the IRT complex. He tried to minimize his physical presence at IRT, since his position there was more precarious than hers. He'd just been added to an electronic system and Dan had convinced an employee at IRT to play along with a minimum amount of information. The last thing he needed was someone wondering why he was there. Cam checked his watch – it was almost time for him to go in. Hannah generally worked until 11:30 and then ate her lunch in the employee cafeteria. She brought her own lunch, but she always sat at the same table, socializing with whoever came by. Today, that someone would be him. While Hannah had focused most of her attention on befriending Quinn, she'd humor Cam for at least a little while, and he could see if he could make a breakthrough on whatever she was hiding.

Women often lied to protect other people and Hannah seemed close to Ben and his team. Maybe she knew about a mistake they made and then covered up. Or maybe she had suspicions about the now-arrested Tim. As far as IRT was concerned, Tim had been fired for making a careless mistake and no one had heard from him since. Truthfully, he was sitting in a jail cell in Florida for the foreseeable future. His calls would be monitored, but there was no sign of external contact with him. It was too bad they couldn't just go shake him down, ask him the questions they really wanted to ask. But life wasn't like the movies – if they showed they knew more than they did, he could send a message out to whoever he was working with. Probably Dmitri, but they couldn't prove it yet. Morgan had asked their local sources to discover what they could about Dmitri's interest in the American space program, but after Quinn quit working for him, they didn't have a very good idea of what he was doing.

Cam entered through the front doors of IRT and, after making his way through security, headed straight for the cafeteria. He checked his watch. Hannah would be arriving in about five minutes. He picked his way through the options and settled on a salmon and quinoa salad. He might as well enjoy the food options that came with being on the West Coast. He paid for his meal and spotted Quinn on the other side of the cafeteria. She winked at him before dumping her tray and leaving the area. Cam scanned the cafeteria and made his way towards Hannah's table. She looked up at him from her sandwich and cell phone. She packed her own lunch every day – a turkey sandwich, apple and chips. She turned the phone off before he could tell what she'd been looking at. "Mind if I join you?"

"Not at all, Cam. Are things getting a little less crazy for you now that the launch is just around the corner?"

Cam shrugged. "They're as calm as they can be. Is your team doing okay?"

Hannah chewed a bite of her sandwich. "I think so. I've talked Ben down, if that's possible. Quinn seems to be settling in, finding her rhythm with the team."

"That's good. How about you? Are things pretty hectic for you pre-launch?"

Hannah laughed. "Oh yeah. For what good it will do. They aren't going to send a software update to the rocket at the last minute, so I don't know why everyone is so worked up. I'm actually taking everyone out for trivia to blow off some steam tonight. You should come – I've already talked Ben and your 'it's complicated' into coming. Bad news, work talk inevitably drifts into the discussion. Good news, they eventually settle down and have a good time. It just takes a couple of drinks sometimes."

Cam grinned. "I'll be there. Any advice for me to move out of the 'it's complicated' zone?"

Hannah packed up what was left of her lunch, even though she hadn't finished all of it. "Persistence. Sorry, Complicated, I have to get back to my desk to meet with Ben. See you tonight."

Cam watched her leave. It hadn't been a complete waste of time. He'd planned on going to trivia anyway and now she'd think it was because she'd invited him. He sat down to eat his lunch and returned to the van for the afternoon.

After a fruitless day, Cam drove them both to Bar 1.01. Before exiting, he turned to face Quinn. "Game plan?"

"Figure out who is the most curious about our trip to Florida."

"Well, let's hope we have more luck than when I tried to eat lunch with Hannah. If she hadn't invited us out tonight, I might have thought she was trying to avoid me."

They entered the bar together and Hannah waved them over. Unlike Cam's first trip to the bar, he now had someone to watch his back. He threaded his way through the large crowd to Hannah's team's table. There were no visible weapons or anyone taking an interest in them, except the people they already knew. Chuck, Hannah and Ben sat together with drinks in hand and Cam caught a waitress to order a couple of beers before they sat down. Chuck and Ben said hello to Quinn and introduced themselves to Cam. Ben didn't usually attend trivia nights and seemed a little out of his element. He drank his beer stiffly and didn't say much.

"So, how does this work?" Cam eyed the slips of paper and short pencils in the center of the table.

Chuck took a sip of his beer. "Simple scoring – one point for each right answer. Team with the most points wins. The announcers usually stick to pop culture or general trivia. If they ask too many science questions, they'll either have a tie between all teams or an argument with an engineer and whatever reference they've pulled up on their phone."

Cam chuckled. "I'll try my best, but I'm not sure I'll be able to help you guys that much. Maybe I can write down the answers."

Chuck tilted his head towards Hannah. "Our fearless team leader usually does that, but maybe she'll let you help today."

Hannah grinned at Chuck but her smile held just the slightest amount of discomfort. Interesting. Cam reached for Quinn's hand and gave it a quick squeeze as the announcer called the first question. Over the tinny sound of the microphone, the announcer asked, "Angel food cake doesn't contain any powered raising agents. What ingredient makes angel food cake rise?"

"Egg whites," Quinn said, with a grin.

Hannah wrote it down with the tiny pencil. Cam watched Hannah write while he took a sip of his beer. He stilled for a fraction of a second. Hannah's neat penmanship was different than most Americans. While his face went back to normal, his brain went into overdrive. That didn't make any sense. Her hand writing looked...no. That was impossible. Unless it wasn't. He took another sip of his beer to cover his surprise. When the announcer said the correct answer, their team cheered and clinked their drinks together.

The announcer played some music, too loud, then lowered the volume. "Okay, smarty-pants out there, let's have you try this question on for size. Gluten-free beers don't use wheat. So what type of grain can they use? We'll take any of the correct answers."

Cam shrugged. "I'm a meat and potatoes guy."

Hannah tapped the pencil against her lips.

Quinn said, "I'm pretty sure they can use rice." Hannah wrote the word and Cam watched out of the corner of his eye. Oh yeah. Her handwriting had tell-tale signs of Cyrillic influence. Unusual for this part of the world. Although it was possible she had immigrant parents, the children of immigrants often lost the accent of their parents and their handwriting was indistinguishable from their peers. If her records said she was American and born to American parents, Hannah herself might be the one with secrets.

"While we're waiting for the official answer, I'm going to take a quick break." Cam rose from the table.

Quinn shot him a wry grin. "You don't think I'm right? Watch guys, he's really going into the bathroom to check my answer on his phone."

Hannah folded the paper in half and stood to deliver it. "Careful, Complicated. This isn't going to help you with the issue we talked about earlier."

Cam chuckled and raised both hands in the air in surrender. His cellphone was in his back pocket and as soon as he reached the privacy of the restroom, he typed a message to Morgan. *Need full background check on Hannah Jenkins. Something is off.*

Morgan's response was instantaneous. *She's an American citizen. We need probable cause, not a feeling.*

Cam sighed. *Her handwriting doesn't look American. Are you sure she was born here?*

Let me see what I can find out without breaking any rules. Can you get a picture?

Negative. But her handwriting looks Cyrillic.

We'll get on it. Good work, Watchman.

Cam nodded with satisfaction. *Thx.* Ideally, he'd get a copy of her handwriting to send to Morgan but there was no way he could do that tonight without blowing a big fat hole in his cover. Cam spoke several languages fluently, and he'd learned to write them from a number of native speakers. Her handwriting was unquestionably different but her nationality was hard to pin down without more writing samples.

Cam returned to the table in his spot next to Quinn. They exchanged a look and he squeezed her hand one more time. He was tempted to talk to her in Morse Code – doubtless she would get it, but the three people most likely to have killed Quinn's partner were sharing their table. Letting her know he'd raised the red flag to Morgan would have to wait. The remainder of the evening, he joked around with the rest of the table and got the occasional right answer. Their team won bragging rights and a gift card for the next time they visited, which they all promised to share. If they hadn't buttoned up this case by then, he'd actually follow through on that. Tonight had been much more productive than expected.

As Cam and Quinn left the building, Quinn threaded her fingers through his. "Thanks, Cam. I had fun."

He slipped an arm around her waist. The rest of the crew was behind them and they had a show to put on. "Do you want to come to my place tonight and talk…strategy?" He waggled his eyebrows and she laughed.

"It's a date."

Once they were safely in their car with the doors shut, Quinn turned to face him. "What happened in there? I saw the weird look. Hannah is putting on a show. I'm not sure if she's doing it to fit in or there is something else involved."

"You got all of that off of one look?"

Quinn shrugged. "Trivia was slow. I had time to think about it. What did you see?"

"Her handwriting looks Cyrillic. What most people don't realize is that each country and even some regions have their own style of handwriting. The way she wrote 'egg whites' tipped me off and 'rice' sealed it."

"Does that mean she's our girl?"

"Not necessarily. It could mean that she came here later in life. I'm asking Morgan to look into it."

Quinn shook her head. "Since she told me everything about herself, including what toothpaste she uses, it's a little odd she failed to mention she grew up somewhere else."

"I'm going to try and spend some time with her tomorrow. Stop by her desk and make small talk. If I'm lucky, she won't be there and I can take some pictures of her handwriting to send to headquarters. Morgan has the analysts getting any more information we can legally dig for without a search warrant. Morgan doesn't think 'Hannah writes her letters different' is sufficient probable cause."

"But what's Hannah's motivation? She barely spoke to Tim while we were at NASA."

"That we saw. She kept stepping away to socialize. We thought we were getting rid of her, but what if she planned it? What if she was happy to be rid of us? What if she found a way to plant the other box without us seeing it?"

Quinn blew out a breath. "Valid points. Still, Tim's in jail now and if she's working with him, she has shown no signs of knowing it."

"Yeah, but if she's working with Dmitri, she's got some backing. She may not need Tim. If Morgan thinks she's an American and she isn't, she's under deep cover. She'd know how to appear completely innocent."

"But that's the problem – another reason she would appear

completely innocent is that she actually *is* completely innocent. Tomorrow, see what you can find out. I'll be close if you need me, or I can stay well away if you want to keep from raising her suspicions."

Cam tapped the steering wheel with his thumb. "I'll see what I can do."

23

Dmitri balled his hands into two tight fists. He closed his eyes as the pain of his nails digging into his palms took the edge off of his anger. Two messages to Tim had gone unanswered and he'd had to go through all of his internet back channels to mask his search before he found confirmation, that Tim had been arrested. He was being held under charges related to property damage at NASA. Fortunately, there was no sign he was being held on a potential espionage charge. Tim wasn't as reliable as his other agents, but he was an American citizen with a price Dmitri could afford. And he'd taken the necessary precautions where Tim was concerned. No mission was without challenges. As long as it didn't put his other spy in Washington at risk.

Dmitri pulled open his file cabinet and retrieved a sheet of paper. Even his allies in Moscow didn't know his cipher, and he would keep it that way. He pulled up an email template and carefully transcribed the digits. He'd never doubted the loyalty or competence of the person on the other end of the email – they would know exactly what to do. Dmitri hit send and resumed his work. There was nothing to do now but wait for the next explosion.

. . .

THE FOLLOWING DAY, Quinn met Cam at the condo for lunch. She had a phone call to make and it'd be easier to coordinate from their home base. Ree answered on the second ring. "Hello?"

"Hey, Ree, it's Quinn."

"Hey, Quinn." Quinn heard some papers shuffling around in the background. "Give me one second. Okay, I'm good. I was just finishing up some grading work and closing my office door. What's up?"

"Can we bounce some questions off of you? Cam's here and you're on speaker."

There was a long pause. "Sure. If you think it'll help."

"Did you talk to Hannah much?"

"Not really. The most I talked to her was when I fed her information to keep her busy."

"Do you think that was deliberate? Was she avoiding you?"

"I didn't think much about it. But now that I think about it…it's possible. How sure are you that it's her?"

"Scale of one to ten…maybe a three? We're working off some handwriting anomalies."

"Hmm. I never thought to look for that. I guess that makes sense. Cam speaks about a zillion languages. Has he noticed anything about her voice?"

"Why do you ask that?" Cam brought Quinn a cup of coffee and she accepted it gratefully.

"She's got some – what do they call it? Vocal fry, I think. Where you end a lot of sentences as if you're asking questions. I wouldn't really notice it much but have been reading some research papers on it – I'm trying to train myself out of the habit. Hers is pretty extreme. And she acts like she doesn't know anything, but works the room like a politician. I just assumed she was one of those people that naturally connects well and sells herself short. I didn't assign any nefarious motive while we were together. Then I got back and realized something was off. But she's the type who wants to be friends with everyone, so it still doesn't completely make sense to me."

Cam leaned into the phone. "Hey Ree, it's Cam. I have a question about the vocal fry. Did it get worse or better the more you time you spent with her?"

"Stayed about the same. She was almost chronically cheerful. Man, you two are a barrel of laughs – I feel like I have suspicions about her for being happy. Or for being both competent and happy."

Cam chuckled. "I promise, we don't arrest people for that. I'm just wondering if she seemed put on or fake. For the benefit of others. If, once she got to know you, it relaxed a bit, I wouldn't necessarily consider it a red flag. But I'm trying to put my finger on what, or who, she might be hiding."

"It's possible she's just more uncomfortable in her role than she lets on. I've definitely seen that before in some of my students. I'd go spend some time with her, see if you can get her more comfortable. Then you can decide if you arrest her for being happy."

Cam cleared his throat. "Fake happy. You're killing our reputation, Ree."

"I don't know, Cam, you're after someone for being too friendly and Quinn gave you a black eye the first day you met. I don't think you need my help here." Ree laughed. "I know it was a misunderstanding, Quinn. But still, it's pretty hard to get the jump on Cam. Parker thought it was hilarious."

"Bye, Ree," Cam said, rolling his eyes.

Quinn hung up the phone and took a few sips of the coffee. "You seem to have a really good rapport with that team." Cam's lips quirked for a second and Quinn almost pressed him on it. But they had things to do and the last thing she needed was to get more personal with Cam. "Ready to go find our bad guy?"

"Or girl. And yes."

"Have you checked the surveillance feed of the gas line recently?" Quinn walked toward the tablet to view the video feed.

"Every day. Also, Morgan has a team doing it remotely every few hours. You can never be too careful."

Quinn took another sip of the coffee and checked her watch. It was time to get back and investigate their newest suspect. She crossed the room and gave Cam a chaste kiss on the cheek. He raised an eyebrow. "Behave yourself."

"I'll do my best." She gave him a cheeky grin.

CAM LOCKED the door behind them before they drove to work, together this time. Quinn was wearing a flowy skirt, her go-to for this operation. And for all he knew, every operation. She ran a hand down the outside of her skirt. He was going to have to have Morgan get him one of the composite knives Quinn had been carrying around with her for his next op. He looked in the mirror to check his appearance. He'd taken care to dress well, but not too well. Since the character he was playing spent a lot of time in the lab, he wouldn't be wearing a suit to work, but he wanted to look nice enough for the office setting. He wouldn't spend very long in the building. He just needed to stop at Hannah's desk for a few minutes. A small camera on his shirt button would record video, so he didn't have to see everything. He just had to get close. However, if she was their IRT mastermind, it was unlikely she'd be so obtuse as to leave evidence in plain sight. At best, she'd use a code with her co-conspirators. Cam snapped his fingers. "We need to see if Hannah ever emailed Tim at work. We can get the analysts to look for any signs they were working together. I don't know if we can get permission for that, but I can have Morgan check."

Quinn smiled. "We don't need permission from Uncle Sam to read her emails. According to one of my many training documents, IRT reserves the right to share email records with whomever they deem appropriate with management signoff. IRT is a private company with its own rules."

"Awesome. Let's see if Morgan or Dan can work their magic on their contacts here to get copies of her emails. It'll be faster than going through the CIA. Do you want to walk in together?"

Quinn thought for a moment. "Sure. It'll fuel Hannah's speculation if she sees us together. Is that the angle you are going with? Dating advice?"

"I tried that once already. Maybe I'll ask her about a report from our trip. If she brings you up, I'll play along. But I'll let her think it's her idea."

"Sounds like a plan."

Cam and Quinn passed through security and Quinn exchanged a friendly smile with the security guard. Quinn's cubicle was near Hannah's desk, so Cam walked with her until she reached it. She sat at her chair and Cam walked purposefully towards Hannah, who gave a knowing smile at his approach. It was too bad she was there – it'd be nice to rifle through her desk and find a definitive answer. But, if they didn't have permission to dig through her email, he didn't really have permission to dig through her desk. He placed his shoulder bag on the ground and leaned against the top of her desk. "I have a question for my favorite technical writer in the Flight Navigation department."

Hannah raised an eyebrow and checked her watch. "The afternoon has barely started and you're already buttering me up. What do you want?" Hannah's body was blocking his view of her computer monitor, but it looked like she was checking emails. Hardly a red flag in corporate America.

"You didn't happen to write up a trip report when we went down to Florida, did you? I'm supposed to get one to my supervisor today, but he has me on at least five other projects. Of course, all of those are incredibly important and can't wait for me to finish my trip report. I was hoping you'd let me copy and paste from yours since Quinn didn't write hers yet."

Hannah sighed. "Okay, just this once, Complicated." She pointed a finger at him. "For you."

"You're the best." Cam gave a quick glance at her desk. A few neat, color-coded sticky notes were next to her computer. Her handwriting shared the same tell-tale signs as the night before, but at work, they were subtler. She might have the time and focus here to eliminate those traces of wherever she was really from.

"Oh, I know." She turned away from him to click at her monitor and he took a small step to the left to look over her shoulder at her email. She was replying to a shipment tracking email but quickly closed it before he could read it. Hopefully, the camera caught it. She clicked a few more times. "It's in your email. Anything else?"

"Nope. That's exactly what I need. Thanks, Hannah."

"Anytime."

Cam walked away from her desk. After making a few turns

through hallways to make it look like he was going back to work in one of the labs, he exited through the front door and made his way back to the van. He pulled up Quinn's video feed – she was alone so they could talk. "Okay, her desk is super neat, not a lot to see on top of it. But her email was up and she was tracking a shipment. Seems odd for a writer. Does she normally manage shipments for your team?"

Quinn pulled up an email, shrunk it down into a small line at the bottom of the screen, presumably so no one behind her could read it. She typed, *"No."*

"I'm going to chase this down with Morgan today. You okay by yourself in there?"

Quinn typed. *"I've got this. She's acting totally normal. I'll let you know if she starts acting weird."* Quinn deleted each word before typing the next.

"Thanks, Q. Watch your back, though."

"I was one step ahead of you, wasn't I? ;)"

"Yeah. The CIA doctors said I probably won't have long term damage, so that's good."

"If you make me laugh, people will get suspicious."

"Roger that. Take care, Q, and I'll be back to pick you up after work."

Cam returned to the condo, unsure if he was going to make a major break on the case or if he was merely going to catch Hannah performing a mundane task in corporate America. He got a fresh pot of coffee brewing and slid the video card into his laptop. When he reached the part of the video at Hannah's desk, he slowed down the footage until her head was out of the way and he could read the email on the screen. He froze it, zoomed in, and enhanced the image. There was a tracking number and Hannah was responding that she had not yet found the package at the IRT building. Once he'd taken a screenshot and emailed it to Morgan, he pressed the button to request a video chat.

"Cam. How's it going out there?"

"I'll say it's going great if you convinced IRT to let us read Hannah's emails."

"It's only been a day. Give me some time to route it through the right channels."

"Okay. I just sent you an image from the email she had up when I was talking to her this afternoon. It appears to be a shipment with a tracking number. Nothing conclusive, but I'd like to see if the analysts see anything I don't. Any luck on getting that check on Hannah's background approved?"

"Approved and complete. She was born in California; she's 37 years old. She's worked for IRT for the past eight years. Always as a technical writer."

"What did she do before that?"

"It looks like she was a freelance writer, no employer listed. She's got a degree in communications. What about her makes you suspect she's involved?"

"Besides the handwriting? It's hard to put my finger on it. But we all think she's putting on an act. It's just that we haven't caught her doing anything wrong." Cam scratched his neck.

"I'm not asking you to back up your suspicions. What's bothering you about her?"

"I think she's playing dumb. She seems incredibly bright, but she often downplays it. Shrugs and has this 'what do I know?' attitude."

Morgan nodded. "Yeah. Some people do that when they're afraid they're going to intimidate people."

"Or they're hiding something. If we can get into the rest of her emails, it would help."

"Cam, our probable cause is really thin on this one. We're trying to charm our way in while minimizing the risk to you both. All I've got is handwriting and a tracking number from a package delivery company."

"Can we get Jordan to help? We'll say the FBI is investigating all shipments to IRT based on a tip. And get access to the rest of Hannah's emails if we can."

"We can try."

"The launch is scheduled for Saturday. Can we do it today?" Cam fought the urge to pace since he was talking to Morgan face-to-face. And she really was doing the best she could under the circumstances – they weren't giving her much to work with.

"I'll see what I can do. Sandy is going to love this."

Morgan hung up and Cam returned to IRT, although this time, he was in a parking lot in the back of the van. He let Quinn know he was back and waited to see what she would come up with.

AFTER CAM WENT SILENT, Quinn waited for Chuck to get his late afternoon coffee refill. If he didn't have a meeting, he'd be back at the coffee pot soon. A few moments later, he rose from his cube and she grabbed her coffee mug. When he got close, she held it up. "Want company?"

"Of course, newbie. Maybe I can tell you about the good old days when the company used to fly us to Florida to watch the launches in person."

"You did that?"

"Oh yeah. Hannah and I are probably the only ones who have been around long enough to remember it. Once we got really big, we all started having huge launch viewing parties here instead. Same party atmosphere, fewer plane tickets."

"So you probably know the folks at NASA pretty well, then?" Quinn tread carefully, pushing a little harder than she would if there wasn't a launch right around the corner.

"Oh yeah. I've mostly worked with Alan Smith, but his project manager, Kiara, is terrific. She's going to probably take on his role when he retires."

Quinn debated on whether to ask Chuck about Tim. At this point, the gossip should have made its rounds. She leaned in, conspiratorially. "Did you know a guy on Kiara's team named Tim? I think he got walked out while we were there."

Chuck nodded solemnly. "Yeah, I heard about that. It's too bad to see anyone lose their job. Tim knew more about their testing than just about anyone else. But between you and me? He was always kind of a jerk. He probably pissed off the wrong person."

"Oh, wow. Well, he tried to be friendly to me, but that was before he was fired."

Chuck stiffened. "What do you mean, friendly? Did he do something?"

Quinn walked over to the coffee pot. Tim had a reputation without her even saying anything. Interesting. "No, not at all. Did he have a problem with that?"

Chuck inclined his head towards Hannah's desk, even though she was out of earshot. "Yeah, I saw him brush up against Hannah a couple of times. I called him out on it and he didn't do it again. Hannah was mortified. She kept insisting it was no big deal. Said he'd accidentally run into her. She didn't want him to get fired when no one got hurt. She was nicer to him than he deserved. But I made sure after that, he kept his distance."

"Wow. I had no idea. I guess I dodged a bullet. Is there anyone else I should be worried about?"

"Not that I know of. But if you ever need anything or have that type of situation, please let me know. We aren't okay with that here. And hey, on a happier note, the launch party is Saturday afternoon. You know where to go?"

Quinn nodded. "Yeah, we will be there for sure."

"We?"

Quinn smiled shyly. "My boyfriend, Cam, and I. He came to the bar with us?"

"Ah, he's been upgraded to boyfriend. Good for you guys. Well, hey, I better look busy. Not much I can do for the launch now that the rocket is going to the launchpad, but I should try to look like I'm doing something." Chuck winked at her and took his full mug back to his desk.

Quinn stood a moment longer, sipping at her coffee. She said into her mug, "You hear all that?"

Cam replied, "Yeah, I did. You think they were doing a brush pass?"

Quinn took another sip. "Possibly. He also could have been just trying to grab her butt. He seemed a couple more conversations away from that with me."

"You should have seen him ogling you when you weren't looking. I was trying to figure out how to subtly punch him if he made a move on you."

"Aw, that's sweet. But you wouldn't have to. I can take care of myself. Back to work. Watch my back, Cam. I don't like where this is going."

24

Parker pulled his car into Ree's driveway. They'd found a cheap flight to Orlando from Indianapolis and were taking advantage of the rare occasion they could travel together. Before he could get out of the car, she was outside and locking the front door. She bounded down the front steps, carry-on suitcase in hand. He patted his pocket to make sure his surprise for her was still there. She greeted him with her light-up-the-room smile before placing her suitcase in the backseat. She slid into the front seat and he gave her a kiss. When she lingered, he said against her lips, "None of that. You'll distract me and we'll miss our flight."

Ree grinned and gave him one more kiss. "Noted. That was the last one. I can't believe we get to go see the launch. With the NASA employees. Not with the tourists, the actual engineers."

"I think it's safe to assume a large number of the tourists who go see rocket launches for fun are also engineers." She swatted his arm playfully. "Ouch. Hopefully, they're nice ones. The one I have in my car is feisty."

"You like it."

"I do." Parker reached his hand across the car and she placed hers in it. "Will you be upset if I tell you that while we're there, I might ask some questions to make sure that we truly wrapped this thing up?"

"Will you upset if I was expecting we'd be asking questions? And that I have a few of my own? Cam and Quinn think this was a team effort and we've only caught one person. I'd like to get a few minutes with Kiara to find out how her team reacted to Tim getting 'fired.' I mean, it's public record that he got arrested, but I wonder if people know."

"A lot of folks wouldn't think to check."

"I wouldn't have if it happened to someone in my lab."

"Well, let's get down there, enjoy the launch and maybe tie up a few loose ends on the case while we're there."

"That works for me."

Several hours later, they had landed and checked into their hotel. The launch would take place the following afternoon, but they'd have some time in the morning to wander around Kennedy Space Center. It would probably be swarming with tourists, but the excited crowd would be half the fun. However, unlike most of the tourists, they'd get to watch from the Vehicle Assembly Building. Ree closed her eyes and tried to relax. After about thirty seconds of trying to fall asleep, she started tapping her hand on her leg. Parker reached over to still it and she snuggled in closer. He generally had a way of calming her down, but tonight, even having him close probably wouldn't do the job. She pulled out her e-reader and read a book until her busy brain became preoccupied with whether or not the hero was going to save the day. Before she found out, she drifted off to sleep.

The following morning, Parker navigated the already heavy traffic to get them into the employee area of Kennedy Space Center. Once they entered the VAB, they passed through the hallway with windows into the now-empty high bay where the rocket had been assembled. Ree smiled a small smile – they had been part of making sure it was ready to fly. Her contentment only lasted a moment when she remembered that it was still possible they'd missed something. Really, she should hold onto that smile until after the rocket had safely delivered its cargo into orbit. They made their way to Alan's office, which was now a hub of activity. A large countdown clock on the wall showed they were almost at the T-minus two hours mark.

"Hey, team – I hope you're just here for the show."

Parker reached out a hand and Alan shook it. "Yes, sir. Thanks for the invitation. No reason to think otherwise on our end. You comfortable she's ready to fly?"

"I don't count my chickens till they're in orbit, son. She passed inspections and went out without incident on the crawler, so hopefully, she behaves herself. Dr. Ryland, nice of you to join us."

"Of course. Thank you for the invitation. It's my first launch. I'd love to get a closer look at a crawler if we have time and you don't mind. It's not every day you get the chance to see a machine capable of delivering a rocket to the launchpad."

"Sure. They have one job and they do it well. All indications are that she's flying on time. The wind is light today, so as long as Ben's team gives us the thumbs up, we'll be go for launch and have engine ignition in about two hours. You guys will love it. The rumble of the engines shakes the windows like you wouldn't believe. Nothing else like it in the world. You should have some time to see the crawlers. I can have someone walk you over there."

"Oh, I don't want to bother you. Why don't you just tell us where to meet you before things get interesting?"

Alan looked as if he was trying to find a reason to disagree, but someone knocked on the door with papers in hand. He raised his pointer finger in the air at the newcomer. "I'll be right with you." He pulled a map of the facility off the corner of his desk. "Go here for the crawlers, but don't touch anything. They'll have my hide if you break something and I wasn't supervising. Then meet me back in this room over here for the launch. Most of my team will be there to see her fly. It'll be crowded but worth it."

"Thanks, we'll do that." Ree accepted the map and fought the urge to thread her hand through Parker's to pull him to the crawlers. She'd always wanted to get a closer look at them. It was too bad she couldn't snap a few images to show her students. The FBI would blow a gasket if they caught her taking pictures of NASA's machines without permission. Her students would get such a kick out of close-ups of the crawler's feet and motors. While they didn't set any land speed records, with a top speed of about two miles per hour, they carried rockets from the VAB to the launchpad without breaking anything on the way. No small feat.

As they left Alan's office, Parker raised an eyebrow. "I'm assuming you have a long list of reasons to go look at these things?"

"Nope. Very short. They are awesome. They take a super heavy rocket from Point A to Point B without breaking anything inside of said rocket. I want to go see the guts of the thing. Unless there is something else we should be doing?"

Parker shook his head. "No, we need to kill some time before meeting up with everyone to watch the launch. I'm fine with staying out of the way."

Ree and Parker navigated the hallways, waving at the occasional familiar face from Kiara's team. Most of them seemed fairly relaxed, if a little surprised to see them. Before they reached the crawler room, they saw Kiara coming around a corner hard and fast, clutching her tablet to her chest. She skidded to a stop when she saw them and her eyes went wide. "Oh, no. Is there a problem?"

Ree laughed. "Now you're going to think I'm only here when something goes wrong. No, Alan invited us to come watch the launch and I didn't want to miss out. Mike couldn't make it."

Kiara let out a sigh of relief. "Phew. I triple-checked everything. We should be good to go. Where are you guys headed?"

"Oh, I was just going to go take a look at the crawlers." Ree raised her hands in the air. "Not because there is anything wrong. I just think they're awesome and wanted to get a closer look."

Kiara leaned in, conspiratorially. "They are awesome. But I wouldn't. Alan has been really on edge lately and I wouldn't want you guys to get into trouble."

"He said it was okay."

"Oh, good."

"But now that you mention it, he's been on edge, how?"

"He probably went into the high bay by himself twice as much as I did. Even though the satellite was covered up and what he could see was limited."

"Oh? Double-checking your work?" Ree crossed her arms and attempted to appear unconcerned.

"I think so. I've never seen him like this. So, don't break anything. Things have been a little tense around here since Tim got fired."

"Yeah, did you figure out why? He got walked out when we were talking to you, but no one told us."

"Alan said it was performance-related. I don't know, though. He was probably the one sabotaging the satellite. But I guess whatever happened is over now. I just have to trust Alan." Kiara checked her watch. "I better go. But hey, tell me if you see something that doesn't feel right. I've got this feeling I don't know the whole story."

When Kiara was out of earshot, Ree raised an eyebrow. "See, sneaking away to be a tourist paid off." She buffed her fingernails on her shoulder and Parker laughed.

"I can't argue with the results. Now, let me take you on the date of your dreams." They walked a little further until they reached the room circled on the map. Parker held the door open and gestured for her to go inside. "Your crawlers, my lady."

Ree took in the sight of the massive vehicles. The area around them was deserted – everyone else was focused on other things. She took her time walking around them, examining the gigantic tracks. The door they'd entered through opened and they heard a distraught voice. Parker pulled Ree around one side of the large vehicle and stood between her and whoever had just come in.

"I can talk now. Look, I wish I could tell you more, but I can't. He just disappeared one day. Literally no one knows what happened. He was walked out, and no one said anything about it." There was a long pause. "I don't know why it matters so much to you. I didn't even think you guys were close. In fact, a lot of people here didn't really like him. He was just good at his job." Parker leaned in just a bit and Ree kept a hand on the back of his shirt. "I'm sorry. I'll let you know if I hear anything, okay? Okay. You too. I'll do what I can. No, of course I understand why you called. Take care."

Ree's heart thudded against her chest at the sound of footsteps. There were only a few before the door opened and closed. Ree whispered, "Did you see him?"

Parker shook his head. "Stay here." He raised a hand and began a sweep of the room. When he returned, he shook his head. "Didn't see who it was. But we did just confirm someone is still interested in what happened to Tim."

"Was that an accomplice?"

"Based on his tone, I don't think so. We'll do our due diligence just in case, but he didn't sound like he wanted to help. He sounded like he didn't want to be bothered, which means Tim's partner is getting desperate. And since they aren't here in person – along with half of Florida – they could be up with Cam and Quinn. I'll see if Morgan can trace that call." Parker typed a quick message to Morgan before putting his phone back in his pocket. "Do you want to spend any more time in here?"

Ree swallowed hard. "No. I think I'm good."

Parker gave her a quick kiss. "Okay. Let's go see that rocket launch."

ON THE OTHER side of the country, Quinn followed her coworkers into the biggest room at IRT. There was a video feed with the sound of mission control along with muted TVs piping in video from several news outlets. The text of the news anchors flowed beneath their cheerful dispositions, with many of them taking a moment to mention the importance of this launch going well. Footage of the last rocket exploding kept popping up, and it was hard to miss the winces from the engineers whenever they saw the fireball, often played in slow motion. Still, the room crackled with excited energy. Quinn glanced at the large countdown clock on the wall. They still had an hour before liftoff, if there weren't any delays. Her team had confirmed the weather shouldn't be a factor, and Chuck seemed to be making a concerted effort to lift the spirits of her team, who were all currently wearing their stress on their faces and sagging shoulders. She scanned the room for friendly faces and realized how few of the employees she really knew. One of them was lying, but which one?

Hannah came up from behind her and tapped her on the shoulder.

She held a glass of pink liquid with foam on top for Quinn. "Hey, Quinn! Can I interest you in IRT's finest punch?"

Quinn made a face. "I'm not really a punch kind of gal. Do they have beer or is that outlawed on the job?"

Hannah shrugged. "On launch day, there aren't any rules about drinking on the job. No one is doing any work anyway." Hannah looked past Quinn. "Especially Chuck."

Chuck appeared at Quinn's elbow. "Quinn, is she giving you a hard time?"

Hannah laughed. "Hardly. I was offering her some punch."

"So, yes, then. Quinn, stay away from the sugar bomb Hannah is holding. They have beer over there – they'll break out the champagne once they're sure the rocket hasn't exploded."

Quinn felt Cam behind her before she even heard his voice. "Did someone say something exploded?"

She made space for him in their small group. "Hopefully, it won't. But they said we get champagne if there is a successful launch. If not, we drown our sorrows in beer."

Chuck rolled his eyes. "You guys, it's going to be fine. We've checked the program so many times, I practically have it memorized. Seriously, ask me what is on a line of the software, and I'll tell you."

Hannah's eyes shifted a bit. "So, you fixed that thing we found?"

Quinn's muscles tensed. Chuck sighed. "Yes, Hannah. I told you we got it. Well spotted, though."

Quinn raised an eyebrow. "Dare I ask?"

"It's nothing," Hannah said. "I just found a little typo. It's my job, after all."

Chuck shifted. "You'll find out next week at our 'Lessons Learned' meeting. Hannah found a part of the code had been commented out. That's why we never found out if the last rocket executed a detonation command or not."

Cam took a step closer. "What does 'commented out' mean? I'm just a materials guy."

"It means that someone put a symbol in front of some lines of code to render them inactive. It's what we do to make a comment in the code that explains to the next person what we were trying to do without goofing up the code. Good code has some explanations of what the programmer was trying to do along the way. Nearest we can figure is someone had commented out that section and they forgot to turn it back on."

Quinn kept her face a careful mix of surprise and disappointment. "Wow. I had no idea."

Chuck and Hannah exchanged a look. Chuck scratched the back of his neck. "The person you replaced was fired over the miss. If they'd been following our procedures, it would never have happened. But Ben didn't want to discourage the team, so he hasn't been sharing that information widely."

Quinn nudged Hannah with her shoulder. "But you found it. Good job, technical writer."

Hannah shrugged. "Yeah, Ben asked me not to spread it around. It didn't get us any closer to knowing what happened to the last rocket, though. At least it's fixed now. And you're here. So some good came out of it."

Someone at the front of the room tapped on a microphone and Quinn startled. She turned in concert with the rest of the IRT employees to face the Vice President of Research and Development, who gave a speech about all they had accomplished. While she pretended to listen, she wondered at this new evidence. Did the person who was fired really make a mistake? If Hannah was behind it, why would she want it fixed? Or had she pointed it out to avoid getting caught? Once the VP had wrapped up his prepared remarks, they had only a few more minutes to wait until the launch. Soon, the rocket engines would be lit, and she needed to look for faces in the room that were surprised it didn't blow up.

PARKER RAN a hand over his pocket when Ree wasn't looking for about the fifteenth time that day. He'd been carrying the ring with him everywhere for the last month, but it hadn't yet felt like the right time. He'd chosen a blue sapphire surrounded by diamonds and hoped she would like it. He was certain marrying Ree was the right choice and thought they were on the same wavelength, but his gut churned at the idea her answer would be anything but an enthusiastic "yes." He was used to working in high-pressure situations – he could do this. He swallowed hard. He could definitely do this. Now, he just needed to find a time special enough to pop the question.

Ree opened the door to the launch viewing room. While there were a number of tourists at the Saturn V Center, the engineers had the best view through the windows of the Vehicle Assembly Building. Alan and Kiara waved when they walked in but quickly returned their attention to a computer monitor, presumably watching real-time data from the rocket. Parker kept an ear out for the voice they'd heard on the phone, but their friend wasn't close by or he wasn't talking. Excited chatter filled the room until the last two minutes before launch, when the whole room went silent. The clock froze briefly, a command was issued over the radio, and the countdown resumed. When it reached ten seconds, the whole room began to count down together, out loud. The main engines were lit, and the whoosh of noise hit the windows with a rattle. When the countdown reached zero, the engines rumbled, and a new wave of sound hit the room. The rocket rose through the air, as if in slow motion, then disappeared out of sight sooner than he expected. Mercifully, there were no bangs, booms, or fireballs. He looked over at Ree. Tears welled up in her eyes and she blinked them away as they were both swept up in the excitement of the room full of hugging people and high fives. Since total strangers were hugging Ree, he wrapped her up in a brief bear hug. "We helped make that happen," he whispered in her ear, "Good job, babe."

He let her go and looked away to keep from making their relationship obvious. The room still buzzed with noise and he tilted his head, indicating they should slip out. It was quiet in the parking lot, not surprising considering all the tourists had been bussed in and everyone else was still celebrating. Parker led Ree to an isolated spot next to the building, and they took one long last look at the plumes of smoke left behind by the rocket, now beginning to dissipate. She squeezed his hand. "I'm really proud of us."

Parker sucked in a deep breath. Maybe for some women, a beach proposal was their dream. But the shine in Ree's eyes told him he'd never have a better moment. He dropped down on one knee, and she gasped and covered her mouth with both hands. His chest tightened and he swallowed hard. "Ree, I'm absolutely nuts about you. You are just as comfortable spending time with me on the couch as you are fighting crime in your spare time. Or your not-so-spare time. You make me laugh, you have a big heart, and you are one of the strongest, most tenacious people I know." Parker reached into his pocket and pulled out the ring. "I've been waiting for the right time to ask you and I realized I don't want to wait any longer. Will you marry me?"

Ree nodded and Parker rose. She leapt into Parker's arms, nearly knocking him over. He laughed and slid the ring onto her finger, and she hugged him tight. "Yes. Today, tomorrow, any day you like. Of course, I'll marry you. And oh my, this is gorgeous."

Parker grinned. "You don't mind I popped the question while we were on an operation?"

Ree examined her ring. "Now that you mention it, proposing after we saved a major rocket launch from exploding isn't nearly romantic enough. Maybe I should take this off and you can have a do-over?"

Parker pulled her in for a kiss. "You're a handful, you know that?"

"Just want you to know what you're getting into." Ree put a hand to her forehead. "Oh, man. Where are we going to live?"

"We'll figure it out – after what we've been through, a creative commuting arrangement will be a piece of cake."

25

The large room filled with IRT employees erupted with cheers as the rocket flew out of sight. Chuck looked confidently smug, and after some quick congratulations, Hannah left their small group to pass out champagne to the other employees. Cam looked for others who might be stressed, but they all seemed either relieved or jubilant. Cam gave Quinn a hug and whispered, "Let's find out who got busted for changing the code."

Quinn nodded as he pulled away and Hannah brought them two glasses of champagne. "Get a room, Complicated."

"Hannah, you're supposed to be the nice one!" Cam said with a grin, accepting the champagne. They waited until no one was paying attention to them, left the champagne on a table, and made their way to the door. Quinn led Cam back to her cubicle. Once they were alone, she said, "There will be a record of who changed the old code. Rory mentioned the fired employee in her notes – Lindsay was her name." Her hands were steady as she logged into the system. Cam stood over Quinn's shoulder with one foot pointed at the door. If someone walked in, it'd be hard to explain his presence. He texted Morgan. *We have a lead. Any access to the cameras at IRT?*

A message popped up. *Will take some time. Do you need me to send in a team?*

No. Just want someone watching our backs.

Cam, abort the op if you're in danger. Nothing is that important.

Will do. Going to push a little harder on this one.

"Got it." Quinn pulled up a bunch of equations and words – this must be the code everyone was so worked up about. While it was really just another language, he'd never taken advanced math courses and it wasn't something he could learn in five minutes. "Definitely a version change from another employee. The woman Rory mentioned in her notes. But her notes didn't say anything about Lindsay getting fired. Maybe Rory found out the real story the night she was killed." Quinn let out a frustrated sigh. "This has to matter. This has to make sense. Somehow." She rubbed her face.

Cam checked over his shoulder. "Quinn, let's stand down. We need to get back in there, pretend everything is normal. Our immediate question has been answered and risk/benefit isn't worth it to keep going right now."

"Deal. Let's go play nice. I'll try not to ask too many questions."

"And I'll go pretend I work here."

Cam's phone began to ring and Quinn jumped. "It's just Morgan." He pressed a button and Quinn leaned her ear close, so she could hear. "Hey, we're alone for the moment. What's up?"

"Cam, we just got into the email system. Jordan charmed his way in. Hannah sent some unusual replies to package tracking emails. The most recent one says that the tracking number should have been sent to Tim at NASA. The tracking slip shows the package originated in Colorado."

"Okay, so what were they shipping?"

"The tracking slip said semiconductors."

"That doesn't make any sense."

Quinn grabbed his arm. "It's not the parts, it's the numbers. This all goes back to Dmitri. Morgan, get with Dan on this. Dmitri had a list of numbers in a file I saw in his office. The Vostok file. We should see if any of them match the tracking number. What was the reply, exactly?"

Quinn leaned into the phone and Cam turned it so she could hear Morgan's response.

"She said that the parts should have been shipped to Tim, not her. She said he knew the parts were coming."

Quinn crossed her arms. "She knew Tim was sabotaging the launch and was confirming the schedule. They didn't have a code, so she had to use dummy email addresses to cover her tracks. Tim may not have known the emails were coming from Hannah. She's got to be our girl. Ugh, this is why I can't have good girlfriends."

"Because they are all Russian spies? How often does this happen to you?" Cam asked, eyebrows raised. He felt immediately guilty when he saw the pang of grief shoot across her face. Damn. Focus on the operation and she'd snap out of it. "Morgan. Find out everything you can about Hannah. View it through the lens that she's working with the Russians and get what you can from Dan. We'll shake her down in person. See if we can find some hard evidence that there is more to this than misplaced packages."

"You got it, Cam." Morgan hung up and Cam turned to leave, but considered Hannah's empty desk.

Quinn grabbed his arm. "Is that a good idea?"

"No. It's a terrible idea. Watch my back, okay?" Cam walked carefully towards Hannah's desk, wishing he had his bug scanner on him. Then he reconsidered. If she was working with Dmitri, he didn't want to give her any advanced warning. He shook his head and backed off.

Quinn pulled on his elbow and they both returned to the celebration. When they arrived, their go-to coworker group had been lost in the mob. Cam and Quinn exchanged a look and they separated, both flicking their earpieces on. Cam scanned the crowd for Hannah, but he didn't spot her. Chuck was laughing with a group of other people – he was definitely a wealth of information. Maybe Cam could figure out more about what had happened by asking him for details. Nah, that was too obvious. Instead, he stared at the news reports, still streaming in, now with talking heads explaining what was next for IRT and the future of space travel. It bought him a little time to process what they'd figured out so far. He cracked his neck.

"Hey, Cam." Chuck appeared at his side. "Seems like you and Quinn are pretty cozy. Where'd you two disappear to?"

Cam shrugged. "I can neither confirm nor deny that we disappeared."

Chuck laughed. "Hey, just don't do anything that would get Quinn fired. She's been a good addition to the team. We're glad to have her."

Cam chose his words carefully. "If you don't mind me asking, do you think it'll be a better environment, now that you've got some success under your belt?"

Chuck considered. "It should be. What happened with Lindsay, the employee Quinn replaced, was pretty bad. It got ugly. She said she didn't make a mistake and Ben lost it. If she'd admitted it, he would have put her on probation and moved on. It's not like she caused the rocket to blow up. It was just a whoops that kept us from getting a signal. But she was super-defensive, claimed she hadn't done it, even though Ben had the evidence to prove it. She was so great – I don't know why she'd lie about it. To answer your question, though, we'll be okay. This will help."

"Wow. That sounds like something out of a soap opera."

"Yeah, it's more politics than we're used to around here. Everyone loved Lindsay. The team was pretty upset, and Ben didn't want to expose Quinn to all of that. It wasn't her fault she stepped into that role right afterward. She seems great."

"So did Lindsay find another job?"

"Oh yeah. I wrote her a recommendation. Look, everyone screws up. In the heat of the moment, she reacted poorly. But she is a great engineer. Hannah was emailing her weekly to see if she landed on her feet. She found a new spot pretty quickly."

Cam leaned in. "Thanks for giving me the inside scoop. Sounds like you guys watch out for each other here."

Chuck shrugged. "It's no big deal. I don't see any point in keeping that kind of secret. Classified stuff, sure. But I don't want Quinn to think everyone's bad attitude is because they don't like her. We just had a lot to get over."

Cam tried to sound as casual as possible. "Anyone in the group still struggling?"

"Oh, sure. But we'll be okay." Chuck clapped Cam on the back and then spotted another friend. He gave them a wave and went over to talk to him. They'd have to do some research on Lindsay, since her name kept coming up. But if she did it, she had to know they'd track the changes back to her. Everything in this building was tightly controlled. It was a minor miracle you didn't have to badge into the break room for coffee. Someone couldn't just change something that big without someone noticing.

Cam felt someone coming up behind him and he turned to find himself face to face with Ben. "Hey, Ben, congratulations on the launch."

Ben gave him a tight smile. "Can you come with me?"

"I'm sorry, sir, but is everything okay?"

Ben looked around him. "I'd prefer to handle this in my office. I'd like you to come with me, please."

Across the room, Quinn's eyes darted until they landed on him. Cam gave her a small nod and she followed them at a distance. Cam checked Ben's person for weapons as well as he could without touching him, considering he could be hiding any number of things under his clothes, like the knife under Quinn's skirt. Quinn stayed back enough that it wasn't obvious she was following them, and Ben led him silently to his office. Cam considered a number of explanations for Ben's behavior and demeanor. If something bad had happened, Cam would be the last person Ben would talk to. Or at least he'd talk to him after Quinn if it was related to their trip to Florida. Ben might have figured out something was off with Cam. Cam flexed his fingers and followed Ben into his office. He shut the door and heard the sound in his earpiece as well. Although he hadn't seen or heard her, Quinn was just outside the door.

"Cam, I'm sorry to interrupt your celebration, but we have a problem. I looked you up in the system since I'd never seen you before and you've been spending a lot of time in our department. But when I mentioned your name to your manager, something didn't seem right."

Cam swallowed hard. He was reporting to a manager who worked in another building to minimize the risk of exposure, but it didn't eliminate the risk entirely. That manager must have come over to see the launch. "I see."

"Can you please explain to me why you are in our systems, but your boss doesn't know anything about you?"

Cam took on an understanding expression. "Ben, I'm sorry to have been dishonest with you. I was sent to Florida as part of an internal investigation. I'm actually a consultant. I frequently work with companies whose projects have had unexpected failures." Ben raised an eyebrow. "Your management thought there might have been foul play and they brought me in. You probably noticed an increased frequency of counterespionage trainings?"

Ben crossed his arms. "I thought that was odd."

"Some things didn't add up after the last failed launch. We had reason to believe there was a criminal in the building and my job was to find them."

"Do you have some sort of ID? This is the first I'm hearing about this."

"Absolutely." Cam flipped open a wallet with ID and a business card to match.

"Do you mind if I call your employer after you leave to check your story?"

"Not at all. You can do it right now, if you like." The number would reach a CIA answering service. If Ben looked up the web address, he would have a similar result.

Ben studied Cam's identification and slid it back to him. He kept the business card. "Does Quinn know about all of this?"

Cam shook his head. "No, sir. We're friends from college and well, we've had some kind of chemistry since the minute we met. I tried to keep my distance, but as you can tell, I don't always succeed."

Ben sat in his chair. "I don't think any of my people are involved."

Cam nodded solemnly. "Most of the people I work with have the same opinion. But I heard you had a coding problem."

"You must have talked to Chuck. I need to tell that man to keep his mouth shut. Even if it isn't confidential, he needs to wait until we present the information to everyone at the same time, so people have all the facts."

"He said the engineer that did it denied it?"

Ben nodded. "Unfortunately for her, the system is tightly controlled. It's easy to prove who made every change. She was furious. But the thing is, she was one of my quieter employees – honestly, I'd been working with her on how to stick up for herself, increase her confidence. I never expected her to lie about a mistake."

"What are the odds she was telling the truth?"

Ben froze. "What do you mean?"

"I mean, do you have a video of her making the change or did someone else use her ID and password?"

Ben put his hand to his forehead and closed his eyes. "No, we just have the electronic record. It had to be her, since we tell them not to share passwords."

"And you yourself follow that rule?"

"Of course."

"And you don't have any post-it notes with your password written on them in your desk drawer?"

Ben laughed. "No. But I've been tempted. Does that happen often?"

"All the time. If someone vehemently denies their involvement, I always ask. Honestly, it's possible someone got it by being nosy and looking over her shoulder."

Ben's face fell. "Any idea who else it could be?"

"Yes. But I need some time to chase it down Do you have any records of the work done on the day your employee made the change? I understand it'll take you a little time to figure out."

Ben shook his head. "It won't, actually. It came up when I fired Lindsay. It was a team-building day – we went whale watching in Seattle. Everyone was there except her. She wanted to finish up some testing to hit her deadline, so she stayed back. That's when she made a mistake with the code."

"Anyone else miss the event?"

"No. Well, Hannah had a doctor's appointment that day, so she stayed in the office while we were gone. But that doesn't help much."

Cam fought to keep his elation from showing. The last thing he needed was Ben connecting the dots. Ben's loyalty to his people would help give him time to get Hannah good and cornered before they arrested her. "Ben, thank you for your time. I'd appreciate you keeping this between us."

Cam left Ben's office and met Quinn near her desk. "It's her. It has to be her."

"Unless it's Ben." Quinn raised an eyebrow.

"Seems unlikely he'd call me out here if that's the case. Let's go see if we can find Hannah."

They quietly shuffled out of the office space. Several hours had passed since the launch and the crowd in the large room was starting to thin out. After fifteen minutes of looking, they both came up short. Hannah had evidently left for the day. Cam found a quiet corner to speak into his earpiece. "Let's go back home and regroup."

Across the room, Quinn nodded slightly. After she'd disentangled herself from a conversation, they left the building to update Morgan.

That evening, after a simple, shared dinner and clean-up, Quinn re-read Rory's reports. The fresh context of the past few days only served to confirm her certainty that Hannah was the missing link in this mess. Somehow, she'd begun working for Dmitri. Whether she was a Russian or U.S. citizen was really irrelevant, although Quinn suspected she had stolen an identity if Cam's assessment of her handwriting was to be believed. Regardless, they needed another couple of days to get the evidence they needed to hand her over to the authorities. Then, convicting her for spying and sabotage would be merely a formality.

Cam sat on the other end of the couch, typing away at a report, which she would likely have to read, edit and approve before sending it to their bosses. Quinn stretched out a leg to touch his and he looked up at her with a smile. Yeah, that was probably a bad plan. She drew back her foot. She'd let herself run out of the big-hitter baking supplies like heavy whipping cream and chocolate in the overly optimistic hope that they might be out of here soon. Although, she had a couple of ripe bananas. She could probably use them to whip up some muffins or cupcakes. She pushed herself up off the couch and headed towards the kitchen. She began to rattle bowls around, and from the couch, Cam said, "So, my other partner doesn't give me black eyes, but he also doesn't bake. I'm starting to think you might be a better partner."

"It was only one black eye!" Quinn shouted from the kitchen, "And be nice or I'm not sharing the muffins."

"I'm going to ask for hazard pay in my report." He read aloud slowly as if he was typing: "Quinn is now withholding food to ensure my compliance." An oven mitt came flying over the couch and he laughed and threw it back. "Throws things when she doesn't get her way."

"Do you want a muffin or not?"

"What kind is it?"

"Banana nut."

"Alright, I won't bring up the black eye incident or report you for demanding my compliance in exchange for food. But only because I like banana nut muffins."

"Any leads from Morgan yet?"

"No, but no night baking for a couple of nights. She thinks we can get permission in time to search Hannah's office Monday and to send in a team to her house. She's rushing the paperwork through now."

"Hot damn. Thanks, Cam. I guess I'll let you have a muffin after all."

After spending Sunday shoring up their paperwork for Morgan, Quinn woke up Monday morning, stretched out, and considered what the day might bring. It felt like a lifetime ago since she found out Rory had been killed. Morgan had a team carefully investigating Hannah's history through the weekend, trying to find if there were any holes. Ben had figured out Cam was up to something. But why had he gone looking for information on Cam but not noticed Hannah's unusual behavior? Of course, Quinn had spent days with her, and without access to the information she had, she'd never suspect Hannah was a traitor. In fact, even with the resources they had at the CIA, they were still working off hunches and circumstantial evidence. She sighed. Today was going to be one of those days.

By the time she made it to IRT for another day of double-checking other people's work, Quinn had the CIA's official blessing to search Hannah's office. However, she was going to have to wait until the end of the day, when Cam would bring his bug scanner along.

After tossing and turning the night before, Quinn made her first stop at the coffee pot. She trudged over, mug in hand, just in time to hear Ben asking Hannah some questions. She poured her coffee slowly. She couldn't hear the conversation very well, but the words sounded tense. She ran back to her desk to print something with a lot of pages and walked to the printer by Ben's office as the pages came out. As she got closer, she could hear Hannah starting to cry.

"Oh my goodness, Ben. I would never get into the code and change it. Why would you even think I'm capable of that?"

"I'm not saying you did it on purpose, Hannah. It's just that Lindsay didn't remember changing it and I wondered if she'd asked you for help. It's okay. We all ask for help sometimes."

Hannah sniffed. "I just helped a little bit. But she promised me she'd check all the changes. I mean, you remember that time. It was crazy around here and we were all just trying to get things moving. I thought I was helping."

"So, the doctor's appointment wasn't real?"

"No, that was real. I just came back to help her. I'm so sorry."

"It's alright, Hannah. I just want you to know you can be honest with me."

"Thank you, Ben. I really appreciate that. I won't let you down again." When Quinn heard Hannah moving around inside Ben's office, she power walked back to her desk, keeping her head down. The white noise of the copier would have blocked a lot of the sound in the microphone. When she was sure no one was behind her, she typed an update for Cam to read on the video feed. He assured her he'd pass it along to Morgan and would be there at 5:30 PM sharp to check out Hannah's desk.

Quinn began working through the list of tasks assigned to her by the more senior engineers. Most of the tasks she could do on her own, but if they started throwing her harder problems, she'd need to start sending them to their contact at NASA. Dan hadn't shared who his contact was, but after their adventures in Florida, she wondered who it would go to on Alan's team. Maybe Alan himself. After an hour had passed, Quinn made her way to the coffee pot for a refill. She had to pass Hannah's desk on the way and she wanted to check to see if

Hannah had been crying crocodile tears or real ones. Her computer was on, but her desk was empty.

Cam's voice crackled in her ear. "She must have stepped out. Give it some time before you check again. Morgan owes us an update by this evening anyway. Hannah might be panicking and I don't want to send her over the edge."

Quinn checked her watch. Usually, Chuck waited an hour or so longer to make his stop, so there was no chance of gleaning any more office gossip from him. Plus, he'd missed the show between Ben and Hannah this morning. Quinn took a sip of the coffee and eyed the donuts sitting on the break room table. They were tempting to take the edge of her nerves but wouldn't be worth the sugar crash later. She sighed and went back to work.

Quinn powered through the rest of her morning despite time slowing to a pace that defied logic. Right after she'd eaten lunch, she heard Cam's voice in her ear. "Quinn, tell Ben you're leaving and get out to the van. Morgan wants to talk." Quinn looked down at her watch. "It's too early to leave for the day, I know. Tell him you have a migraine or something."

Quinn considered visiting Ben in person and settled on sending him an email. She fired it off quickly, gathered her things, and walked as calmly as possible to the parking lot. Cam was parked close to the door and she hopped in the van. Once the door was closed, he said, "Morgan wants to talk."

"It can't wait?"

"She said no." Cam drove the van down the street to the parking lot he'd been using for the day. It was pretty full and they both climbed through a small door into the back for privacy. Before Quinn was fully settled, Cam selected Morgan's name on his tablet, and after it routed through secure channels, her face appeared on the tablet.

Cam leaned in. "What's going on, Morgan?"

"Good afternoon. I wanted to let you know that we were able to link Hannah to Dmitri using the cypher Quinn found in Dmitri's office. Hannah sent several emails that were suspiciously similar to those Tim received from his mystery sender."

"You guys have been putting in the hours."

Morgan's eyes were weary. "Quinn, I've talked to Dan and we're concerned you're at risk. If you worked for Dmitri and you have been getting close to Hannah, there's a chance she knows who you are. Did she act differently around you today?"

"She wasn't in the office much this morning."

Cam rubbed his neck. "We need to check the surveillance video of our condo. She might have connected the dots." Cam pulled up the feed and scrolled along the timeline. A body popped into the frame and he froze the time. "Shit. She was at our place at…9:15."

"Did she go inside?"

"Negative. But she did tamper with the gas line."

"That's it. Let's go get her. Morgan, can you send us her address?" Quinn checked her knife and Cam passed her a gun. He then took one for himself.

"Yes. And I'll send a crew to get the gas to your place turned off and to undo whatever she did. Do you need me to send backup to Hannah's house?"

"Yes. But give us a head start. I'd like to see if I can get her to talk to us. I want to find out what she knows about Dmitri."

When they reached Hannah's small house, the need for backup became irrelevant. No one was home. They peeked in the windows, but nothing screamed "spy." But of course, nothing at their place did either.

Cam selected Morgan's name on his phone. "Morgan, check the borders and airports. We need to know if she went anywhere. And you can send in a team to check her house without us – I doubt you'll find anything if she was this careful. But I'd send them in anyway. Just in case." There was a long pause and then Cam began rubbing his neck. "Yes, ma'am. You call Ree and I'll coordinate with Parker. Then get me a charter as quick as you can out of Seattle. We'll leave for the airport now. Let's try to intercept her." Cam hung up the phone and began running towards the van, speaking Parker's name into the phone. Quinn followed after him. He turned, tossed her the keys, and jumped into the passenger's seat. "Drive us to Sea-Tac. Hannah is after Ree."

26

Parker's phone rang, pulling him away from the evidence board for his latest case. He was training a new agent and was finally at the point where the newbie could take over. Still, he didn't want to just set him loose with no help. He looked down at his phone and was surprised to see Cam's name pop up. He was still supposed to be deep undercover. With the FBI no longer needed on the operation, the CIA wasn't volunteering any more details – no surprise there – and his brother wouldn't be calling him unless it was important.

Parker answered with, "What's up, C?"

"We figured out who was behind the explosions at IRT. It's Hannah. Bad news is she figured us out first. We have video of her tampering with our gas line this morning."

"Shit. Where is she?"

"She landed at Chicago O'Hare two hours ago, headed southbound one hour ago towards…"

"Enterprise. Shit."

Parker sprinted to the car while Cam filled him in on all of the evidence they had against Hannah. Anyone who was capable of hiding her true motivations that skillfully was likely formidable in other ways they hadn't yet considered.

"Quinn is driving us to the airport now. We'll take a charter direct to Enterprise. Bring in Alexis or Scarlett if you need to. They're all cleared for this on a need to know basis."

"Got it. I'll call them in if needed. I'll also warn Mike. First, I'm driving down to get Ree."

REE LOOKED up from her equipment and rubbed her eyes. The last student leaving the lab for the day gave her a wave and she managed a small smile. She'd spent the better part of the afternoon troubleshooting this machine. While she was proud that she very nearly had it working, she was almost as proud that she hadn't uttered any expletives at the thing in front of her students. To avoid any distractions, she'd left her phone at her desk. She smiled at the ring on her finger. She should take it off to do lab work so it didn't get scratched, but she wasn't quite ready to do that just yet. She'd just been careful to avoid nicks and dings.

Ree yawned. She needed to power through just a few more minutes. Unfortunately, she'd cut herself off of coffee mid-afternoon so she had some hope of sleeping tonight. Ree began to gather up the tools she'd brought back into the secure lab with her. Matt would be leaving shortly, so she'd need to head home soon as well. After her adventures with the FBI, Ree made it a point not to stay in the lab alone anymore, gun in her purse or not. She was probably more paranoid than she needed to be, but what was the old saying? Just because I'm paranoid doesn't mean that someone isn't following me? She chuckled to herself and stretched her arms over her head. She pulled a wrench back out of her toolbox. Maybe she could squeeze in one more thing and then call it a night.

PARKER TIGHTENED his hands against the steering wheel and pulled his car onto the highway. Traffic was heavy, but moving. It was pretty common for Ree to let her phone go to voicemail when she was engrossed in her work. Usually, it wasn't a problem. After trying her desk phone and cell phone with no success and leaving a message with

Mike, he dialed his brother's number and hoped to hell he had a backup plan. If he didn't, Parker was calling the local police to storm the place in riot gear. It wasn't ideal – Hannah could have gone anywhere. There would be no easy way to unwind the kind of attention that generated front-page news. Cam answered before the phone processed half a ring. "Cam, Ree isn't picking up her phone. I'm getting ready to call local law enforcement for backup."

"Stand down, Parker. I've got someone closer."

"How close?"

"In the lab. Matt works for me occasionally. No one knows that but us, and I'd like to keep it that way."

"Matt Brown? As in Dr. Matt Brown? And you didn't tell me this sooner?"

"Need to know, P. Let me call him and I'll get there as soon as I can."

R EE BIT back a curse while attempting to loosen the sticky bolt on her equipment. While many people believed test machines were inanimate objects, incapable of having a personality, Ree had worked among them long enough to know better. Like people, machines all had their own unique quirks. This one had stubborn bolts. She pushed a little harder on the end of the wrench and screamed when she felt a tap on her shoulder.

"Easy, Ree. It's just me." The reassuring face of Matt Brown generated relief even as her cheeks heated. She was known for being a bit jumpy. She wasn't easy to panic per se, she was just extremely focused. When there was an external stimulus, she had a larger than normal reaction. Or at least that was what she told herself.

"Sorry, I'm a little high-strung today."

"I guess." He smiled an easy smile. "Do you have a minute?"

She wiped her hands on her pants to get the grease off and then cursed her stupid decision. She'd worn dress pants instead of jeans and it'd take a good half hour to undo the damage from the seconds she just saved. "Sure. What's up?"

"Why don't you come with me to the office area?" Ree made eye contact with Matt. Something in him had shifted. His ever-present smile was gone and his head swiveled, as if searching for something. In place of his pleasant disposition, a purposeful tension had settled around his shoulders. Ree followed him, looking for the cause of his alarm, but they were alone. When they made it back to their desks, she looked around the area for an explanation but came up with nothing. The only thing out of place was that the door to the hallway was shut, and locked. Matt had been a friend and ally as long as she'd known him, but his behavior had finally raised enough red flags to ring alarm bells. She put herself between him and her purse. Just in case.

"Matt, you're freaking me out. What's going on?"

"Ree, get your weapon out of your purse. I hope we don't need it, but we might."

Ree froze. "How do you know about my gun?"

"Well, two minutes ago, I didn't, but my friend Cam just informed me you're packing." Matt raised an eyebrow. Ree took a step backward and swallowed hard. The only Cam she knew was Parker's brother and a CIA officer. Not only was she not to even indicate that she knew Cam was CIA, she generally avoided mentioning his name at all.

"Cam who?" Ree hedged.

"Cam Mitchell, your soon to be brother-in-law. I work for him when he needs me. We go back a long time, back to the Navy. One of the IRT employees you met in Florida just skipped town and is headed this way. It looks like she knows you through the work you did at NASA and you're in danger. Parker's on his way, but Cam asked me to help watch your back until he gets here."

Ree walked over to her desk and saw her phone light up. Four missed calls from Parker and one from a private number. One text. *Go with Matt. He's one of the good guys.* Ree raised her eyebrows. "This is too weird. Do we stay here?"

"No way. We get out of here while there are still people around. I'm going to walk you back to my house and watch your six until the cavalry arrives. Cam and a friend of his hopped a plane a few minutes ago. They'll be here later tonight."

"Jeez, Matt. Have you been CIA this whole time?"

"Only on occasion. If it makes you feel any better, I was pretty shocked when I found out you were moonlighting for the FBI. Let's talk about it when there are fewer windows around, huh? And seriously, grab your gun. Hopefully, you don't need it, but I'd feel better if one of us was armed."

"You want it?"

"No. I'm more prepared for hand-to-hand than you." Matt dropped a few heavy textbooks into his laptop bag, testing its weight before hefting it over his shoulder. He left his laptop on his desk. Ree's eyes widened.

Ree retrieved her purse and unlocked the office door. "I'm too scared to challenge you on that right now."

Matt took the lead, checking each hallway before Ree followed. Students were leaving classes and the crowd would help them blend in. Matt raised a hand and looked both directions before opening the door that led outside. "We'll walk calmly, a few blocks, to my house, as if nothing is wrong. You ready?"

Ree swallowed hard and nodded. They walked as casually as possible through the crowd of students until they reached a newer home with navy blue siding and white trim. Matt took one last look behind them and unlocked the front door. Once inside, he flipped the deadbolt and closed the curtains over the windows. When he returned to where she was standing at the front door, she put her hands on her hips. "Are we safe now?"

"As safe as we can be. Apparently, our perp likes to blow up houses."

Ree cleared her throat. "Hate to point out the obvious, Matt, but we're in a house."

"Yeah, but if I can work in front of you for a few years without you knowing I'm CIA, I've got to think someone who's never met me won't figure it out on short notice. Highest probability is that she'll go to your lab or your house. Any idea how she knew where to find you?"

"I went in as myself on this one since we were looking at a rocket. It was a risk, but it was riskier to lie about it and then get caught. Man, she was so friendly. I thought she was protecting someone. I didn't think she was our mastermind."

"Some people are good at hiding it." He leaned against a wall and raised an eyebrow. "Speaking of, how did the unassuming Dr. Ryland end up working for the FBI?" Ree was nearly fooled by his casual manner until she realized he was standing between her and the door.

"Yeah, that's complicated. And probably confidential. Or classified." Ree ran a hand down her face. "Or whatever you people say. But long story short, there was a threat in the lab and they thought it was me. Once they figured out it wasn't, I offered to help them out from time to time. While we're on the topic, I'd like to know how the unassuming Dr. Brown ended up working for the CIA. I guess not so unassuming if you served with Cam…"

"Yeah. He was on my SEAL team. I was there the day he got hit. I took some damage to my back. It accelerated my retirement and I went back for my Ph.D."

"Jeez, Matt. I had no idea. I'm sorry."

"Don't be. I was doing what needed to be done and I'd do it again. And I'm happy now. I like what I do. It's a low-key lifestyle."

"When you're not working for the CIA."

Matt lifted a corner of his mouth. "Yeah, there is that."

Ree smacked a hand to her mouth. "Simon. You reported him. *You* were the anonymous tip."

Matt laughed. "Technically, I just reported the boxes."

"Ahh, you reported ME."

"I reported the deliveries. But yes, they were addressed to you. I personally didn't think you were involved. I figured they'd get to the bottom of it and prove it."

"I can hardly hold it against you. I wouldn't have met Parker otherwise."

"Parker the 'writer?'" Matt made air quotes. "Funny that Cam always talked about his brother but it never occurred to me he'd come sniffing around on campus to follow up on a lead. Small world. I just assumed when Simon left, they confiscated his equipment and reported him. I didn't realize they'd sent someone in person."

Before Ree had a chance to decide if she should tell him that Alexis the grad student also wasn't who she seemed to be, her phone buzzed. "Speaking of, that's him. Hey, babe. I'm here with Matt. Yeah, crazy, right? Oh, good. Be right there." Ree hung up the phone. "He'll be at the door in 3...2...1."

Matt checked the peephole and opened the door. He let Parker in and swiftly closed the door behind him. Ree rushed over to give him a hug. He pulled away and reached out a hand to Matt.

"Parker Mitchell, FBI. I'd appreciate it if you don't spread that around."

"Matt Brown, but you already know that. And understood. I'm a friend of your brother's."

"You're not just a friend of my brother's. You're the man who saved his life. And now you're helping keep Ree safe. Thank you. On both counts. I owe you one. Two, actually."

Matt shrugged. "Just doing my job, Parker. Have you heard from Cam?"

Parker nodded. "He's with another operations officer. They'll be here as quick as they can. From what I understand, they're on a government charter and getting a little impatient to arrive."

A few hours passed, but it felt like longer with the awkward small talk and constant perimeter checks from the two professionals in the house. Ree had pulled up her security system on her phone, but the camera on her front door didn't show anyone and there was no sign of forced entry. The highway cameras had last spotted Hannah outside of Chicago, headed toward Enterprise. If she wasn't coming, where she had ended up was anyone's guess. It was entirely possible she was following an escape route out of the country and they were overreacting. A loud knock on the door made Ree jump. Parker checked the door. "It's Cam."

Cam entered and shook Matt's hand. "Hey, man. I owe you one."

"You don't owe me anything, Watchman. You're all paid up." Matt nodded at Quinn and they introduced themselves by first name only.

"Hey, brother." Cam thumped Parker on the back.

Quinn lifted an eyebrow. "Brother. Of course. That's why Parker looked familiar. And Dr. Ryland, it's nice to see you again."

Parker eyed Cam. "You told Quinn we're related? That's big."

Cam shrugged. "Any sign of Hannah?"

Parker crossed his arms. "Not yet. I don't know if she's on her way here or not. My guess is she wants to pump Ree for information or she's cleaning up her mess. Ree isn't the obvious choice, she's just the easiest to find. You two were supposed to be dead this evening. She'll want me and Mike next. Or she's skipping town."

"And you warned Mike?"

"Of course. He's used to it. He'd be here, but he was farther away than you, working undercover. Told his wife too, but she's a profiler who can handle herself."

QUINN STOOD awkwardly outside the group until Cam gestured with his head for her to join them. Despite the circumstances, this was a group that was comfortable with each other. If she didn't watch herself, she could get comfortable too. "Why don't we keep Ree here and go over to her house? We can set up a camera and wait out back or close by to see if Hannah shows."

Cam raised an eyebrow. "Don't want to wait inside the house?"

Quinn shook her head. "With a perp who likes to blow things up? No, thanks. I'll pass. I'll take my chances outside."

Cam looked at Parker. "What's the cover like in Ree's front yard?"

Parker winced. "Not great. Some small bushes. We can get you access to her front door camera if you're willing to wait out back."

Quinn nodded. "That'll work."

Cam crossed his arms. "It's as good as settled then. Ree, Matt, you wait here. We'll go see if Hannah decides to make an appearance."

Quinn and Cam followed Parker to Ree's house. She lived within walking distance, no more than a half-mile away. However, they went through the back alley and found a well-covered place to crouch behind her AC unit. It wasn't the most pleasant place to sit, but they had an eye on the gas line and hopefully, Hannah would make her appearance soon. Parker had Ree's security feed pulled up and Quinn and Cam listened for car noises.

A half-hour later, a car pulled up in front of the house. Quinn crouched low and peeked past the side of the house to see who it was. Cam followed closely behind while Parker monitored the video. Quinn looked back at the boys and nodded. The car door slammed and they crept around the side of the house, trying to time their approach perfectly. Quinn scanned the streets, but Hannah had come alone.

Parker watched the feed and a few seconds later, whispered, "Okay, guys. On my count. Three, two, one." They came around the house just as Hannah pressed the doorbell.

Within seconds, Quinn had rushed the front porch and pulled Hannah's hands behind her back, pinning her against the side of the house. "Care to tell me why you are paying Ree a visit?"

Hannah's voice was pure shock. "Quinn! What are you doing? I...I was just in the neighborhood and wanted to pop in and say hello."

"Nice try, but I don't like liars. And bad news, Cam likes them even less. I know you're working for Dmitri and I know you've been coordinating with Tim. So, I would recommend you tell us everything you can and we'll give you the same deal we gave him." Hannah froze. "That's right. We know all about your contacts, all about how you coordinated with him to sabotage the rockets. We just need some information on your boss."

"They were blackmailing me. They threatened my family if I didn't help. Just let go of me, and I'll explain."

Quinn exchanged a look with Cam. He shook his head. "You can talk right here." Hannah's face was pressed against the house, but she remained silent. Apparently, she hadn't thought her lie through well enough because she didn't have a follow-up prepared. "Why don't you come with us and we'll have a little talk. On the record."

Parker pulled a pair of handcuffs from his pocket and snapped them on Hannah. Cam shook Parker's hand. "Thanks, P. We'll take it from here."

Quinn turned Hannah around, checking the street to see if anyone noticed the small drama playing out on Ree's front porch. Out of the corner of her eye, she saw a movement on the roof of a house down the block. Quinn didn't even remember making a conscious decision before she lunged forward to block Cam and the world went black.

27

Quinn woke to the sound of the high-pitched, regular beat of a heart monitor. And pain. A lot of pain. She groaned before she could stop the sound from coming out. She forced her eyes open, blinked a few times, hard, and took in the room around her. She tried to take in a deep breath, but a sharp ache stopped her. Her last memory was of movement on a rooftop and the sight of a black, silenced muzzle. She felt a squeeze on her hand, and with some effort, she turned her head and met Cam's eyes. "You're here."

Cam smiled. "Of course, I'm here. Where'd you think I'd be?"

"On to the next op?" Quinn's tongue was thick and Cam looked at her with affection.

"You're insane, you know that?" Cam smiled, rubbing the back of her hand.

Quinn closed one eye. It was too much effort to keep them both open. "You're going pretty easy on me. How much pain medicine am I on?"

Cam grimaced. "More than you were happy about the last time you woke up, I'm afraid. But you had some pretty major damage to patch up. You borrowed a few units of blood from the hospital."

Quinn moved a hand down her stomach and clenched up with the pain of that small movement. Just a small area of stitches, but even that slight touch hurt like a mother. "What happened?"

"Well, lady crazypants obviously chose the wrong accomplice. He was aiming at me and Hannah, but you took the bullet intended for me and kept it from being a kill shot."

Quinn blinked her one open eye. "That's good, right?"

"I don't love that you have a hole in you, but we're both alive. The CIA is hunting down the accomplice. Your only job right now is to recover."

"If it wasn't a kill shot, why do I feel like I'm going to die?"

"The docs had to dig around to get all the shrapnel out. You're going to be okay, but they wanted to keep you unconscious for a while to recover. You were a bit of a handful for the medical staff. Kept telling them you were fine and would leave on your own two feet as soon as they stitched up the damn hole." Quinn laughed and pain shot through her stomach. "You're lucky they didn't shoot you with a tranquilizer dart. I mean, they pretty much did, but at least they put it in your IV." Quinn threaded her fingers through his and looked down at their joined hands. Cam raised an eyebrow and she shrugged. He pulled her hand close and kissed the back of it. She gave him a little tug. He laughed and sat carefully on her good side. "Does this mean what I think it means or are you just on some really good drugs?"

"I'm definitely on drugs. But I think we've moved past a summer camp fling. I'm crazy about you. I want to see you again. I'd love to tell you that when I'm sober, but I think that's a few days away yet."

Cam leaned in a little closer. "Something tells me you'll have the same opinion when you sober up. I'm pretty crazy about you too. I still think you're a handful. But it's kind of hot."

"I haven't ever fallen for someone like this before."

"There's a first time for everything. And I mean, I think I'm getting the better end of the deal. Not every guy has a woman willing to take a bullet for him."

"I'd rather not do it on a regular basis, if it's all the same to you."

"I'm on board with that plan. Watching you get hurt was one of the worst things I've ever seen."

"This is going to be tricky, you know," Quinn said.

Cam smiled. "The best things usually are."

NOTE FROM THE AUTHOR

Thank you, dear reader, for joining my characters and me on this adventure! If you enjoyed this book…

1. Leave a review on Goodreads, Bookbub, or your favorite book retailer. Even a short review is a great way to help other readers find this book!

2. Sign up for my newsletter for exclusive content and news about new releases at: https://ktleeauthor.com/

3. Follow me on social media:

    Twitter: @ktleewrites

    Instagram: @ktleeauthor

    Facebook: https://www.facebook.com/ktleewrites

4. Check out the rest of The Calculated Series! An excerpt from Calculated Reaction is included at the end of this book.

Calculated Extortion (Prequel Novella)

Calculated Deception (Book 1)

Calculated Contagion (Book 2)

Calculated Sabotage (Book 3)

Calculated Reaction (Book 4)

Calculated Entrapment (Book 5)

BONUS MATERIAL

If you enjoyed Calculated Sabotage, please enjoy the following excerpt from Book 4 in The Calculated Series, Calculated Reaction.

1

Special Agent Alexis Thompson scanned her surroundings for threats, but saw none. To find the explosives hidden in the deserted industrial park, she needed a specialist. Alexis leaned down and whispered, "You ready to go?" Her partner replied by thumping his tail on the ground. Alexis checked behind her to make sure they were still alone, then straightened. "Okay, Waffle, let's get to work!"

Waffle lowered his nose, snuffling along the ground. Alexis kept the leash loose, giving her canine partner the space he needed to do his job. The click of his claws against the concrete broke through their otherwise silent surroundings. Alexis kept one hand near her weapon, a habit developed after years of working for the FBI. Despite walking through an area potentially riddled with explosives, Waffle's tail wagged as he tried to locate the dangerous objects. When they approached an empty oil drum, he sat and looked at the large container, then glanced up at Alexis. Alexis took a careful step closer and spotted the offending item inside. She gave Waffle a red rubber toy and told him what a good boy he was, even as her heart began to pound. Technically, she should flag it and call in the bomb disposal team. But it clearly didn't have a detonator. What was the harm in just getting the job done? Alexis leaned into the oil drum to retrieve the small package.

The door behind her opened and Alexis whirled around, reaching for her weapon. She relaxed when she spotted the K-9 unit supervisor coming through the doorway with an approving smile. He reached out a hand to shake hers. "Great job, you two." Alexis accepted the praise and gave Waffle the command to lie down. He settled on the ground and gnawed on his toy, looking up at their instructor. "Waffle will be back to work in no time. And you handled him like an old pro." He pointed at the package in her hand. "Glad you trust me enough to assume that isn't really going to blow up, but why don't you leave it where you find it next time? Don't want you to get in the habit of grabbing bombs with your bare hands. Even in practice."

Alexis acknowledged the praise and gentle correction with a small nod. "That's fair. Old habit of jumping right in to get the job done." She leaned down to scratch her dog behind the ear. "Waffle did well, though. I didn't even see him limp today." While it wasn't obvious from the day's performance, Waffle was healing from ACL surgery. He had ruptured the ligament playing with an overly-exuberant fellow trainee. Waffle let his toy fall out of his mouth. He watched it roll along the ground for a moment, then snatched it back up again.

"He's not the only one on the mend. Your arm is looking better too." He nodded at her right arm. Alexis had been protecting a witness when she'd been hit by a sniper bought and paid for by Russian politician Dmitri Yeninov. Instead of wallowing while she was benched, she'd been training Waffle and researching the man who shot her. Alexis had missed out on the CIA's latest attempt to stop Dmitri and his hit man while she was recovering. She didn't intend to let that happen again.

Alexis rolled her shoulder. "It feels better, too. I'm ready to get back out there."

"I bet. You two are working great together, Alex. If you ever want a job in my department, just give me a call."

Alexis smiled. "Thank you. I'll definitely consider it. And Waffle is still assigned to me, at least for a little longer, right?"

He nodded. "His training isn't complete yet. I'd like to have you take him all the way through his final tests. If today is any indication, I think Waffle will pass with flying colors."

Alexis beamed like a proud parent. "Awesome. I'd like that." Alexis's watch buzzed. "Sorry, but we need to get going. I have a meeting I can't miss."

The trainer raised his hand in a wave and Alexis left with Waffle trotting faithfully behind her. When they reached the car, he jumped into his spot in the back seat. Waffle's huge head was visible in the rearview mirror and his happy doggy tongue lolled out one side of his mouth. Waffle was a giant red Labrador who apparently didn't read the pamphlet that said Labrador Retrievers didn't usually get much bigger than eighty pounds. He tipped the scales at one hundred pounds of good nature, wagging tail and expert nose. He was affectionately known around the office as Alexis's bomb-sniffing elephant.

HALF AN HOUR LATER, Alexis and Waffle arrived at the FBI Chicago office. It was Alexis's home away from home, whenever she wasn't working undercover. She made it to her desk with a few minutes to spare for her meeting. After Waffle had greeted all of his friends at the office, he settled onto the floor next to her. While the FBI didn't allow pets at the office, Waffle was more of an employee than a pet, and he went everywhere with Alexis.

Alexis petted Waffle absently with the side of her foot and printed off a single copy of the report she would need for her next meeting. She rubbed her now-healed arm. Dmitri and his hit man, Andrei, had been busy. Thanks to a combination of intelligence the FBI had gathered and some information provided by the CIA, she actually had an idea of where they were going to strike next. The only problem was that she didn't know what they were planning to do. Unfortunately, she was merely detail-oriented, not omniscient.

The door to the office space opened, and Alexis and Waffle looked up in tandem. Her team lead, Special Agent Parker Mitchell, walked in, closely followed by his brother, Cam Mitchell, their ally in the CIA. After discovering the capabilities of Parker's team, Cam had begun engaging them in the CIA's operations whenever their skills were needed. The FBI was happy they were demonstrating successful cross-agency collaboration, and Alexis was always willing to help out.

Cam's projects were virtually guaranteed to be more interesting than the investigations that usually landed on her desk.

Now, all she had to do was convince Cam to let her chase down the lead she'd discovered. Alexis rose from her desk to greet him, report in hand. She fought the temptation to shake out her shoulders and bounce on the balls of her feet as she often did before sparring in the company gym or warming up for one of her half marathons. There was no way she was going to let the Mitchells pull her off her case because she only just got released from desk duty. She could probably even make Cam think it was his idea to bring her further in.

Waffle trotted over to the two men, beating Alexis by just a few seconds. "Hey, Cam. Nice to see you in person." Alexis reached out a hand, and he shook it.

"Hey, Alex. Good to see you too." Cam reached down to pet Waffle. Waffle was a working dog, but he was relaxed in the FBI office unless Alexis told him it was time to work. Even though Cam wasn't part of the normal crew at the office, he'd been by a few times. Waffle had quickly learned that the intimidating Mitchell brothers weren't too tough to resist a dog who had perfected the art of getting petted.

Waffle pushed his head up into Cam's palm. Alexis eyed the dog, who responded to her judgmental side-eye with a goofy doggy grin. Alexis looked at Cam. "Sorry about Waffle. He's shameless."

Cam gave Waffle a good scratch behind the ears. Waffle thumped his backside right on top of Cam's shoe and leaned into the scratch. "It's no problem. How's the arm?"

"The arm is great. Doc says I'm all healed up now."

Parker raised an eyebrow. "Alex is shooting better than she was before she got hit. I think someone is trying to make a point that she's well enough to go outside the office again."

Alexis crossed her arms. "Letting me lead the security team at your wedding this weekend doesn't count. I'd do that with or without your permission."

Parker laughed. "See what I mean? I think there is going to be more security there than at a state dinner."

Alexis waved a hand. "I may have gone a little overboard, but you all deserve to relax on your big day. You and Ree are going to focus on getting married without wondering if someone from an active investigation will use a public gathering as an opportunity." Ree Ryland wasn't just Parker's fiancé. Ree consulted for their team on occasion, including the most recent occasion that brought Dmitri's hit man as close as her front porch.

Parker looked at her with concern in his eyes. "I don't know. Maybe you should let someone else take the lead. Give yourself a little more time to rest and relax. Just to make sure you're truly okay. I wouldn't want you to overextend yourself." His mouth twitched, just a little.

Alexis slugged Parker in the arm. "I'll sic my dog on you."

Parker chuckled. "He's a lot less scary than you." Waffle thumped his tail.

Cam tipped his head towards the conference room. "We've got some things we need to talk about. Better get to it since we all have a full schedule this afternoon. Is your bomb-sniffing elephant coming?"

Alexis whistled at Waffle, who took his place at her right heel. "Sure. He can sit in the corner. It'll be good practice for him. Let me grab my laptop. Want me to bring in anyone else?"

Cam shook his head. "Let's not, for now. I'd like to compartmentalize our next steps, if we can."

Alexis raised her eyebrows at her team lead. "You heard him, P."

Parker rolled his eyes. They'd worked together for years and had developed a good-natured, older brother/little sister dynamic. "Very funny. Go get your stuff and let's tell Cam what you found."

Alexis settled in at the conference room table and her heart started to race, as it often did at the start of an investigation. There was also a small undertone of nerves, unusual for her. However, this operation was personal. Alexis took a breath. "Okay, I'd like to start by saying that, while I've done a lot of research, I'm coming to you with less than the full story."

Cam shrugged. "Welcome to my world."

"That's what Parker said you'd say. I spent some time mapping out the first two attacks Dmitri masterminded. I started with the assumption that our Russian politician must be following some sort of pattern or method, beyond just causing chaos. Subject matter expertise doesn't seem to be an issue for Dmitri – he picks people who know a lot about the weapon or tool he is using and convinces them to take the lead, and therefore, the fall. His last two attacks have been related to newsworthy technologies. Blowing up a rocket hit the headlines, and if he'd been successful with his bioweapon, that would have, too. Killing people doesn't seem to be his primary objective, but he also doesn't mind if people get hurt or killed when they're standing in his way. Obviously." Alexis gestured to her own shoulder.

Cam nodded. "We have the spy Andrei tried to kill on Ree's front porch in custody. That checks out with what she's told us."

Alexis frowned. "We've been chasing Dmitri, but every time we get close, we find Andrei doing all of his dirty work. Since Andrei left the country without us catching him *again*, Dmitri has to know we're getting close."

Cam folded his hands on the table. "I think that's a good assumption. I also think Dmitri will want to up the ante to prove himself if he thinks he'll be discovered. But Andrei doesn't leave much evidence behind for us to work with."

Alexis straightened the report on the conference room table. "Along that line of reasoning, after you asked me to get involved, I started going through the old reports to see if we missed anything. Remember the employee who was fired from Innovative Rocket Technologies, the one the CIA concluded was an innocent bystander?" Alexis carefully sidestepped that Cam and his partner were "the CIA" on the operation.

Cam winced. "Yes, I remember her well. Lindsay Campbell."

Alexis exchanged a look with Parker. "Lindsay is now working at the Future Energy Laboratory, a government-sponsored research lab out in Colorado. She's received some calls we haven't been able to fully trace back to their source. They happen at the same time, once a month, but it's a new phone number every time, and the phone numbers used on past calls are no longer active. The FEL is working on solar, biofuels, nuclear energy, you name it. Dmitri could be using Lindsay to gather materials, or simply steal government information on new technology. Regardless, I think it'd be prudent to send someone to check it out. I mean, it could be nothing. Unless it's not."

Cam let out a low whistle. "She's probably reporting to someone." He gestured to the report. "Okay, I'll definitely take a closer look at this and consult with the operations officer I was working with on the last op. If Lindsay wasn't an innocent bystander, she'll want to know." He took a moment to choose his words. "She is every bit as invested in this as I am. This is really great work, Alex. We appreciate it."

Alexis slid the report across the desk to Cam. "So you know we should send someone in person to investigate, right? And, if it's a dead end, I'd hate to waste your time."

Cam laughed. "First of all, you don't think it's a dead end, or you wouldn't be tapping your foot while you talk to me. Second, if there is an opportunity and I'm convinced we can do it safely, you're first on my list. If the FBI lets me, that is. They may be more hung up on you getting shot last time you tried to help me catch Dmitri than you seem to be. Let me run this by a few people and I'll let you know what our next steps are." Cam reached out a hand to shake hers. "I'll see you both again soon."

Once Cam left, Alexis turned to face Parker. "Alright, what did he leave out? His jaw clenched a little when he was talking about the other officer. I mean, I could tell from the reports she was injured on the operation. But what else?" Parker's mouth twitched and Alexis swatted his arm when he remained silent. "You know what he didn't tell me, don't you?"

"I wish I could tell you. You'd love it. But you know how those guys are. They're worse than us. I think they issue them a cloak and dagger when they start at the Agency."

"Did the CIA figure out how to make super humans or something?"

Parker laughed. "It's a good story, but it's not quite *that* interesting. Don't worry, you might still find out. Cam knows you're available if he needs you. And he's thinking about bringing you in. Good job, Alex." Parker opened the conference room door and held it while Alexis led Waffle out. "Don't you need to get going?"

Alexis nodded. "I do. It's bad form to miss a bachelorette party you helped plan." Alexis studied her nails. "Hey, before I go, I need to talk to you about something else."

Parker narrowed his eyes. "What did you do?"

"I may have performed a very small background check on the guests coming to your wedding." Parker lifted an eyebrow and Alexis raised her hands in the air. "A tiny search, really. Public records only. All above board."

"Well, did you find anything?"

Alexis bit her lip. "Nothing to worry about. Well, nearly nothing. You have an uncle that got a DUI."

"Yeah, already know about that one. He's spent some time in meetings and seems to be making some progress. Anything else?"

Alexis sighed. "Dr. Matt Brown is invited. While he passed the public records screening, anything I would actually want to know about him is still under lock and key, per our boss, who remains immovable on the topic. If he's no longer a suspect in an investigation, I'm not sure why it matters anymore." Matt had worked with Ree since Alexis and Parker met her while investigating a weapons smuggler on campus. While Matt had initially been on their list of potential suspects, their boss had very quickly taken him off the list and told them to stop investigating him immediately. And she'd still never been given any further information about Matt.

"So, you didn't try to find any information, right?"

Alexis sighed. "I didn't go looking where it wasn't publicly available."

"Wow. That's impressive."

Alexis glared at Parker. "I can behave myself. It doesn't mean I have to like it. Look, I know Ree thinks the world of Matt, but I don't like having unknown factors when it involves you guys. Especially since Matt's on the guest list." Parker's expression was inscrutable. He knew something. She could work with that. Contrary to popular belief, intimidating someone wasn't always the best way to extract information. She made sure he met her eyes. "But I'm *assuming*," Alexis drew out the word, "that you've asked your brother to make sure Matt isn't a threat to your future bride, or you wouldn't be comfortable with Matt working with Ree on campus every day." Alexis let the words hang in the air.

Parker smiled. "You are correct that I would be concerned if Ree was around someone who would be a threat to her safety. I don't mind that Matt is there. Also, I believe you're supposed to read me my rights before delivering that level of questioning, Agent Thompson."

Alexis rubbed her hands together. "Ah, perfect. No further questions. For the record, you are welcome to tell me the actual truth about Matt whenever our boss allows it. I hope you don't mind that I did some digging."

"Not at all. Thanks, Alex." A grin played at the edge of Parker's mouth.

Alexis put her hands on her hips. "You already knew I was doing it, didn't you?"

Parker laughed. "Oh, yeah. I saw you researching the guest list a couple of weeks ago. Why do you think I didn't beat you to it? Thanks for covering that for us – saved me some time, so I could help Ree with seating arrangements. Which is definitely worse than just about anything I do here." Parker winced. "I will happily conduct surveillance any day I don't have to decide which aunt has to sit next to which cousin and get debriefed on which relatives aren't speaking to each other at the moment." They returned to their shared office area and Parker slipped into his jacket. He flipped his keys in his hand. "I have a wedding to-do list to finish, too. See you tomorrow. Have fun with Ree this afternoon."

Alexis grinned. "You got it. Congrats, friend. I'm excited for you both. Let me know if you need anything else."

"I think we're all set. I'm assuming you're coming armed?"

"Please. Do you have to ask? Fortunately, your future wife selected a dress with a flare in the skirt, so I can hide it. That was thoughtful. You picked a good one, P."

"Yeah, I think she's pretty great, too. Thanks, Alex. I'll see you tomorrow." Parker raised his hand for a fist bump and Alexis returned it. She went back to her desk to grab a bag filled with Waffle's toys and food before she led him down the hall to drop him off with Jordan, her good friend, and the FBI's local cybersecurity expert. This weekend, he'd also volunteered to be her dog sitter. With Waffle taken care of and all of her FBI business well in hand, her next mission could begin.

2

Lindsay Campbell paced the empty workspace at the Future Energy Laboratory with her cell phone in hand. Large pieces of manufacturing equipment sat dormant in the large room, waiting for the day to truly begin. Alone, the room seemed cavernous, but when the rest of her team arrived, it would be abuzz with activity. She was typically the first person there in the morning. Getting fired from her last job continued to be a powerful motivator for her to get to work a little earlier than everyone else. Unfortunately, she'd been in such a rush this morning that she hadn't checked her calendar. She had a regular call scheduled that she would prefer to take privately. Well, this room would work in a pinch. The man she spoke to once a month would have questions, and she wasn't about to ignore his call.

Lindsay jumped when her phone buzzed. She swiped the screen to accept the call. "Hello?"

"Good morning, Lindsay. How are you?" The voice on the other end of the line was butter smooth, with just a hint of a Boston accent.

She forced herself to make small talk, even though she was itching for an update. He didn't need to know how nervous she was. "I'm good. Settling in with my crew, doing meaningful work."

"That's good to hear. Is now a good time to talk?"

She looked out of the windows of the lab into the connecting office. It was still dark. "Of course. What's going on?"

"You know that project we were worried about? It turns out we need some help on the ground. Specifically, Lindsay, we'd like your help."

Lindsay closed her eyes. She could do this. In fact, it could be argued that there really wasn't anyone better positioned for the work than her. But after her most recent failure, why would they still want her to help them? What if she messed everything up again? No. She wouldn't let self-doubt win this time. Lindsay rubbed her neck and the words tumbled out, almost without her permission. "Yes. I'll help. Just tell me what you need."

"We'll send you instructions and will be in touch again soon."

"Okay. That's good. I can do that. I think."

"Thank you, Lindsay. Welcome to the team."

THE MAN SITTING across from Dmitri Yeninov turned off the audio recording of the spy they now had in place in Colorado. Dmitri exchanged a look with Andrei, who gave a nod of approval. Dmitri smiled. He had been right about the woman on the other end of the call. Properly motivated, anyone could be convinced to help. Of course, the man in front of him believed he was critical to Dmitri's team, and there was no harm in letting him believe it. The man's name was of no relevance, but he knew a piece of Dmitri's true plans, so Dmitri had to make him feel useful, at least for a little longer. Dmitri stared down his nose at the weasel, looking so smug about his little recording. Dmitri offered no additional comments, and the man had the good sense to fidget in his seat.

Dmitri let him squirm for another moment, then reached for the small recording device. "This is good. For now. I would like for you to continue to be our contact point for Lindsay."

The weasel sat up a little straighter and began motioning with his hands. "I'm glad you liked it. I've actually been working on how we approach Lindsay to make sure that she…"

Dmitri waved his hand. "The details are insignificant. We just need to have her compliance. I'll expect more updates as our little project moves along. That will be all." Dmitri stood to dismiss him and Andrei showed him out, leaving Dmitri alone with his thoughts. More people than he'd cared to involve were aware that he was working on something, but no one person knew exactly what would happen except him. Andrei knew more than any of Dmitri's other allies, but even he did not know the full plan yet. Dmitri hadn't made it so long in his position by being foolish. And he'd made sure to be in a very public location whenever his people were making their contributions to his project. He cracked his neck. Yes, there had been a few setbacks, but nothing that he couldn't handle. And now that his plan had been set into motion, success was guaranteed.

Calculated Reaction is now available at your favorite book retailer!

ACKNOWLEDGMENTS

I am so grateful, as always, to my friends and family for your support. Thank you to my mom, who went above and beyond to provide feedback on early reads, including the fight scenes! Thank you to my husband for being an amazing source of support and valued sounding board for plot details. Thank you to Darcy, as always, for her great eye for plot and strategy. Also, thank you to Jenni, who gave me super helpful feedback with her writer's eye! I am always very grateful for Emily, both for your friendship and for all of your help on technical questions. Last but not least, big thank yous to my two fabulous editors, Laura Anderson and Bridget Fryman.

ABOUT THE AUTHOR

K.T. Lee is a writer, mom, and engineer who grew up on a steady diet of books from a wide variety of genres. When K.T. began to write the kind of books she wanted to read, she mixed clever women and the sciences with elements from thrillers (and a dash of romance) to create The Calculated Series.

Made in the USA
Coppell, TX
17 July 2025